HEARTS OF CLAY AND TEMPEST

Elizabeth Hunter

HEARTS
of CLAY
and
TEMPEST

A Litttle Mermaid Retelling

Nymeria Publishing, LLC

First published in the United States of America by
Nymeria Publishing LLC, 2022

Nymeria Publishing
PO Box 85981
Lexington, SC 29073

Visit our website at www.nymeriapublishing.com

Print ISBN 979-8-9851572-0-8
eBook ISBN 979-8-9851572-1-5

Printed in U.S.A

To Kindred Spirits

Acknowledgements

THERE ARE SO MANY folks who have been virtual or real hugs for me on this journey. Writing a book isn't a solo time and if I thanked everyone who pushed me over the finish line, we'd have a whole other book to write. My internet fam on social media, every kind comment or supportive DM has meant the world to me. I've made incredible friends on this journey and want to thank a few important people to me.

To Tiffany Chiang, aka Read by Tiffany. You support me through heartbreak and joy and have rooted for me every step of the way. Thank you for being the kindest friend I could ever ask for.

To Karen Haxton, I started sharing this story with you during finals week and we brainstormed about Darcy for too many late nights. Darcy wouldn't exist on page without you!

To my sister Tammy - you deserve the world. Thank you for being the first person to hear my stories.

To Sarah, thank you for sticking by my through thick and thin and always rooting for me.

To Zoe, I'm so glad you were the first person to hear my book news.

To twitter mutuals, aka book twitter, aka the best corner of the internet. Y'all have kept me motivated!

To my Disney fam who always help me believe in magic: Shay, Sienna, Sofi, Lindsey, Taryn, I hope Darcy's story helps you capture your dreams.

To my Granny Hunter, who always believed in me. I miss you all the time Granny and wish you could be here to hold a copy of my story.

And for my parents, my dad for asking to read my writing, and my mom for all the Rod and Staff English lessons. Diagramming sentences paid off.

Chapter One

Darcy

TONIGHT, THE CLOUDS HIDE the moon. I rest my elbows on the harsh wood of the window frame, absently picking dirt from my cracked fingernails. It's been hours since the sunset, though dense fog meant the day was short, dark as dusk. Rain still threatened, and we're likely to wake up to soaked grass and another short day of fog and clouds. Late winter thunderstorms, ending with water dripping off our roof's thatch and pooling puddles at our doorstep.

As if in answer to my thoughts, the sky rumbles. I raise my chin, glancing at the clouds. They weave their way past, covering my favorite stars. The same stars my Uncle Kian is using tonight as he sails home.

Wind rustles my hair, and I squint past the sandy cliffs. My cousin is still out there. Anya can't sleep without a late-night walk on the beach even though her walking leaves her hair drenched with salt and ocean spray.

I turn from the window, releasing a sigh. I unpeg the heavy cloth, letting it shut out the evening. I don't need to see the dark sky tonight to worry over my Uncle's trip. Anya would be the first to tell me to go to bed and not wait up for her. If my Uncle or cousin caught sight of me now, they'd both roll their eyes at my worry. I could almost hear my Uncle Kian chiding me about chewing my nails, his quiet, constant reminder that the ocean isn't a monster to fear. Yet even with his calm voice, I can't picture the ocean as anything but a threat.

He said as much when he boarded his ship ten days ago. Uncle Kian longs for the end of winter, the end of the deadly storms that lash our coasts. As soon as sunshine starts to coat the water, the bite of winter air lessening, my Uncle is ready to sail. Every spring, my Uncle and a half dozen men from our village leave for weekly trips across the miles-wide bay that separates our coast from the rest of the world.

Anya says spring is a sign of promise. The sunshine and warmth mean the ocean is safe again. Even when the seasons change, when few are scared to sail, I'm still terrified for Uncle Kian. The sea is frightening enough in the daylight, sparkling innocently in the sunshine. The sparkle hides the menacing dark depths of cold water. I don't know how Anya can stand it, how she paces on the beach at night. Black, deep, never-ending waters. There's nothing innocent in the inkiness of the ocean. Anya swears there's nothing prettier than the waves breaking on the rocks, the white caps glistening in the moonlight. I can think of prettier things – the rocky, windswept cliffs at noon, the sunset glittering across a field of golden wheat, or best of all, a clear, dark sky splashed with tiny pricks of light.

Thinking about my Uncle sailing makes me nauseous on stormy days like this. The water takes so much; I can barely stand to hear the waves breaking on the beach. With my Uncle gone, half the village treading the waves, my stomach is tight with worry. While a chance late winter thunderstorm storm simply drenches our village and wheat fields, the unexpected storms can easily take my Uncle's life.

Anya could slip on a rock, fall into the cold waters. The ocean takes without a second thought.

At least, the wind hides the sound of the waves tonight. I sink unto the bench, brushing my hands over our loom.

Weaving will take my mind off the ocean. Voyaging keeps us fed. But the cloth Anya weaves keeps us comfortable. We aren't as wealthy as some of the new towns cropping up with the Saxon settlements. But my Uncle trades the cloth for iron kettles, leather for shoes. Next year, he promised to bring back glass for our open window.

I look up as my cousin swings the door open. Her eyes are wide, flecked with fear, and my hands still on her loom. The wheel rocks back and forth, my feet steady on the pedal, "What is it," I can barely breathe the question, my cousin's face frightening, whiter than a midday cloud. I've only seen her white like that once before, the day her fiancé jumped into the rough, icy water to drag out a screaming child.

The child survived, his thin arms caught around his savior's neck. Anya's love died, his lips nearly frozen blue, eyes still like ice.

She stands trembling in the doorway, "Darcy," She repeats my name. I watch her hands clutch the door frame, wind raging behind her, "You can't hear her?"

I feel my heart skip a beat, "Who do you hear, Anya?"

She steps over the threshold, hands fisting into her skirt. The door slams shut behind her, wind howling incessantly. I keep my mouth tight, watching her. She stops in front of our hearth, stooping until her knees brush our dirt floor, "I hear her, Darcy." She whispers, barely loud enough for me to catch the soft words.

My cousin doesn't need to elaborate. With the bare fear on her face, I can read my cousin's thoughts. I stand, the stool scraping on the dirt floor underneath me, "If we were to lose anyone," I set my hand on her shoulders, "I'd hear the Banshee too."

She shivers violently. "Don't say her name." She looks up at me, her eyes wide. The Banshee is a childhood story, a ghostly woman who screams when someone you love is dying. I'm sure the Banshee had a human name at some point, before whatever magic cursed her to spend her days screaming in children's nightmares. Anya catches my hand, and I search for something to distract her. Anything to calm her fear of the wailing woman, "It's just the wind." We hold our hands together, her calluses rubbing into my palm. Her fingers are freezing. I squeeze her palm, and Anya whispers, "I know the wind."

Outside our cottage, the gusts shriek louder. My heartbeat remains steady, but my cousin is still catching her breath. She glances at our gapping windows; with winter ending, we've loosened the oak boards keeping the frost away. "He'll be home soon," I offer the words. She looks back at me, and I can almost see her thoughts. Uncle Kian out on the sea, he's gone for nearly two weeks. The men should be back in a day or two, or even a whole week. We both know how the voyaging works.

She drops my hand, bending back to the fire. Reaching for the pot of gruel, muttering about the wind as she stirs the mixture of wheat and milk. "We aren't the only ones with loved ones' voyaging," I speak softly, trying to find a way to comfort her. To see her lips curve into a soft smile, the tension loosening from her shoulders, "If anyone else in the village heard the banshee, we'll hear about it in the morning."

Anya purses her lips, brown eyes flickering in the light of the fire, "Papa didn't hear," She hesitates,

"She cried when mother died. No one speaks about her, Darcy."

She meets my gaze, chin lifting, before she asks, "Have you ever heard anyone else mention her wailing? Ever?" I don't want to answer. Anya has always insisted that she heard the Banshee the night her mother died of a raging fever. When Uncle Kian spoke to our village seer, Isolt, whispering about the voices Anya heard, the older woman assured him that Anya didn't hear things. Anyone should be able to hear the forlorn wailing — especially those who listen. The Banshee, Isolt explained, lives to warn people.

Still, Anya is the only one I know who has ever heard the dreaded wailing. If anyone in our village has ever heard the Banshee, they've kept quiet. Anya's gaze lingers on me, fingers twisting around the edge of her skirt, "You always have answers, Darcy. You're the one always telling me how dangerous the ocean is."

Anya doesn't need me warning her about the sea; we've both avoided mentioning her dead fiancé for nearly two years. I don't intend to break my silence on his memory just because she's hearing things tonight. "It's just the wind, Anya." I speak firmly, sinking into my pallet, "Uncle Kian will return. The wind is just tricking you."

I hear her stir the fire again before she sinks into her pallet. Her voice is soft in the still room, "I know the difference between wind and death."

I don't have an answer. I can't believe Anya truly heard the Banshee cry, not when all I heard was the wind shrieking outside our thin walls. Uncle Kian is as much my family as he is Anya's Father. If the wailing woman decided to warn us about his life, we'd both hear her cries. There can't be anything more than the wind. Not tonight.

↓

Anya and I don't speak of the Banshee again. She's gone when I wake up the next day and doesn't return till near nightfall. It's a smart way to avoid me, spending an entire day on the ocean. She knows I won't willingly head down to the beach, not without a bit of coaxing.

When she comes back in the early evening, I want to ask her if she is still concerned, but she brushes me aside every time I start to ask. Besides, I already know the answer. Her lips pressed together, eyes nervous, her restless tossing all night long.

Instead, I chatter about the wheat planting or my weaving, or even the next time we might travel to a Saxon estate. Anya stares at me, worry still caught in her eyes. She picks at her weaving, but her hands tremble too much to finish the delicate patterns she usually works out with our cloth. I want to reassure her, promise her everything will be fine, but fear isn't something you can talk away.

Two days later, the voyaging party returns. Anya and I race to the sea, her face white, lips chewed through. I scan through the familiar returning faces, our neighbors Fergal and Hugh, Iollan, and Quinn.

Their faces are rugged, unshaved with a week of hair. Clothes tattered, they're dragging their feet.

I look past the men, noticing the frayed sails, signs of the rough voyage. Usually, the men would have crates of cloth and salt, trades from the fish they catch. But they leave the ship empty-handed; the crates must have been thrown overboard during a storm.

Quinn walks up to Anya, looking at her white face. I can see the news in his pinched eyes. He doesn't even look at me, "I'm sorry, lass." He touches Anya's shoulder. "The sea is fierce. Your Father," he looks down, "a good man, he was."

Before he even finishes speaking, I catch Anya in my arms. She lets out a wail, her voice a shrill scream in the hushed throng. Another man passes by, murmuring an apology. Anya is crying violently, hot tears. The village clusters around us.

Our oldest neighbor, Isolt, steps to my side. Her gnarled fingers curl together, she lowers her head, raising a cloth over her face. As Anya weeps on my shoulder, Isolt begins to keen, high-pitched wailing.

Other women edge closer, raising their voices. The wailing rings around me, a steady show of grief. I press my lips together, holding Anya. I keep seeing her face, pale, the fear in her eyes. The unspoken words, *I heard the Banshee.* The Banshee only cries when those you love are close to death. A warning. The keening continues around me, wailing. Sobbing. More wailing. I should be keening too, but I can't. Not with Anya in my arms. I should clasp my hands together, lungs burning as I wail for our loss.

But I can't. Not while Anya's tears soak through my wool dress. Not when I didn't believe her, when

I only heard the wind. I close my eyes, tears burning. Kian was the only Father I ever knew. The Banshee should have cried for me, too. She should have warned me. I loved him—just as much as Anya. A childhood nightmare has betrayed me.

The sea crashes, thunder rolling. Someone pulls Anya from my arms, urging her to come with them.

The village will care for us tonight, make us a meal. We'll sit for seven days, mourning Uncle Kian.

Then, we will burn his things and throw the ashes into the sea.

The women walk with Anya, still wailing. I stand on the edge of the beach, the sun hidden behind clouds. I wrap my cloak around my shoulder; my chest wet from Anya's tears. I rub at my cheeks.

I know Anya heard the wailing. It wasn't the wind. She heard the Banshee when her mother, my Aunt Nuala died. But that was years ago. Anya's three years older than me. I was too young to listen for the Banshee when Aunt Nuala died. And my mother – she died when I was a baby. We were both too young to hear the Banshee then.

My shoulders start shaking, my teeth chattering. I look out over the sea, curling my toes into the stiff sand.

All I can hear is the wind. But I ache to hear more. I raise my palms, my shoulders still trembling. I rub my hands into my eyes before falling to my knees. Uncle Kian is dead. The Banshee cried. And I must have been deaf.

Brendan

Flavian hates the mountain, and I have to admit, it doesn't make for a pleasant hiking trip. He kicks at the various rocks lining the path carved into the mountain's sides, muttering about the blasted Finn. They are forcing us to meet them at the borders of earth and sea. I look behind me, nodding at the dozen guards trailing behind us. They silently climb behind Flavian and me, feet skidding on the slippery rock path.

"Tell me again, Brendan," Flavian grumbles, "Why I have to traipse into the mountain just to collect the taxes?"

Hiking takes much longer than taking to the skies. I'm sure every one of us would rather abandon the earth and spreading our wings in the crisp mountain air. But the cliffs are too steep; we can't sweep into a landing in these deep mountain passes. I ruffle my wings, wanting to roll my eyes at his complaining, "I didn't hire you just to spend extra mornings in bed. Besides, what better way to learn a bit of diplomacy?"

Some of my men must have heard my last question. They chuckle, laughing at the idea of learning diplomacy from the Finn. Collecting taxes should be simple. Like everyone else in the Fae Court, the Finn, the Goblins, Fauns, and Leprechauns should send a representative to the Court. Each year, the various clans deposit the yearly taxes and promise fealty. However, the Finn's specialty is being difficult. They won't come to the Queen's Court, so every year, a squadron from the Court has to hike into the mountainous yawning cavern adjoining the Fae territories to the Finn oceans. This year, it's our turn. I drew the unlucky straw, forcing my squadron to wake up far too early this morning to hike into a mountain.

We reach the bottom of the trail, the ground leveling out into the stone path leading into the mountain's center. The sun is just beginning to peek above the craggy mountain peaks when we slip into the cavern. The dark walls glisten, ancient riddles etched into the stone. Supposedly, the riddles prevent the Finn from ever crossing from their ocean waters into the land. I suspect that's a bedtime story to comfort restless children, frightened by stories from the wars. I grew up on the stories, my Father grumbling about fighting Finn warriors before the Finn king reluctantly swore loyalty to our Queen.

I think that's when the mountain was carved, two hundred years ago. Since then, the Finn haven't crossed into Fae lands, refusing to visit the Court or walk past the boundary separating their ocean territories and the rest of the world. "I hate this place," Flavian sighs next to me,

"Nothing like darkness to eat away thoughts of breakfast." "You haven't had breakfast yet," one of my men instantly reminds us.

"Exactly," Flavian barks back, "And if you're not careful, you'll be my breakfast." Our laughter echoes down the dark cave, the sound reverberating around our footsteps. We reach the end of the long hall, filing into the circular room. Dim light flickers from lit sconces inlaid into arches carved with the faces of legendary Fae. I've been here once or twice, but my skin shivers when I glance around the dark cavern.

The legendary sacred alter sits at the center of the room, a glittering path of crystal leading to the dais.

The Finn are already present, standing at attention, webbed hands wrapped tight around their spears. I step unto the crystal, walking towards the altar.

"Gods' blessing on you." I clear my throat, addressing the Finn standing opposite from me. He is silhouetted by the dancing darkness of the wall of water directly behind him. The water is the final border dividing the Finn from ourselves. It's been a hundred years or so since any Fae have visited the Finn Court. My mother told me the last visitor to the Finn Court went mad. He clawed off the skin from his face, and the Finn dropped him off at a beach, abandoning his starved body to the seagulls.

As I step closer, I can more clearly see this Finn warrior's golden armor; the metal etched with swirling patterns. I bow my head slightly.

"Our Queen sends her greetings to your people." I'm not surprised by the Finn's snarl, his long teeth flashing. The others hiss, stamping their spears against the stones. The sound fills the hollow chamber, and I can imagine Flavian wincing, the sound too loud, too close.

I deliberately keep my eyes on the center Finn, though my men shuffle uncomfortably, fingers moving to the pommel of their swords. Their stamping subsides, and the leader hisses at me, "We take no part in your Queen's blessings." I try to process his words, thinking through what veterans told me at the Court. The Finn detest the Fae Court and hate paying the yearly taxes. Be as quick as possible, take the tax money, and leave.

Don't delay or accidentally insult them. My palms are already sweating, and I tighten my hand around the hilt of my sword. But before

I can speak again, the Finn leader takes a step forward, "We won't be paying tribute to Oona. Not this year. She knows what we demand."

They can't refuse the tribute; the yearly taxes bind the lands together, prevent the threat of war,

"Impossible." I force my breathing to remain calm, my voice steady. "turn over the tribute."

The Finn sneers, "Or else what, Brendan, son of Riordan? My men outnumber yours, and you are not prepared to fight." I can't return empty-handed. "Brendan," Flavian whispers, edging forward on his toes.

"They're just testing us. Don't let them."

I don't plan on letting them. I eye the Finn, noting the bag hanging from his belt. It must be the taxes. He's coy, but he has the gold coins. For a moment, I wonder if he's acting on his own or with the blessing of his king. "Hand it over." I jerk my chin towards his belt. "Don't be foolish."

His teeth glitter, while around him, his men lower their spears into a fighting position. Behind them stands the massive wall of water. Behind my men and I, just the long hall and the inside of the mountain.

The Finn can jump into that water, escaping instantly. Without the Queen's magic, we cannot follow them. I glance at Flavian, and he reads my thoughts. Get the bag of tribute and get out. Fight them into the water. Don't let them insult us into leaving.

The moment the Finn lowered their spears, my men have been on guard, unsheathing weapons. I speak one more time, "Hand over the tax."

He sneers again, "I don't obey Fae boys." That nearly makes me wince, but at least the insult confirms what I'm thinking. He's simply testing me. I shout a command at my men, and we rush forward, our swords an arc of metal. The spears rattle against us, whacking into our armor. Flavian yanks down a metal helmet, a tassel of silver cords trashing from the top of his helmet as he twists around, swinging his sword in around flash of metal.

My feet skid on the soft stones, but I press forward towards the Finn leader. One of the Finn guards jabs into me, knocking me backward. The Finn lifts his arm, bringing his spear nearly on top of my head, and I block it with a jolt. His face twists, and I pull my sword back before swinging forcefully up. He raises his spear, and I step closer, quickly shoving my sword into his face. It cuts across his head, slashing a clean line at his neck. I watch the blood split the green skin across the side of his neck as he stumbles back. He drops his spear, yowling in pain. I immediately kick, shoving my foot into his chest, slamming him to the floor. I lean over him, stabbing my sword through a chink in his armor between his arm and chest. He twists under my foot, trying to throw me off. I push harder, my hand a fist around the sword as the metal tears through his skin.

I step off the Finn, his arm now a useless limp of torn nerves. The Finn leader still has his bag of gold, he shoves his spear at one of my men, the tip slashing at anyone who dares come close enough. I slam my shoulder into another Finn, shoving him towards Flavian. Flavian grins, leaping towards me, eagerly slashing at the guard with his sword.

I duck another guard, now feet from the Finn leader. He hisses as he sees me, his rows of teeth glinting. I grit my teeth but press on, weaving a circle around him. Quick stabs at him, trying to find an opening. His eyes are murderous, a vicious green, as he screams curses at me. He answers every thrust with a quick hit from his spear. Water splashes on my boots, and I realize the Finn are falling back, diving into the ocean. The Finn leader must realize this as well, for his eyes narrow as he snarls at me. There's no way I can bring this Finn to his knees. Not in this space, in the few minutes left of this fight. Instead, I swipe across at his waist, cutting the cord tying the tribute bag to his belt. I don't get a chance to see his reaction before he brings his spear down. Hitting me across the head, the wood snapping heavily against my skull.

I crumple, biting my tongue hard enough to draw blood. My sword falls to the floor, clattering. The room spins, and I slide my palms across the cold floor, spitting a curse. He might have taken the chance to run me through, but Flavian jumps in closer, stabbing him across the face. Blood splatters on Flavian's arms, splashing on the stones and into my face. The Finn howls, cursing as he whacks at Flavian. Flavian parries with him, driving him backward. He shouts in his own Finn language, a harsh guttural cry before he spins and dives into the water.

I'm still on my knees, my head throbbing, blood gathering at my lips. I feel Flavian, his slender fingers curling around my shoulders, asking if I'm alright.

"I'm fine," I struggle to stand, clutching the bag, "I've got the tribute." My men circle me, congratulating me for collecting the taxes. "Just like we heard," One of them exclaims, "They're just like we heard."

I want to smile, but my aching tongue twists my face into a grimace instead, "Let's not draw the short stick next year." My men laugh, grinning feistily. Flavian hands me my sword, and I slip it back into my holster. He meets my eyes, an edge of concern in his gaze. "Are you truly alright, Brendan?"

"Yes," I nod, ignoring the wave of nausea building in my gut. "Should've known they'd fight about handing over the tribute."

"But you weren't expecting it," he comments. "We have the tax," I hold up the heavy bag; the room is still shifting under my feet. I close my eyes, "That's all that matters." My men give a half-hearted cheer before grumbling about the troublesome Finn. Several of them are bruised from the short fight and more than a little annoyed at the Finn's stubbornness. Flavian grabs my shoulder, scowling, bothered by the Finn's choice to fight us. I'm bothered as well, but I don't want to talk about this in front of our men. "I don't know about all of you," I manage a slight grin, facing my men, "But I am quite ready for breakfast."

"Next time," Flavian growls at me, "wear your helmet."

"Of course." I take in a shuddering breath. "If I'd known we needed to fight them, I would have come battle-ready." It's an easy enough excuse, and Flavian doesn't argue. We reach the end of the mountain tunnel just as the sun spills over the edges of the cliffs, flooding the canyon with light. We can't land in the canyon; the cliffs stand too close together, the paths steep. But we can take off, fly our way out of the mountain valley. My men spread out, fanning pearly wings into the air, before bounding into flight.

"Is the sky still spinning?" Flavian flaps his wings. "I was ready to bet you were going to lose your stomach back there, but then I remembered you hadn't had breakfast."

I groan, gingerly touching my bruised head. "It's fine."

"Kind of wished you had eaten," he teases. "Imagine that story back at court." He's laughing as I send him a short glare. "My head hurts abominably. And you're plotting to ruin my reputation." I spread my wings. "What kind of friend are you?"

He doesn't answer as we take to the skies, him flying just to my left. I glance at him, the wind ruffling his white hair, "I suppose they've played that trick on every squadron's first time."

Frustration rises in his voice, "It's not right, Brendan. The least anyone could have done was warn us." I can't disagree. But I don't want to encourage his irritation. "It was a test, Flavian. And you almost stayed in bed, anyway." Flavian tips his wings, executing a swift barrel roll. He comes up right under me, snorting, "At least now we know who can't win a fight without me." I snort at his retort, catching my tongue with my teeth, my face pinching into a wince.

Flavian must take my silence as agreement because he lets out a casual laugh before swooping further away. "Brendan," Flavian calls back, his words catching in the wind, "You're a prig." He flaps his wings, diving. I watch his pale hair, his wings beating as he descends. He is practically racing me back to the Court.

I signal to the rest of my men, pulling the rest of the squadron into formation. I lower my head, descending. I'll be damned if Flavian beats me to the throne room. He won't waste a moment to brag about saving me from near decapitation. Not that the Finn would have done anything more than knock me out.

I leave the rest of the men at the barracks. Several of the men are bruised, and while my head still aches, I'm relieved the Finn didn't do much more than batter us. Flavian is waiting for me at the foot of the throne entrance. Still in uniform. I glance around, checking if the Prince is close by since Flavian has already carefully hidden his wings, hiding what Edric can never have.

"You take a nap?" I pull to a stop in front of my second, noting the way his hair is carefully combed.

"You look entirely too refreshed."

His mouth pulls into a grin as he brushes his hand along his polished leather jerkin. "I thought you were the one sleeping. Took you long enough."

HEARTS OF CLAY AND TEMPEST

"Just stopped by the barracks." I wince involuntarily; my tongue is beginning to throb.

"You're going to start slurring soon," Flavian comments, leaning forward. "He didn't clip you in the jaw. Yet your tongue is twice its normal size."

He grins at my slight scowl, lips quirking. "Who was it that said helmets were a bother? Oh, that's right," He mimics me, "All they do is dull your hearing and make you half blind."

"They still make you half-blind," I mutter back, holding up the bag of gold, "I'm never drawing the short straw again."

The coins clang together, and Flavian reaches for the bag, "You think it was worth it?"

I drop the bag into his hand, repeating his question, "Worth it?"

He sighs, "Worth fighting us. Why did they do it?" My head is starting to ache. This is strange because I didn't know it could hurt worse than when I practically collapsed back at the cave. I pass a hand over my thick hair, grimacing at the lump forming on my scalp, "If they wanted to antagonize us, then yes."

He snorts, before grinning at me, "They could have just asked me. I know faster ways to get under your skin."

"Sure, you do," I grumble, taking in a breath, "Next time, tell him not to hit me in the head." We step forward together, walking into a crowd of Fae. Flavian leans toward me, voice low. "Believe me; I have plenty of other ideas where he should have whacked you."

If my head weren't aching or my tongue throbbing, I might be able to come up with something witty.

But I'm still trying to think of a retort when a Fairy girl inches forward, balancing on her toes. Her brown ringlets dance across her plump breasts, and she grins widely at me, flapping her silvery gossamer wings.

Flavian clears his throat, and we share an amused glance. The girl tilts her head, mouth parting open.

I keep my eyes straightforward, though it's tempting to reach up and nudge her pile of curled hair. Just to see the elaborate wig fall to the marble floor. It makes no sense to me, the blatant attempt to grab my attention. If she were the only one, I might think she was simply daft. But lately, every girl at Court keeps stepping in my path.

Flavian likes to tease me, joking about the uniform. Draws a girl's attention, he says, the dark green cloak, the gold tassels on my shoulders, and the knee-length red boots. As if Flavian would know anything about what girls notice.

Not when he can't take his eyes off Edric every time the Prince steps into a room.

Besides, I should think my dress would do the opposite. The uniform carries so much, announcing my role in bold colors. Brendan, son of Riordan. A general's son, commander of the palace winged squadron.

Even if I enjoyed one of the flirting Fae girls, I have no choice when it comes to marriage. I'll marry someone worthy of my Father and my family. Worthy of a life devoted to the Court and our Queen.

Preening lips and batting eyelashes are the last things on my list. Not that I have a list. I'm a soldier. Not a suitor. We pause at the massive doors, waiting just long enough for the guards to swing them open. Someone announces my name, "Brendan, Son of Riordan, palace squadron commander. Accompanied by his second, Flavian, Son of the accursed." Flavian stopped flinching at that title a long time ago. But it still makes his teeth grind together. A constant reminder of his family, who he hasn't seen in years. As long as

Flavian serves at my side, and he can't visit his banished family. Flavian would be banished too, if not for being my second, though now his friendship with Edric keeps him tied to the Court.

It's fifty paces to the throne, and the room is lined with courtiers. Along with a half dozen or more soldiers, guards from other squadrons. A few grin mischievously, obviously guessing that the Finn tried to knock us around. The room isn't quiet. Chatter echoes around the arches, the balconies crowded with more onlookers. We walk through the center of the room, barely enough space to squeeze through the crowd, before coming to stand before the empty throne. I weigh the bag of gold in my hands, my head throbbing incessantly.

Queen Oona isn't sitting on the throne. But it's barely past sunrise. I wasn't expecting her. Flavian takes in a breath, and even over the murmur of noise, I can hear him. Prince Edric should be sitting on the marble throne, taking his mother's place for our morning meeting.

An official duty. One he barely started last year, part of his mother's plan for him to step into his place as Prince.

Flavian looks at me, his already pale face whitening. I don't need to ask him if Edric had other plans; Flavian would have mentioned that. We both know Edric needs to be here. He shakes his head, shifting from right to left. "He knew we were coming this morning."

Flavian must have told him last night, right after I issued our orders. I know he spent the night away from the barracks, holed up in Edric's room. He probably had to wake up a half-hour earlier than the rest of us to meet before we took off for the mission. As if reading my thoughts, Flavian whispers, "He couldn't sleep. He went for a walk but then told me to catch some sleep before the raid."

I look around me, keeping my voice low as I ask, "Did you remind him before you left this morning?"

His fingers twist together. "He was awake, and he knows he should be here." Not exactly an answer to my question. My mind runs through possibilities: Edric awake, taking walks in the middle of the night, Flavian rising an hour before dawn. The two both awake, sharing a kiss, a quick tumble. Edric falling back asleep, exhausted. Currently sleeping now.

Minutes pass. The murmuring is louder. Everyone knows the Prince is supposed to be here.

We planned on depositing the gold to Edric. As disgruntled as he was to wake up far too early, Flavian was almost giddy about a court appearance for Edric. Edric spends so much time hiding away, recoiling from the spotlight, Flavian was thrilled for this morning's audience. A safe way for Edric to remind the Court who he was. No duels or contests. Simply sit on the throne and receive the Finn's taxes.

"Brendan." I stiffen at my Father's voice. "You should return in the afternoon." His boots clink on the stone behind me, words low, speaking directly to me, "Staying here only heightens this fiasco."

I turn slowly. Not only is he my Father, but he's also my commander. "Sir," I dip my head forward, trying not to wince,

"As you command." I look up to see him cutting eyes at Flavian, lips twisting into a scowl, "He should have known the Prince wouldn't bother. Waking up at dawn," My Father looks back at me, "You pander too much to these boys." If my tongue weren't throbbing, I might spit an answer back. Remind my Father that the Prince isn't a boy, and we're not catering to him. It's Edric's right to receive the taxes. Still, it's my decision where to take the tax money. I could have taken it directly to the treasury, avoided a morning audience. My Father holds out his hand, another option to deal with the money. Though now it's not an option. I dump the bag of gold into his palm.

The room shifts, the crowd is gasping as my Father pockets the bag. I can almost hear the whispers; the

Prince must still be sleeping. I keep myself from grimacing at the harsh words, the quick condemnation of Edric. Flavian snarls at my Father, his face reddening. "Boys." My Father smirks. "I'm surprised the Finn didn't run you through." His voice is a touch lower, "Oh, I forgot, the Finn can't touch the Prince's darling."

My stomach tightens, "Father," I whisper, "Don't." Everyone can see how Edric looks at Flavian and how their hands stay grasped together whenever the Prince leaves his room. The Court can say whatever they want about Flavian, but I know he is more than Edric's heart. The Court only sees him tied to Edric's side; they've never seen his quick angry flashes in battle, the way he turns into an absolute beast of temper.

"He is our Prince," Flavian's voice is sharp with anger as he steps closer to my Father, "At least I give him the respect he deserves." I open my mouth to dismiss Flavian, sending him away from my Father. Before this argument can get any worse. But Flavian doesn't wait before shouldering past my Father. He shoves his way through the crowd; arms crossed across his chest. His cape swings back and forth, and I watch the green color fade. Storming away to Edric. I can almost picture him dragging Edric out of bed, scolding him for sleeping the morning away. He'll be angry for a day or so, but he cares for Edric too much to stay angry.

"You should have stopped him." My Father's voice is low, and I turn my attention back to him. "You can't mix love and politics. It'll disgrace the squadron."

We'll always disagree about Flavian and Edric. I won't have Flavian resign just because he's in love.

My Father wants me to denounce Flavian and his romantic notions. I don't. "The Prince's commands, Father. Flavian remains on my staff." His dark eyes meet my look, and he flashes his teeth. A moment, just long enough to express his displeasure, "That boy will destroy this court."

He turns his back to me, swallowing into the crowd. I'm not sure which boy he is referring to, Prince Edric or Flavian. Knowing him, he might be talking about both of them. Courtiers pounce on him; as a general, my Father is always a well of information. Courtiers are digging for information or asking for favors. I've been asked dozens of times for a place in the squadron or to mention a problem to my Father.

I don't doubt what he'll talk about now: another long rant about Edric. The Prince is a wastrel. Inept. A fool. He disgraced my son, abandoning him to wait at the throne. He'll hold up the gold, reminding them all why our family serves as the Queen's commanders. The respect owed us. My teeth ache. I need to get out of here. Check on my men. Eat some food. Take something to dull the constant aching, throbbing lump on my head. Courtiers press in around me, snagging at my cloak. I ignore my raw tongue, snarling a command to leave me alone. It takes a few minutes, maybe half an hour, but I finally thread my way to the throne room entrance. Another crowd awaits me here, gathered around the threshold. These people make me choke, sucking all the air out of a room. I suppose that's why I look over their heads, my eyes flickering to the massive stairs.

He's supposed to be in Edric's rooms, checking on the Prince. Instead, Flavian is tearing down the balcony. Running down the stairs, sunlight streaming through the windows behind him. His hair is white, falling around his face. I push the courtiers out of the way, shoving my way through the crowd. I reach the bottom of the stairs as Flavian comes to a gasping halt. He grabs my shoulders, panting, "He didn't come back last night."

His eyes are so wide; the white flecked with his blood vessels. His words pour in a rush, "They don't know where he is," Another yank of breath, "I don't know where he is."

"Flavian," I shake his shoulders, trying to keep my voice soft, "What are you talking about?"

"Edric," He grabs my arm, twisting my hand away from his shoulder, "Brendan, the prince is gone."

Gone? I stare at Flavian, repeating his words. Edric is probably in the gardens. His woodshop. Maybe even his mother's rooms. "He's disappeared," Flavian continues, looking about wildly, "Someone's taken him."

I yank back away from Flavian, "Of course, he's here." I stare at my second, "You've barely checked his rooms, Flavian. His highness does live his own life without your permission." But Flavian is still pale, even as I turn away. He is scowling at the watching crowd. Edric has simply lost track of time, carried away in his work. Not asleep as we all assumed. The crowd, however, is already whispering.

Flavian's words, *he's disappeared*, swirl outside the throne doors. Ridiculous. A Fae Prince simply can't disappear.

Chapter Two

Darcy

WE THROW THE ASHES into the sea next week. There's pitifully little; the sea swallowed Uncle Kian's body. Following tradition, we burn his bedding, his walking stick.

I shudder as the waves consume the ashes. Anya steps into the grey foam, touching the sea as if to say goodbye. I simply can't. I know if I ever step into the sea, it will eat me alive. The waters are a constant threat, a promise to drag me down to a watery grave just as the waves have taken Uncle Kian.

I'm still standing on the moss-covered rocks when Anya walks back to the house. The wind is shrieking again, but I
can't go back. I feel heavy, weighed down.

"You'll get sick out here, child." I turn at Isolt's voice. The oldest woman in our village, her skin wrinkled and yellowed.

"The wind isn't my enemy, Isolt," I force false cheer into my voice, "It's just the sea we have to fear."

"We've nothing to truly fear," Isolt replies, taking another step toward me. Isolt hobbles on her cane, "Death comes for everyone."

I nod at her words. Isolt is old. Old people talk about death. It's like they've forgotten that living is a good thing. I suppose when every step aches, and you've outlived even your own children, death is a friend. When life is still good, I shiver at the thought of dying.

"You're bothered, child," Isolt keeps talking. "We'll see that you and Anya are taken care of. We won't let you two starve. And you can still weave; I've seen your patterns. They're beautiful."

Not as beautiful or delicate as Anya's intricate weaving. But I smile wearily at her compliment; my cheeks are aching. Isolt loves talking. Some call Isolt a seer, but I think she simply collects stories. When you've lived long enough, you've probably heard enough stories and seen enough mistakes to guess people's futures. Uncle Kian would send Anya and me to Isolt's cottage often. Along with almost every other child in the village. We all grew up hearing Isolt's stories. Tales about Queen Oona, and the merfolk, and the Slaugh.

I take in a breath. If anyone were to know, it would be Isolt. "Do you ever hear the Banshee?" Isolt sucks in a breath, and my cheeks redden. "I'm sorry," I stumble over the words. "I didn't mean—"

"Nah, child." She turns to me, grabbing my shoulder. I wince. "Each of us hears the Banshee more than we care to.

You heard her?"

"No," the words tumble out before I can hold them back, and I feel my eyes watering again. "Anya heard, but I never did. It was just the wind." Isolt's fingers are still tight on my shoulder. "Perhaps you didn't listen well?"

Her question is accusatory. I pull away, my neck heating. "I loved Uncle Kian. I would have wanted the Banshee's warning." My throat burns, "I didn't just want it, I needed it." Then I step off the rock, my bare toes scrapping over the moss. Isolt hobbles after me, but I don't turn back. She doesn't know how hard I tried to listen, how I wanted to believe Anya.

"Child, Darcy," Isolt wheezes my name, and I pull up short. I turn back toward her, the wind playing with my skirt. Isolt lifts her head, chin wobbling. She speaks firmly, her voice more confident than I've heard her sound. "They say only the pure can hear the Banshee."

The pure, my eyes narrow at her words. I've heard the word most of my life, though Anya tried to keep it from me. But the rumors about my father always came back to me—the children who refused to sit next to me during Isolt's stories. She keeps talking, "Only a true Irish soul can hear her wailing. Not even the Saxons can. Only we Irish." "I'm Irish," I blurt the words, my cheeks hot.

She stares at me a moment before continuing. "I never knew your father. Maybe he was a Saxon lord." I feel as though she's stripping me naked in front of the entire village. No one ever talks about my father.

Not in front of me. And if Anya were here, she'd be furious. Tears bite at my eyes. It doesn't matter about him. He's a dead scoundrel. But he had to have been Irish. The Saxon lords don't wander into our seaside villages. We're miles and miles from an estate. I've only seen a Saxon once in my life, a proud, pale man prancing on a pony through our village. His blonde hair long enough to brush his shoulders, Anya and I laughed at his curls.

Like a wee girl's hair, Anya used to have golden curls, while my hair has always been orange. It is burnished red now.

Anya's hair is dark auburn, and I'm as Irish as Anya. As Isolt. As anyone in the village.

I turn away from Isolt. "Anya needs me," I start walking away, "Good day, Isolt."

I kick at the pebbles on our lane, bunching my hands across my chest. Isolt is just a crazy old woman.

I didn't hear the Banshee. Maybe I wasn't actually listening. Perhaps I didn't want to hear the Banshee.

↓

Quinn is leaving our cottage as I walk back in. I glance at Anya; she's standing stiffly by the fire.

Quinn nods at me, murmuring a sympathetic word.

I look at Anya, waiting till I hear Quinn's steps fade away. "What did he want?"

Anya lets out a sigh, she runs her hand through her thick auburn hair, "He suggested I marry."

Marriage. I knew, even if I hated the plan, that's what the village would insist on. At least marry Anya off. "You can't," I blurt the words, "There's not any man here worthy of you." "Killian's wife died," Anya starts, and my cheeks flush.

Killian. His name brings up a million different images. Wavy ginger hair, arms corded with muscles, his grin, and constant laughter.

I followed him for weeks, blushing whenever he looked my way. I tried to find a way to speak to him, laugh at his jokes. I was craving his easy company and kindness.

Until that day, I was standing on the edges of the sheep pastures, watching Killian and his friends sheering. A friend elbowed Killian with a glance at me. Killian's voice, a touch high, *And what should I care that she's mooning over me?* My cheeks reddened, and I turned slightly, averting my eyes. But their voices drifted to me, Words mixed with laughter. *She's not ugly, Killian.*

She's a bastard. That's ugly enough.

Of course, I should have known he thought that. But I didn't realize he would have cared. I've heard the whispered words my whole life. *Bastard.* Anya's cousin. *Without a father.* And her unmarried mother, dead when the girl was born.

My chest fell into my stomach; I couldn't laugh with Killian. He'd never smile at me, never walk me home. Never pick a garland of flowers, or dance with me at Samhain. I ran home, tears sliding down my cheeks. My girlish dream, a friend, someone I could admire, someone who wanted to talk to me. It was just a dream. Killian was handsome, funny but beyond me. I was nothing to him, worse than nothing.

Despised. You can't despise nothing.

I've ignored Killian for the last couple of years. Of course, he married a docile, sweet wife. I don't think I ever heard her say two words. But she laughed at Killian's jokes. Her thin, pale hair braided with flowers he picked. They danced at Samhain, her face pressed into Killian's broad shoulders.

Dead of a fever. Early this winter. Left Killian with a six-month-old babe. And the baby needs a mother. Of course, Quinn will tie Killian and Anya together.

She's worse than ugly, a bastard.

"You don't love Killian," I stalk over to her, forcing her to sit down. "I'll find a way out of this.

You're not ready to be a mother and wife all at once."

She looks up at me, her mouth opening. "But how? Our weaving won't last us through a winter."

I chew on my lip, pulling my hair back. "Tomorrow." I cross my arms, thinking aloud. "I'll walk to a

Saxon estate. Offer our services."

"Leave the village?" Anya whispers, "The sea?"

I hate the sea, but I can't say that to Anya. All the sea does it take, and take, and take. But Anya, like every fool here, loves the damned ocean. She longs to hear the waves crashing on the rocks, the wind shrieking on the sea. She loves dashing out into the spray on the first warm day of spring, splashing herself with the salty water.

But one look at the ocean, and I feel weighed down. The ocean is threatening to choke me, devour me whole. I twist my hands together. "An estate's safer than the sea, Anya. We won't have to lie awake at night, worried our men aren't returning."

It's the wrong word to say. Anya's lips quiver, she raises her voice, "I don't blame the sea, Darcy. And I won't have you doing it neither!"

"Fine," I talk to my pallet, falling to the hard ground, "But our future can't be here. Tomorrow, I'll walk to an estate. See about finding us work."

Anya doesn't reply. I wait for an answer, but all I hear is the shrieking wind. The waves are pounding against the rocks. I roll over, pressing my eyes closed. I have a long walk ahead tomorrow. I can't think about banshees or wind or Killian. Not tonight.

I must turn sometime in the night, the moon's light hitting the very edges of my pillow. I roll over, stiffening.

My cousin is gasping, wretched sobs muffled in her pillow. I slip my bed sheet off, clamoring over the cold dirt floor. She doesn't stir as I slip into bed beside her, "Anya," I whisper her name, drawing her close. Her skin is hot on my bare arms; she buries her face in my chest. Her shoulders are shaking. I rub soothing circles over her back, her hair sticking under my chin.

"He's gone." Her voice is muffled against my chest. "They're both gone."

"Shh." I bend my head, whispering into her ear, "Go back to sleep, Anya. It's alright."

Her fingers dig into my arm, a sob breaking from her lips, "Why." She's trembling, her voice coming in heaving sobs.

"Why do I have to lose both of them?" I hold her tight, my throat burning.

Compared to my sweet older cousin, my heart is light. She's lost both her childhood love and her father in less than two years. I brush the hair from her damp forehead. "I'm here, Anya. We're together."

"I still miss Silas," she whispers, a muffled sob of her lost love. "And now, father," her voice fades into a choking sound.

The sea has taken everything we love, my uncle. Anya's fiancé, her childhood love. I clasp my hands against her back, still trying to comfort her. She pulls back from my chest, lifting her head, eyes gazing up at me. Tears shimmer on her eyelashes, "We can't lose everything."

Her lips are trembling, "We won't, Anya." Our foreheads touch, her tears dripping unto my cheek, "I won't let the sea take anything else."

Anya's eyes flutter shut, she draws in a breath, gulping for air. Her shoulders are still shaking. I run my hand over her frizzy braid. "Go back to sleep." I kiss her hair. "Sleep, Anya."

My eyes close, weary with all the promises I've just made. Find us a new home—a new life. And finally, most frightening, keep the sea away, far away from everything I love.

Dawn stirs me from my dreams, and as I always do, I hold unto that last touch of drowsiness. I can't remember what I was dreaming of, and I snuggle deeper into my covers, my nose brushing Anya's arms. Her skin makes me jolt awake. I roll away from the sweltering heat of my cousin's sweaty body. Her face is still red, her skin hot. I pull my hair away from my neck, fidgeting with my loose braid. Anya's thick frizzy hair never leaves her careful plait. The hairs clump together, the frizzy ends sticking to her sweating face. My own finer hair tangles into a mess, a knot of twisted knots and clumped strands.

Usually, I'd try to be quiet, pulling at my hair, braiding back the curls. But I need to talk to my cousin. I yank my messy hair into a bun, hardly bothering to combat the tangles before I'm stabbing at the fire, the metal poker hitting the edge of the fireplace. Anya groans, rolling over. I stack the metal pots, clanging them together. She can't go back to sleep now. I won't leave without her promise. Anya finally sits up, yawning.

"You can't marry Killian while I'm gone." I speak quickly, "Don't let Quinn pressure you into saying yes."

She yawns, rubbing her crusty eyes, "Killian is dependable, Darcy. And I can be a mother."

"I didn't say anything against Killian," I go back to stirring the fire, "And sure, you could be a fine mother. But he won't be happy to have me in his house."

Anya stands up, brushing her skirt out, "If you're talking about gossip, you're foolish."

My cousin's tone is light, but my fingers still on the fire poker, "Killian and any other young man in this town won't have me," I turn to her, "His mother wouldn't let me even speak to his sister." I can't tell her about the insults, the jeering from Killian and his friends. Still, my lips are trembling. "There's a reason we have to take the cloth beyond our village to sell."

Anya's face is fallen, her shoulders slumping. "Darcy, I can't believe."

"People are cruel," I bite back at her, my teeth catching on my chapped lips. "Just last night, Isolt said my father was probably a Saxon."

"A Saxon," Anya breathes. "How could she?" Anya stamps her foot. "It's not true, Darcy." Her hands ball into fists, and she presses them to her eyes before releasing a sigh. "You can't believe her."

I never planned on believing her. Saxons are horrible enough, and I shudder at the thought of being related to the priggish landlords. But at least Anya is riled now. "I can't stay here," I press my cousin, pushing back a guilty twinge. She's still wary with grief, but this is too important to leave alone. "No one's going to marry me, and most of the village despises me. I have to move to a Saxon estate for work." Tears slide down my cousin's cheek, and I reach for her arm. Our hands catch, my voice softening. "I don't want us to be separated."

"Of course not." Anya squeezes my hand. "I just hate to leave our home," She sniffs, tears hovering in her voice, "Our friends."

The whole village claims to be Anya's friend, any fool who smiles at her is instantly a friend. The smiles never come my way. Hanging on Anya's skirts, sitting beside her, listening to her friend's chatter. "We'll make new friends." I pick up a piece of corn cake, biting off the edge. "Just wait till I come back from the estate."

On the estates, no one will know that my father is missing. No one will care who my parents are. I'm grateful for the distance from our village, the miles from rumors and gossip.

Though with that distance, the walk there can take a full day. I will probably spend the night on the

Saxon's lord's land, sleeping in a barn full of hay, before coming home tomorrow. Anya seems to realize

I'm leaving. Anya lets out a sigh, rubbing at her eyes. "You won't be gone more than two days.

We'll decide what to do then."

I roll my shoulders, swallowing the rest of the wheat cake. I'm sure I can find a job on the estates. Uncle Kian sold my cloth to the landowners; if anything, I can work for a weaver. I give Anya a warm hug and then set out. Most of the village is still asleep. The animals are just now waking up, chickens clucking. A goat whines as I pass, sheep skittering awake.

I have two options, walk along the road, or climb the cliffs. The road cuts between massive cliffs, rocks jutting out on each side. I detest how it hems you in, so I opt to skirt the cliff face, jogging up through grass and piles of rocks. I look out over the sea; the sun is rising in full force now. Gold sparkles on the waves, glinting. I blink away, looking down the rocky cliff unto the road.

I pause, my eyes narrowing. A golden cloak catches my attention. I'm hunched over the side of the cliff, looking down as close as I can without falling off the rocks.

Massive red curls, horns are jutting over the hair, large bare feet, bark growing between his toes. And his gold cloak. An actual leprechaun. I blink, sure my eyes are playing tricks on me. But the magical creature is still there. I feel like if I breathe, he'll hear me and disappear.

I've never seen one of the fabled little folk before, but I am certain this creature is one of the gold-bearing men. I squeeze my eyes, biting on my teeth. Then I blink them open again.

The creature is still there. I'm not seeing things. I pinch my toes into the soft earth, blessing the soil for my luck. All I need is to do is catch this leprechaun. I can almost taste our fortune stretched out in front of me, a glimmering idea of happiness—gold enough for a warm cottage, perhaps even a boarded floor instead of dirt. Work on an estate, gold to keep us fed and warm. Gold enough to move from the ocean. Into one of the larger towns growing inland, away from the sea. The thought is enough to drive me into action. I whip up my skirts, tying into a knot above my knees. Then I dart back up the cliff, scanning for the creature. The leprechaun is still there, his golden cloak glinting in the dawn. I inch along the ridge facing, now nearly directly overhead. The leprechaun is ambling, lumbering. He doesn't look up, and I take in a breath. I wiggle my toes, take another breath, and then jump.

For a moment, I'm hanging in the air and falling, falling. And then I ram, landing on top of the leprechaun. Screeching, he's screaming at me. My legs tangle in his arms, my hips bruising. The leprechaun tries to shake me off, but I lean on him with all my body weight. He's scrambling, clawing at me. He pushes me away; his weight is heavier than mine. I can't let him go, not this easily. More shrieking as I grab his legs, yanking him back down to the hard earth. He fights me, and I fall forward, holding his neck. My nails dig into his leathery skin. He claws at me, but I spit back at him, "I've caught you," the words come out in a gasp, "And I won't let you go, not without gold."

He stills underneath me, and I wait for his reply. When he doesn't answer, I shake his shoulder, "Did you hear me?"

"I'm not deaf." His voice is deep, gravely. "And I'm not rude, either."

"Then you'll give me gold?"

He glares at me, his face bunching into a fierce scowl. "How can you even see me?"

It's my turn to stare, the strange question throwing me off guard. "What do you mean?"

"Human,' The leprechaun's words drip in distaste, "Humans only see my magic when rainbows brighten your senses."

That doesn't matter now. I don't bother looking for a rainbow; he's just trying to distract me so he can escape. "I want my gold. And then I'll let you go."

"You haven't caught me." His voice is distractingly deep.

"Course I have," I stumble for words, "I've got your neck in my hands."

"And I'll disappear any second, you git."

His words shake me; of course, he can disappear. I'm human, and he's a magical creature. My shoulders slump, my throat catching, "Please, I need your help."

He shoves me off him, flicking at his clothes. "You can't simply catch me," he sneers, "Only riddles can tame magic."

A riddle. Of course, I lick my lips. "If I give you a riddle, you'll give me gold?"

The leprechaun looks at me, blinking slowly. His eyes are so green; they're like sunlight dancing in the grass. I can't help staring. His lips draw together in a fierce frown. "I've got no gold for you. The Fae Queen hoards the gold."

His words hit me, the mention of the fabled Queen. I gasp, trying to remember the stories I've been told. "You serve a Queen?"

"Queen Oona." The leprechaun brushes a hand over his cloak. "If you want gold, you have to go see her."

"Then take me to her," I'm so close, so close to securing our future. I'm not going to throw it away because of a miserly leprechaun.

"A riddle," he says, "and I'll take you to the Queen." He raises his chin, and I lean back on my heels, knees digging into the dirt.

He speaks again, slowly as though I were a child, "A riddle I can't answer, and I'll take you to the Queen."

I nod. He raises his hand, and I take it. His skin is rough on mine, leathery, thick. He grips my fingers, his hold so tight, my fingers ache. He speaks, voice low, measured, "For an unanswered riddle, I promise you safe passage to the court of my Queen, Her Majesty Queen Oona of the Fae."

The leprechaun tightens his hold on my hand, and the air around us grows tight. I feel my heart catch, and I can taste something sweet yet cold. Then the leprechaun releases my hand, and I'm trembling. I flex my fingers, green stains on my palm. I look up at the creature, and he's waiting. A riddle. This magical creature wants a riddle from me. What kind of question has he never heard? All the stories my people tell, he would know them. He probably even knows who wrote them.

This riddle has to be about me. My story. This creature doesn't know me. I lick my lips, the sweet taste of magic still clings to my tongue, "This controls my life, yet terrifies me."

The leprechaun stares at me, then he grins, teeth flashing. "That's an easy one." I blink, my stomach falling. "A day with you, watching you, I'll know the answer."

"A day," I stupidly repeat his words. The leprechaun grabs my hand, dragging me to my feet. He begins to march, and I follow, "What do you mean?"

"I might not know the answer now." The leprechaun glares at me, snarling, "So we begin our journey.

But when I know the answer, our agreement is done."

I fumble for his meaning. "You aren't guessing?"

He snorts, "Safe passage for an unanswered riddle. When I answer your riddle, you're on your own." He's Fae. I should know this. Leprechauns are lesser fairies. Tricksters. He can do anything with words except actually lie.

He turns suddenly, grabbing my hands. I stand limply. "What are you doing?"

"Passage," he mutters, holding just one of my hands now. Then he snaps his fingers and the world shifts. One moment I'm on the familiar lane, surrounded by green cliffs, the ocean only feet away. The next, I'm in deep darkness. The darkness presses down around me, and my breath knocked from my stomach in a gasp.

I fall to my knees, my legs hitting stone. The cold reverberates through my bones, and I jump back from the leprechaun's touch.

He's still here; that's consoling. He's standing just in front of me, his teeth white against a veil of darkness.

It's the only thing I can see, his white teeth.

I look around, blinking. But the darkness is so complete, and even my chest feels heavy with the inky blackness.

I whisper my question, "Where are we?"

The leprechaun snorts again, the sound making my skin crawl. I can't stand his sneering, and I barely know him. "The borders of the Fae Court, human."

He brushes my shoulder, and I stumble to my feet, trying to keep up with him. I can hardly see, much less make out his steps.

At least the path isn't rocky; smooth stone press into my feet. I skitter my toes across them, feeling the cold stone.

Laid out brick by brick, we must be on some sort of road.

I take another step, yelping as I run into my guide. He growls at me, pushing me back. "I couldn't see," I protest, my voice loud, echoing in the dark. "I don't have your stupid fairy eyes."

"Shut up, human," the leprechaun snaps at me, poking me in the stomach. I grit my teeth together, my skin flushing. He's rude, just as all the Fae are in the countless stories Isolt regaled us with. We used to laugh at her tales of the arrogant, pompous Fae. I silently promise to thank Isolt when I see her again. At least she warned us the Fae were terrible jerks.

"Hoyt," A voice booms, and I jump again. "What have you brought back?" Light floods the darkness, and I blink, my eyes watering.

"A human girl," my guide, Hoyt, is talking. I look past him, looking over another leprechaun. He's also wearing a gold cloak, but he carries a lantern. I instantly like him better.

"Has she news of our Prince?"

"She has nothing," but I don't hear the rest of Hoyt's reply. My mind puzzles over the question, wondering if the two are chatting about a leprechaun prince. Or the Fae prince from Isolt's stories.

"We don't have time for her," the leader is talking. "Answer her riddle and be done with her."

"I can't, Shane," Hoyt replies, and his answer is so miserable, I feel a stab of pity. I'm forcing him to drag me around, and the thought makes me shift uncomfortably. But this is for Anya and our future.

The leprechaun steps closer, raising his lantern. His eyes flick over me. "Was there a rainbow?"

Hoyt shakes his head. "I've no idea how she saw me."

The lantern rattles, and I look away from the leprechaun's fierce stare. He reaches for my arm, pinching me so quickly, I don't have time to jump back.

I yelp, trying to pull away. The leprechaun laughs, "Human. Her skin's soft as a newborn."

I rub at my arm. It's going to bruise now. I glance up at him, holding back my thoughts. His skin, even in the darkness, I can see the rough edges. Thick as bark. You can't pinch a leprechaun. It would likely hurt your fingers much more than his skin.

My lips ache to scold him for touching me, but I can't afford to offend him. I've no idea where I am. I can't make an enemy, not now.

He swivels the lantern away from my face, "Well, take her to the colony tonight. And the Queen in the morning. The Queen will know what she truly is. I'll send word to the court."

Hoyt grabs me by the elbow, yanking me past the other leprechaun. I stare at the lantern, wishing he would give it to us, dreading the idea of stepping back into the darkness.

Then Hoyt pauses, and I hear the scraping sound of metal hitting metal. Creaking, and he pushes a door open. I stoop, lowering myself to follow him through the doorway.

The darkness vanishes, my eyes squinting at the bright light. My mouth falls open, my hands trembling. Green plants, soft pink skies, and sunlight. I raise my hand, shading my eyes from the brilliance. The ground beneath my feet is so soft, and it's like walking across a row of sheep. Not that a flock of sheep has ever let me dance across their backs.

As the grass tickles my feet, I imagine this would be the feeling.

Hoyt yanks insistently on my elbow, his fingers pinching at my skin. "Well, come along. We don't have all day." "What is this place?" The question falls on the still air as I turn in a circle. I can't help staring word choice: consider something else everywhere. I crane my neck, trying to look at everything. The endless sky stretches as far as I can see. Flowers dot the hills, fading into everlasting hills. Even what I can't see sounds beautiful. Water must be flowing nearby. The sound is musical, almost like tinkling bells.

Along the road, I reach up, my hands brushing fat berries hanging over my head. Hoyt doesn't seem to object, and soon my fingers are sticky. I'm used to the berry patches in the hills, blooming alive in spring with dark blue, tart tiny berries. These berries are rounder, softer, and fall off the vines easily.

I lick my finger, and it's so sweet, sweeter than the tart summertime berries. I glance back up at the green leaves, the clusters of blue, shimmering with a dusting of silver. Fae fruit, I nearly jump. I cough, my eyes watering. The fruit is enchanted far too sweet; I've heard of the dangers of eating Fairie fruit. But I'd never imagined the sweetness of the clinging flavor. It coats my tongue even as a swallow, the sweetness sticking in my mouth. Even as I spit the taste away, my hands itch to reach back up and shake the branches. A slight tremor would shower me with the sweet berries.

My stomach growls, but I won't risk enchantment. I've heard what happens, how humans have gorged on Fae fruit, then were overwhelmed by the sweet magic. Fae fruit can drive you to distraction, and you'll end up forgetting your own name. Goosebumps rise on my skin and I shiver involuntarily.

Forgetting who I am, why I'm here. Losing my mind, the stories make my skin crawl. I can't lose myself to Fae enchantments.

I'm thirsty now, my lips sticky, and my mouth dry—the fruit blooms around me, a constant temptation. We walk in between the brambles, Hoyt batting back thorns, berries falling to the ground beside us. I bite my lips, tucking my hands together. Enchanted sweetness tickles my senses, and my breath catches as another cluster of berries gets knocked to the ground.

"Safe passage includes not eating the fruit," Hoyt snaps back at me. I look away from the fruit, refusing to think about how thirsty I am.

"Where are we," I stumble after Hoyt. It's hard to tear my eyes away from the verdant beauty. The berry patches grow in between taller trees. I gape at the white blossoms, the branches swaying in the light breeze. And even the strange colored birds, purple and blue feathers in-between the tree branches.

Another childhood story, birds who can peck out your eyes and whisper your secrets to your enemies.

Deceitful beauty, everything here is tinged with danger.

"This is the land of Fae," Hoyt finally answers. I know that answer, but he doesn't provide more details. What court we've entered, whether I bargained with Fae trickers who tolerate humans or Fae who trick and hate humans. I wrack my brain, trying to remember everything I've heard from Isolt. The Queen Holt mentions, she rules over a Faire Court. And the Fae lands are divided between two courts, the Seelie and the Unseelie. One of those groups hates humans and would sooner eat my heart than hand over a gold pot. I don't even realize I'm chewing on my nails, thinking through everything I've ever heard. In one of the stories, I'm pretty sure it's the Unseelie. They hate humans and sometimes capture people as slaves. Goosebumps hit my neck, and I shiver at my thoughts. *Please*, my eyes are burning, and I gulp in the warm air., *Let the Queen be one of the nice Fae. Just please give me my pot of gold.*

A day for the pot of gold. Hoyt said he'd know my riddle's answer by the end of the day. Then he's either give me gold or send me home.

I can avoid the too sweet berries, the deadly beautiful birds, and cruel Fae for a few more hours.

Enough time to keep my riddle and claim my gold.

Hoyt's steps are lighter. His fingers twitch, and before we go too much farther, he is snapping his thumbs.

Add to his snapping, music comes. Not the twinkling silver sound of the running water. But fiddles, drums. Pipes. At first, it's a faint noise.

As we walk further, the sound is more precise, louder. I can't help but grinning, and the music is just like I'd thought it would be. Lighthearted. Cheerful. Magical.

I expect we'll run into a dancing set of leprechauns any minute. After all, ever since I can remember, that's what I've heard leprechauns do. Dance until their toes fall off.

The road is growing steeper, and I clamber after Hoyt. If possible, he's walking even faster now. How is it even possible for such a short man to move so quickly?

We pass a bough of trees, and Hoyt stops. I come to stand beside him, gaping.

A cluster of stone cottages, a stone fence. And smoke curling behind the roofs. The smell, well, it's irresistible.

Sausage, and cabbage, I can almost taste the incredible meal.

But I'm not staring at the cottages. Instead, I'm entirely caught watching the musician. The music is so rich, so full, and I could have sworn there must be multiple instruments.

But it's not. The music comes from just one leprechaun, with a violin on his shoulder, a flute in his mouth. His feet tap as he dances round and round. He is playing faster and faster.

He pulls his bow back, and the flute is clear, high, and sweet. I close my eyes, swaying at this melody.

It's as I imagine angels sing.

Then the music stops. Abruptly, in the middle of the tune.

I open my eyes, blinking at the small musician. He tucked the violin under his arm, his flute between his fingers. He's staring at me now.

"Had to bring her back," Hoyt is talking, explaining. "Taking her to the court tomorrow."

"We've never had humans here," the leprechaun's voice is soft, delicate compared to Hoyt's roughness.

"First time for everything," but I don't hear Hoyt. I'm staring, caught up by the leprechaun's face.

He's smiling, his smile genuine, almost kind.

"His name's Galen," Hoyt barks up at me, and I look down at my guide. "One of our best musicians." "But he looks so young," I gasp the words, unthinking. His red beard is hardly more than stubble, his curly hair hiding his short horns.

And his skin, it's barely wrinkled, still nearly smooth. Almost white, while Hoyt's skin is dark and leathered. This leprechaun, I look at Hoyt, my words even in the air.

As usual, Hoyt is a grouch. His thick eyebrows are drawn together, his teeth bared, "At least the Fae Queen can teach you to hold your tongue."

He stalks off, and I look down at the young leprechaun, "I'm sorry." I run a hand through my greasy hair. "I intended no insult."

His green eyes shimmer. "Humans." Even the way he sneers, it's kinder than Hoyt. "You can't teach them much about politeness."

I could have guessed he'd also insult me. But I am still curious. Why is he so young? The leprechauns are ancient Fae; they've no wives or children. They should all be the same age; I look at his feet. Roots are just beginning to grow along with his toes, but his feet almost look human at first glance.

My eyes stray back to his violin. He cradles it, green-tinged fingers stretching across the strings,

"Suppose you'll be wanting dinner." He jerks his chin. "Follow me."

My stomach growls, but my fingers clench—Fae food. Only salt can protect a mortal from enchantments. Spells are woven into the food. If the leprechauns offer me food without salt, I should turn it away.

"You know." Galen pauses at the threshold of the cottage. "I've never met one of you."

I meet his intense gaze. "Well, you're only the third leprechaun I've met. I haven't figured out what

I'm supposed to be thinking about you."

He snorts, the casual way he speaks masking the edge to his words, "You're still here. You haven't run away yet. It looks like you're not thinking about us at all."

Chapter Three

Brendan

MY DREAMS ARE VIVID, an endless cycle of the Finn's sneering face. I'm lunging for the bag of tax money—the floor cold against my hands. Only when I raise my hands, blood coats my palms. My eyes sting with my own sweat, and I have to bite my lips to keep from throwing up. I've failed. The gold is gone. I'm dying, the Finn's spear piercing through my stomach. The blood pools around me, and all I can hear is my Father's voice, sighing in disappointment at my failure. I try to breathe, but I'm choking on my own blood.

The door slams open, and I jerk awake, blinking at the harsh light spilling across my small room. My sheets are all tangled, damp with my sweat. I raise my hands; my palms are white, a stark contrast to the bloody vision I'd just dreamed. I'm still breathing heavily as I try to clear my thoughts. The endless nightmares that plague my sleep can't last forever. I force myself only to let my mind dwell on one thought; we will find Edric.

I roll over, grunting. My eyes inch open, taking in the figure standing in my door. His heavy breathing, hands twisting together. Dusty light flickers around his blonde hair.

"Flavian," I mumble my second's name, rubbing my crusty eyelids. "This better be important." He might have woken me from another horrifying nightmare, but it was the first chance I've had to sleep in three days.

"It is," I grimace as Flavian stomps across my small room, boots loud on my wooden floor. "The leprechauns have a human."

"A human," I sit up too quickly, my vision blacking. The room is spotty, and I shake my head, "Which leprechaun clan?"

"Hoyt and his men, the eastern clan," Flavian replies quickly. "Shane came to Court this morning, told the Queen that Hoyt brought her in from the border. She must have something to do with Edric."

"A woman." I push out of bed, shoving the blankets out of my way, reaching for my boots. "Did they say why she is here?"

"Hardly a woman according to the message," Flavian growls, "A girl. Caught Hoyt close to the western coast." I've only met the leprechaun envoy once, and he didn't speak to me then. Most leprechauns avoid Fae guards like myself and Flavian and only visit the Court during yearly fealty vow ceremonies. The leprechauns live spread out around the kingdom and are among the few Fae that enjoys visiting the human world. I think they probably blend in better than most Fae, with their short legs and scruffy beards. It's easier to hide stubby horns in a leprechaun's messy hair than to hide my wings or pointed ears. Besides, the fact that Fae, like Flavian and me, stands taller than most humans. Even then, most leprechauns won't travel without magical protections, and humans can't see them unless there's a rainbow. Rainbows distort magic, breaking the cloud a spell casts over a Fae traveling in human lands. I ask Flavian if the leprechauns mentioned a rainbow. Most of the time, they'll mention how a human caught them. Flavian shrugs, "The message didn't say." Sleep still clings to my head, my thoughts slow as I mull over Flavian's words. I reach for my bucket of water, picking up the wooden pail. I tip it up, splashing water on my face. The leprechaun Flavian mentioned, Hoyt, lives closer to the ocean. Rainbows are common enough beside the water; maybe he thinks mentioning the rainbow is too obvious. There's no other way for a human girl to see Fae like the leprechauns.

"I think we should go get her," Flavian speaks all at once, his words rushed together. "She must know something, might know where Edric is. We can't waste another moment."

"It's a human." I shake my head, water dripping on my shoulders. A towel hangs on my wall; I reach for it, patting my skin dry. "Probably just a coincidence, a mortal wouldn't know anything about our Prince or Court."

"The gods curse coincidence," Flavian snorts. "I don't believe that for a second." Flavian's pale cheeks are tinged red, his green eyes sparkling. The flush of color doesn't hide the deep shadows forming, and he hasn't slept for the past week. Restless without Edric, sick with his fear. Even if he could sleep, I'm sure his nightmares would be worse than mine. I lay a hand on his shoulder, and his leather armor is cool on my skin. "If you truly hope to help Edric, you need to rest. I'm awake now, and you need to sleep."

"But the leprechauns," he starts, all ready to argue. I don't let him continue. "I can deal with them on my own. If the Queen sends us to fetch the human, you are to stay here. And rest."

Flavian yanks back from my touch, sputtering. His hands shake and his words an incoherent protest.

Without sleep, Flavian is emotionally wasted. Combined with his fear for Edric, his distrust of the mortal, I can't allow him near her. Not before he's rested and eaten and thinking more clearly. I speak again, "That's an order, Flavian. You need the rest; I can't afford to have you completely drained right now. I need you to be ready."

His skin is translucent, and I glance at his thin hands, the knuckles swollen before I ask another question, "And when was the last time you ate?"

He tucks his arms together, looking down at the wooden floor. "How can I," he says, his voice is thin, etched with pain. "How can I eat, not knowing if Edric even breathes?" Flavian speaks brokenly, shoulders hunching. He doesn't look at me, and in-between his soft syllables, I can hear my men shuffling outside the doors.

"You will be of no use to Edric wasted with worry," I speak firmly, ordering him to eat some porridge. I'm not sure if he needs sleep or food more, but I think a gust of wind could knock him over right now. Flavian glances up, his face bleak. His skin is stretched taut over his cheekbones, his lips pale.

I incline my head towards my bed, reaching to grab my cloak from the hook by my door. "Sleep, Flavian. Eat something. I will be back."

He doesn't say a word as I step out of my door, closing it behind me. A Queen's messenger, golden shamrocks tattooed to his cheeks. He holds out a slip of paper, inclining his head. The paper is etched with shamrocks, the emblem of the Queen's household. I cut it open, scanning a dozen words. Nothing else. Just a summons. No details about leprechauns or a human mortal. The short message might not say anything, but my men have already heard.

They've gathered outside my doorway, watching as I read the brief summons from the Queen.

"Are we fetching the mortal?" one of the questions. "Do you think this has something to do with our Prince?" I've barely heard about the mortal, and they're already asking about her. I'm always impressed by how quickly news spreads, especially at Court. I glance at my men, feeling their weariness.

We've been on constant patrol the last sixteen days—snatches of sleep, days without time for food.

"I don't know anything." Their feet shuffle at my words, released sharp breaths. Disappointment hangs in the air, and I clear my throat. "I've been summoned to the Queen. Be ready for patrol."

They glance at one another, and I feel their ripple of unease. A mortal appears while Prince Edric has been missing for the last two weeks. All of my men are still in armor, and I doubt any of them have slept more than I have, just an hour this afternoon. "Be sure and eat." I tap one of them on the shoulder as I walk past them. "Find some food, and I'll be back soon." The men disperse, heading to the kitchens. A few glance back at me, their eyes dark with exhaustion.

I've tried telling my Father that this is too much for my platoon.

We may be the Queen's guardsmen, but we're not invincible. I need sleep. My men need rest.

My Father won't hear of it, of course. As long as the Prince is missing, we must be searching. Or at least, appear to be looking. As it is, we've no idea where Edric might have gone. I've spent the last two weeks organizing search parties, hunting for hours each day.

At least we're doing something. Even if my gut tells me our actions are entirely useless. This isn't hunting Goblins, waiting for the right moment to strike. There are no clues, no enemies to shake down for information. As Flavian said, the Prince has simply vanished.

The Queen remains shut in her rooms. I've not seen her once in the past two weeks. I crumple the paper in my fingers. At least I have an audience with her Majesty. I'll be able to see her face, gather what she's thinking. Soldiers have been coming and going to the Queen's rooms every day, so my presence doesn't attract that much attention.

The guards open the Queen's doors, beckoning me through the hallway.

A few soldiers are leaving the Queen's room, and one salutes me. I return his salute, nodding at the others. The Queen's doors are open, and I step over the threshold. The Queen stands at a table, head bent over a map. I wasn't expecting my Father. He nearly towers over the Queen, looking over her stopped shoulder.

He looks up at me as I step into the room, snapping fingers, "Brendan," his eyes flash, "I'm sure you've heard about the mortal and the leprechauns."

"Aye, sir," I nod, looking toward the Queen. She hasn't raised her head, leaving her hands flat on the mahogany surface of the table.

"I'm going to meet the leprechauns," My Father continues, drawing my attention back. "You will stand by the Queen until my return. Follow her commands."

My thoughts flicker with questions, and I can't help wondering why the Queen isn't issuing orders.

Despite my questions, I keep my gaze on my Father, meeting his icy eyes, "Aye, sir." I answer quickly, "As you wish."

He snaps his boots together, speaking to the Queen, "I will gather my wing battalion. We'll fly to the Terebinth forest."

The leprechauns cannot cross into the sacred boundaries of the Court, not with their mixed blood of

Fae and angels. They will bring the mortal as far as the forest floor, the ancient meeting place between the Queen and her subjects. The forest is frightening enough; I hide a grimace. I hated the dark wood as a child, and I knew that my mother's spells and my magic probably kept me safe. Even then, whenever we traveled through the forest, I would read a book and try to avoid the darkness outside our carriage.

I've rarely even gone through the Terebinth Forest after I moved to Court, only visiting when we're required to meet the Leprechauns once a year or so. The mortal will hardly be prepared for the trees, the black witch wood, the spirits who choose to speak to travelers.

The human will already be terrified, and even more when my Father arrives with his troops.

My Father's wing battalions are clawed beasts, creatures he has personally spent centuries training. Some would argue they aren't Fae, but my Father ignores those arguments. It does not matter to him that his personal winged forces cannot speak. I learned as a child that my Father's winged creatures are his most treasured possession. They obey. They fly. They can capture enemies in their claws. And unlike his son, the winged beasts don't disagree or fail at following commands. My Father salutes the Queen before leaving the room. He barely looks at me, hardly needing to remind me of his orders. I look to the Queen. Her golden hair tumbles past her waist, curls escaping from her braids. I've never seen tangles in the Queen's hair like the knots I see today.

"Brendan." She looks up, her lips pale. "The leprechauns are threatened."

"Your majesty?" Her words take me by surprise "The leprechauns?"

"Each other." She stands up from the table, holding out her palm. "Your Father sent Shane away before you walked in. He came to tell me of the human."

I must look startled because the Queen just said a leprechaun was in this room. I feel like my words are stupid; the

Queen just said he was here. Still, I blurt out what Flavian told me, "I thought he sent a message."

The queen shrugs. "It is best if the Court doesn't know who I can allow within my walls. The prejudice against the leprechauns." She levels her gaze at me, and I feel my palms sweating. My Father is often vocal about his disapproval of the hybrid creatures. The leprechauns, not entirely Fae. In his words, a blight on the country. Unlike his winged beasts, the leprechauns have their own minds, follow their own orders. Mixed Fae who can disobey and make their own way in our world apparently offends his idea of an ordered society.

"Of course, majesty." I swallow, trying to think of something to say. "The leprechaun was here?"

She taps her long nails on the table. "Shane is concerned. Hoyt picked up the girl. All the clans are searching for Edric." She takes in a breath. "The timing is noticeable. The human arriving at the same time Edric leaves." "The mortal threatens our lands?"

The Queen almost smiles, her pale lips twitching. "What would your father say, hmm." She meets my eyes, "We are not afraid of mere mortals."

I've heard my Father say that same phrase before. I incline my head. "I'm certain the mortal is quite terrified of our lands." My Queen raises her eyebrow, raising her hand to brush thick ringlets of hair back from her face, "You are most certainly right, Brendan." She sighs, her words almost mournful. "The poor mortal is quite unprepared for our court."

Nothing can truly prepare anyone for Court; even after years of visiting, the Court still manages to chill my blood. I've seen Fae pull out each other's horns over dinner, scratch each other bloody, and banish their own family from the palace.

"You know your Father, Brendan, son of Riordan." The Queen turns her gaze on me, and I shiver involuntarily. With her bright eyes, piercing gaze, I sometimes wonder if the Queen can read my thoughts as I double-check my own protections. The mental guards my mother always reminded me to keep around my thoughts. I blink quickly, visualizing my mind, gritting my teeth together. Repeating the protection spells that I keep wound around my heart. "I cannot send your father to the leprechauns lands," The Queen speaks softly. "He revels in war, as my commander should."

I don't argue with the Queen's opinion of my Father. She might have placed him in command, but he is bloodthirsty.

My whole life, I've heard him conjuring up possible battle plans, envisioning future wars.

"You are not your father, fortunately for me, Unfortunately for him." Her words pull me away from thinking about my Father's plans for war.

I dare not raise my eyes to the Queen's gaze. A breath passes before she speaks, "The leprechauns will be at odds over this human. Fighting to claim her, have the honor of presenting her to the Court.

Gather your men. If fighting breaks out, ensure my kingdom's peace." The Queen pressed her glowing palms together. "Go to the leprechauns' village, disperse any fighting. Punish those who disturb my kingdom's peace."

"Majesty," I fall to one knee, rising quickly. "As you command."

My men suit up quickly, buckling their swords into place. Flavian stumbles from my room, brushing his blonde bangs back from his face. Shadows still line his eyes.

"You're supposed to be asleep." I yank on the belt around my shoulders. "Under orders."

Flavian grins. "It was enough." He touches the straps on his shoulders, the sword hilt right next to his face. "I need something to do."

"Sleep is something to do." I can't help snapping back at him, "Watching over a pack of leprechauns is hardly an adrenaline rush."

"No nightmares involved." Flavian rolls his shoulders, his tone deceptively light, "I'll be at the landing." I watch my second stalk off, his sword glinting in the evening sunlight. If he had a nightmare, he didn't take a draught. He's too strung out to sleep without help. When we return from the leprechauns, I'll see that he sleeps for at least an entire night.

My men gather at the landing outside the palace, standing in formation. Their faces are grim, shoulders tight. Despite the edge of exhaustion, their eyes are bright. We're doing something tonight.

The shadow of the Queen's Fortress stands behind us as I turn to address my men, "We're to maintain peace." I repeat the Queen's orders, "My Father is meeting the mortal. We're to ensure that the leprechauns obey the terms of the treaty between the clans."

My wings flare behind me. "There's no need to let the leprechauns know our presence. We'll remain shadowed around the leprechaun village unless conflict demands our interference."

Heads nod, their wings following my lead, unfolding. The last rays of the sun glimmer across the feathery tips, feathers are shimmering in the fading light. I turn away from the sunshine, raising my hand to signal. My lips utter the prayer, the words my mother taught me before my first flight into battle.

"Guardian of hearts, be with my men. May our words carry your glory."

My feet step forward, I leap off the landing. Wind rushes at my skin, whipping through my hair. My feathers catch the breeze, and I'm soaring. Flavian pulls to my right, his blonde hair bright in the evening darkness. His wings shimmer, the feather's fighting the glamour he keeps them under. Though without Edric around to watch us soar, I'm surprised my second still insists on hiding his wings. Loyalty is a fickle master. It either controls you, or you master your own heart.

My Father's words flash through my thoughts, our oft-repeated family motto. "Loyalty to the deserving." He would sneer at Flavian's loyalty to Prince Edric. Call it misguided, emotional, undeserving.

As though my Father would genuinely know anything of deserving loyalty. Cavorting with any woman who catches his fancy, exiling my mother to our estates in the Far North. I haven't seen her since before Edric swore to become my Second. Cold air bites at my lungs, I rein in my thoughts. My fingers are tight, I unroll my knuckles, forcing my thoughts away from my Father. Away from his constant sniping about Flavian and Edric.

We skirt the edges of the Terebinth Forest. My skin crawls even at the heady, magical smell of the forest.

Dead, but still alive creatures. As a child, my mother told me stories of the tree's spirits. The nightmares they can spin in your minds. She never called them wraiths, but I imagine that's what the creatures truly are. Whatever you might call them, I'm secretly relieved my Father meets the leprechauns in the forest. Even if the leprechauns brawl, I'd rather be breaking up fights than treading the eternally dark forest.

Once we pass the forest, the mountains dip into gentle hills. Evergreen, fruit-filled valleys. Streams filled with gold nuggets, leprechaun mills, and cabbage fields. Light flickers on the horizon. The Eastern clan's village. Where Hoyt is keeping the mortal for tonight.

I signal my men, a motion of light in the night sky. My squadron falls into formation around me, wings beating as we hover together. The light I noticed earlier is brighter now. Not the soft light from lanterns. Blazing brightness. Fire.

"Flavian," I jerk my head at my second, "Take two men, report on the village."

Flavian flaps his wings, grabbing two of our men. He dives forward, racing towards the village.

I fold my arms, watching the dancing light. It is flames, I decide. We're too far away for me to make out shapes in the fire, but something is certainly happening—something besides dinner.

The shields around my mind tighten, Flavian signaling me. I lower my guards, my second speaking into my mind.

"Warring leprechauns."

My wings flare. "Information," I command, "Break up the fighting, do not kill unnecessarily." The squadron replies in unison, a single voice. We dive forward, our wings whistling.

Darcy

I can smell the cabbage as I step into the leprechaun cottage, the smell thick, hanging in the air. Leprechauns hover around the table, shoving each other aside to grab plates. They dump bowls of cabbage and sausage onto their wooden plates, swallowing the food in ravenous bites: my mouth waters, but my brain protests. I cannot eat this food; there's no way for me to protect myself. Not without salt.

Hoyt startles me, grabbing my elbow. "You're hungry."

I barely nod, and he presses something into my hand. A small brown pouch, leather strings knotting it closed. "They shouldn't touch the food with magic, but if you're worried." I tug the leather strings open, the loose knot unraveling. The gaps open, revealing crystal white grains. My shoulders nearly sag with relief at the sight of the salt. I lick my finger before touching my fingertip tip to lump of white. I need to taste the crystals just to be absolutely sure, but a quick taste confirms. Hoyt has gifted me with the one protection a human can rely on in Fae territories. While the salt can't stop a spoken curse or a magic spell, it can block any magic laced food.

Another leprechaun shoves a plate into my hand, a ladle dumping a steaming blend of cabbage and sausage on my plate. I take a pinch of the salt, sprinkling it across the plate. Then, I tighten the strings to the pouch, tying it to laces crisscrossing the front of my dress. I can't lose the one protection that lets me eat in peace.

The food is thick and spiced with both my salt and herbs—pepper and sage, with a creamy sweet sauce for the sausage. I gobble up the plate, and then another leprechaun ladles a second helping of food on my plate. I yank at the pouch, pinching out more salt. This time I eat more slowly, taking smaller bites of the sausage. Anya and I have only had sausage once or twice a month, after the village feasts at Samhain. We save for months, working all summer to buy one animal from the butcher shop. Anya bargains with the butcher, bringing home links of sausage. If I were in charge, the sausage might all be gone by the winter solstice. But Anya is more frugal, locking the sausage in the rock cellar behind our house, partitioning out small links for months before we run out of the meat by midsummer. Anya spices apples and mashes berries to go with the sausage, but even her jams pale compared to the leprechauns savory meal. There's just so much meat, more than I've eaten in six weeks.

The leprechauns chatter, their voices deep and gruff, much like Hoyt's. I can't catch much of what they say, and as the meal progresses, someone lights a dozen candles spread around the table. The cabbage is nearly all gone, chairs scraping back as some leave the feast. Hoyt reaches for a glass, uncorking another bottle of wine. The younger musical leprechaun pushes back his seat as he reaches for his fiddle.

Someone starts tapping a hand against the table, calling out roughly which song he wants to hear. The musician grins, "Ah, I think our guest should pick." He winks at me, "What do you want to hear?"

I'm chewing, and I swallow so quickly, I almost choke, "What," I sputter, "I don't know your songs."

He shrugs amused, lifting his harmonica to his mouth. But before he can start playing, the door slams open, a leprechaun storming in. His voice booms around the crowded room, "Fagan's coming round, at least half a dozen of his guards with him."

"That dog," Hoyt spits the word, knocking his chair back. His wine glass topples, the dark juice spilling across the messy table. I grab up my plate, the wine flowing under it, spilling over the edge of the table. Only a bit splashed unto my plate, and I look at my sausage and gravy in dismay.

"Human," Hoyt grabs the back of my chair, yanking me back. I drop the plate, startled. The glass crashes to the floor, shattering.

"I'm sorry," the words tumble out, but Hoyt pulls me away from the table. Leprechauns shove past us, and I whip my head towards the door as several of my hosts shove their way outside. Hoyt lets go of me, reaching behind me to open a cabinet. "Here," I can barely hear him. The room is too small and loud. He pulls back, shoving a scabbard into my hand.

"It's iron," He reaches back into the cabinet, pulling out a helmet and another scabbard. He pulls the helmet over his head, his horns are jutting out on the side like a goat.

"What's going on?" I gasp the question. "Are you fighting?" The scabbard sits heavy in my hand. But

I can hear Hoyt now, as most of the leprechauns have headed outside. "They must have heard about you," Hoyt growls, "Everyone thinks you'll know about the Prince. And Fagan wants the Queen's praise more than anyone else." He says these names as though they mean something to me as if I should know who this Fagan is or that I care about this Queen and her son.

I want to ask more, but Hoyt doesn't wait. He turns from the cabinet, heading towards the door. The table sits in the middle of the room, littered with remains from our dinner. Overturn wine glasses, the bowl of cabbage now cold and nearly empty. The sausage is all gone. My plate sits in broken pieces on the floor, and I flush at my carelessness. Anya wouldn't have dropped her plate, and if she had, my cousin would have already cleaned it up. Anya would be cleaning up this whole mess right now, washing dishes and wiping up the puddles of wine. She wouldn't be standing here, fiddling with a knife.

But I'm not Anya, and she'd be the first to laugh at my attempts to clean up anything. The knife weighs heavy in my hand, and I pull it out of its scabbard—the iron glints in the candlelight. I've never held something so delicate. The handle is carved golden, emeralds set into the side. And the metal is tapered into a slight edge. I take the scabbard, adjusting it around my waist. It fits a little loosely, made for a Fae with wider hips. I almost slip the knife back into the scabbard but stop short. This knife has killed people; I realize with a shudder. I'm supposed to kill with it. I'm not supposed to be standing here thinking about Anya and home. These leprechauns fed me, shared their music and home. Even Anya would be outside trying to find a way to help them fight this Fagan creature.

The cottage is shaking with the shouting and stamp of leprechauns fighting outside. Hoyt is out there, slashing at someone named Fagan with his short sword. The cottage door is closed, but I can still hear the screaming and stomping and the leprechauns deep-throated growls. I can't just stand here, staring at this messy table. Not while these short elves die over me.

Overturned chairs flood the room, I walk through them, edging them out of the way. The door is heavier than I expected. I grimace, pulling open the heavy wood. The noise is overwhelming, but my eyes take a moment to adjust to the dark courtyard. A large moon shadows the fighting. Not just one, I gape. Two beautiful moons. The moonlight skitters the fierce faces of the leprechauns.

Darkness falls around them. The leprechauns grapple with each other, slitting at arms. Biting, clawing.

I quickly see Hoyt, straddling another leprechaun, carving his knife down the fellow's back. The cloth tears, blood gushing. It spurts over Hoyt's arms, coating his face. The leprechaun's screams are horrendous. My stomach turns, my fingers clenching harder around my knife.

My brain is frozen, and I can't seem to take a step into this fight. Whoever this Fagan is, I can't tell him apart from the other leprechaun. They're all short and thick-skinned with wiry goat-like horns. I'm still standing there, unsure what to do when a leprechaun rushes at me. He grabs at my legs, screeching words I can't understand. The leprechaun's nails are digging into my thighs; he's trying to drag me down with him. I kick at him, but he prepared for that. He's ready for my hand, whacking him over the head. My fists do little good against his helmet, though I can feel my knuckles tearing.

But the knife, I gasp as my fingers grip tighter around the weapon. I've never hunted, never fought anyone like this. I curl the blade between my fingers, fighting to stand balanced against the leprechaun's weight. My first instinct is to smash the knife into the creature's head, but it won't do any good against his helmet. Instead, I plunge it into the leprechaun's neck.

Then I jerk back, dragging the golden knife with me. The leprechaun flails, mouth gaping, eyes widening. "You human dog," he coughs, "Iron," he spits the words as he falls backward, hitting the earth with a thud.

I stumble over his body, he convulses on the ground, spitting and cursing as his blood seeps into the soil. "I'm sorry," I choke on my own words, hardly believing my knife did this. "Human dog," I can see the words on his lips, but before I can respond, a shout startles me into turning away. I move my head, a scream in my throat as another leprechaun barrels down on me, "You killed him," he's shouting, his eyes flashing as he lunges at me. I trip backward, nearly falling over my own skirt. He raises an ax, bringing it over his head, and I spin away— barely evading another sweep of his ax. I can't seem to get out as he bears down on me. The next time he pulls back, ready to chop at me, I leap forward, slashing my knife as close to him as I can get.

His beard brushes against my arm as I jerk the knife across his face. Blood gushes over my hands. I stumble back again, my stomach lurching. His blood is spurting, his scream an agony of pain. The ax falls from his hand as he claws at his face. I'm shaking, hardly believing my knife is making him bleed out in front of me, when a leprechaun grabs my free hand, his fingers curling around my bloody skin.

Instinctively, I almost stabbed him with the knife. But my panic lets up as I realize it's the musician, the young leprechaun who has winked at me and played songs all evening. He yanks at me, dragging me away from the fighting. I stumble after him, holding the blood-soaked knife to my chest, cradling it, even as Fae blood soaks into the ground.

The leprechaun drags me behind the cottages, and then we're running, running faster than I've ever done before. His feet barely skim the ground while I'm dragging in gasping breaths. My lungs are screaming in protest, but I fight to keep up. We cross a hill, and I dare a glance back. Fire blossoms against the dark sky, the thatched roofs of the cottages ablaze. The cottage where I just had dinner, the table filled with food and wine and friendly leprechauns. It's going to be destroyed, and I don't need to ask why. Hoyt said these men were looking for me. I stumble again, my legs aching in protest. I rub my hands against my skirt, trying to get the blood off. The red stains are starting to dry.

I spit at my hands, rubbing them together. The blood needs to go away. The leprechaun is now on top of me, screeching at me to run. Never mind the blood; he's yelling the words, urging me to keep running. He grabs my arm again, yanking on the fabric. It tears, but I hardly notice as I fight to keep my feet moving. I keep running.

Brendan

As we crest over the flaming cottages, I immediately see my second. Flavian stands out, a foot taller than the whole clan of Leprechauns, his feathery wings bright in the chaos on the dim, chaotic courtyard.

Flavian is already cutting through a leprechaun, his hair bright in the flicker of firelight. His jaw clenches as he swings his long sword, deftly turning it towards a leprechaun's sword hand. Blood splatters around him as the leprechaun howls in pain, falling away.

His two men are clubbing at other leprechauns, and the creatures continue to scatter, clawing at each other, running short daggers into their enemies' eyes, ripping out beards.

Darting out of my men's way, but still fighting.

My eyes scan the village, my nostrils scenting. A northwestern clan by their smell. Fiercer than the clans closer to the Court. Stubbornly fighting, even as they're outnumbered. If they don't surrender soon, my men will cut through their ranks, destroying the whole clan. We're here to stop the clans from fighting, not kill off a whole family of leprechauns. There's only one way to stop the fighting instantly. My fingers wrap around the blade, and I pull it from my sheath. The blade is weighted with spells, tying my family's magical light to the runes carved into the hilt. Holding the metal makes my heart beat faster, my muscles straining with the magic. My mother taught me the incantation, and now I murmur the words.

My face starts burning, my skin hot with the magical light. I close my eyes, wincing at the heated pain. When I first learned the spell, I clawed at my skin, begging my mother to take it away. Now, my hand grips tight around my blade, sweat dripping from my fingers.

My men are still flying with me, but as we land, they break away from me. If any of them looked directly at my burning face, the light might temporarily blind them. The sword in my hand is now a blazing beacon, and I hold it up, the blue flames dazzling. My face is bright white, brighter than the fire shooting from the cottage roof, and my whole body is shaking from the intense heat. The burning has spread from my face to my neck and arms. In a few minutes, my entire body will be a blend of sharp white pain. Most of the leprechauns come to a standstill, awed by the light. My men spread out, breaking up individual fights. I can hear the howling as they grab leprechauns by their hair, yanking them off each other. Daggers and swords clatter loudly as my men throw them into a pile.

"In the name of Queen Oona the Blessed." My voice falls around the village., "Protector of the Fae Court, Chosen of the Gods, I command peace. Your fighting must stop."

More weapons clatter to the ground. My wings beat as I take a few steps around the fray. One of the cottages collapses behind me, the largest rafter falling in, flames licking at the remaining walls. A cloud of sparks fill the sky, embers raining down around us.

Someone throws a dagger down, cursing the ruined cottage. I force my fingers to relax around my own blade, pushing it back into my sheath. My hands are dripping with sweat, but with the weapon and its spells now put away, the burning brightness starts to ease. I force my eyes open, looking around at the sight of crumpled leprechauns, the injured curled into balls, moaning in pain., "Who led this attack?"

The creatures glance at one another, lips curling, muttered growling. They speak in their language, though Flavian and I both know their dialect.

A lumbering leprechaun steps forward, eyes flashing., "Cut off my ears, Fae," he spits, "Or my tongue."

Fagan, I've seen him once or twice. At diplomatic meetings, he's always the last to arrive, the first to protest. He was complaining about the Queen's justice. The Seelie order, our way of life.

I jerk my chin at my men. Two of them step forward, grabbing Fagan's arms and looping a golden rope around him, tying him tight. They yank off his cloak, and my eyes wander over the midnight blue cloth. Silver threading on the back, the outline of a star. Seven points.

One of my men lets out a gasp, dropping the cloak. His eyes meet mine, an ember of fear.

The star is long dead, the symbol of the wicked, the slain Court of the Unseelie.

A subtle shake of my head and one of my men stoop down, catching up the cloak. He throws it into the fire. Green cloaked leprechauns wrestle more blue cloaks away from Fagan's clan, throwing them into the inferno. A flurry of sparks soars up into the night sky.

"Fagan, I cannot forget you," I speak quietly, but I know the leprechauns can hear me. Even with their half-Fae blood, they still have excellent hearing. More cloaks thrown on the fire as the leprechauns spit at the fire, cursing the Unseelie Star.

I step closer to Fagan., "Never content to live within the boundaries of the Queen's justice."

"Seelie Justice.," Fagan's lips curl, he spits. "The Slaugh take your justice."

I ignore Fagan's insults while my men glower. The leprechauns shuffle, knowing that Fagan's own words condemn him. "The Queen's Justice has lasted a thousand years." I step closer to the leprechaun., "Your discontent cannot disrupt the entire order of the kingdom."

Fagan isn't stupid. He knows I don't intend to leave him alive. He spits again, but at least his aim is low. My boots are still spotless.

"The Slaugh take your prince, your queen, your Seelie Court."

Leprechauns and Fae alike jerk back at his words. Cursing the Queen, and our Prince, my blood boils as his words and how he brandishes the forbidden, treasonous symbol.

"Silence," I snarl, nodding at my men. Two of them grab the leprechaun, shoving Fagan to his knees.

My sword drifts higher, wavering in my hand., "Your actions condemn you. Your words curse your soul. As you have rejected loyalty in life, may death itself betray you."

The curse rolls my tongue, words I have never spoken, the curse is chosen for Unseelie betrayers., "May your soul remain unseeing, the land of Promises hidden to your feet, and may the Gods reject your prayers."

Fagan's eyes flash, but I won't let him speak. Not another cursed, traitorous word. I swing my sword, it whistles before thudding against his neck, the blade slicing through leprechaun skin. The skin tears into bone, my sword crunching through the leprechaun's neck.

Blood splatters my boots, the head falling, rolling across the ground. I look away from Fagan's snarling lips and his narrowed eyes. The leprechauns are gasping, not protesting.

Shocked, but not angry. The body lies in a heap on the ground, and I turn from it, my fingers still tight around the hilt of my sword.

Blood stains the silver metal. The blood of a traitor, I remind myself, one who dared to curse my Queen.

I stoop slightly, running my sword over Fagan's coat, smearing his blood off before sheathing my blade again. One of my men reaches for the corpse, hoisting the head and limbs into the fire. Flames hiss, licking at Fagan's body.

"Have you taken the mortal to the forest?" I turn to the crowd, my questions falling quickly.

Nods and affirming words. My wings flare., "You are witnesses to Fagan's treason.," I look over the watching leprechauns, "I trust you keep Queen's Order."

"Aye, sir.," One leprechaun steps forward., "But our clan is now missing a leader."

I share a look with Flavian; his eyes are wary. He must catch my eagerness to be off because concern rolls off him in waves.

"In a fortnight," I reply to the leprechaun., "The Queen's representative will meet you at the

Terebinth forest. We'll select a new leader then."

The leprechauns nod., "In the meanwhile," I look back at the leprechaun, "You lead the clan until then."

His mouth falls open, but I don't wait for more questions. I turn away, signaling my men. Two steps, wings flapping, we're airborne.

The squadron rallies away from the village. Flavian pulls up next to me, itching to ask questions.

I bank towards the forest., "My father's creatures will take the human," I shout at Flavian.,

"Frighten the mortal to death."

"And you're going to intervene." Annoyance filters through Flavian's voice. But I don't disagree.

I look at my squadron., "Take the men back to the barracks, Flavian. See that everyone gets a meal and rest tonight." Flavian nods at the order before leading the squadron out of my path. The bank to my right, swooping away from the forest. Darkness coats my skin as I pass over the forest. My skin is shimmering, my own light fighting against the forest's creatures.

My eyes furrow as light flares in the distance—my Father's battalions.

Darcy

We run through dark woods, and I trip over tree roots. The leprechaun barely waits for me. I slash at my skirts with the bloodied knife, cutting the fabric away below my knees. I still trip after my guide, but at least I'm not stumbling over my clothes. I can barely manage to stay beside the leprechaun as we jump through the crystal creek, my body stiffening at the touch of the icy cold water.

We forge ahead, ignoring my gasping breaths. The air is too cold, burning my lungs. I can't hear the fighting anymore, though my breathing is so loud, I'm not sure I'd be able to anyway. I'm desperately hoping we've run far enough because I simply can't go much further. Roots dart across my path, I trip over one, landing in the moist dirt. Mud clings to my palms now, blood and soil sticking to my arm, the wet earth damping clothes along with the blood. I barely keep from stumbling again, skirting the gnarled roots. I lean against a tree, fighting to catch my breath when my guide pulls up shorts. The bark is rough, and I lean against it, pressing my fingers into the wood. The air is cold on my lungs, my stomach suddenly churning. It's cold air and my hot skin blending all at once. Now all I can see the leprechaun I stabbed, his blood shining and hot on my skin. I jerk forward, acid clawing at my throat like a hand wrapped around my neck.

"Here," the leprechaun grabs my hand, pulling me out of my panicked daze. "You don't have time to fall apart now." His gruff tone speaks directly into my ear; he's shaking me, "We've got to get up these trees. Our friends will meet us."

His words are a jumble, and though I can hear him, his instructions don't make any sense. I try to gasp out a question, but my throat closes tighter, and I can't seem even to open my mouth. "Let's climb," The leprechaun urges me, and I turn into the tree, reaching up for a tree branch. If I stand here any longer, I'll end up losing all of the food I ate just a half-hour ago.

The bark peels into my hands, needles tearing my palms. My toes press into the rough bark, and I hoist myself up branch by branch. I look down at the leprechaun, wondering how his short arms are following me. But of course, he's more prepared, and he's pressing a pick into the trunk, pulling himself up step by step. The tree wavers underneath our weight, and now my chest and throat are as tight as the cloth Anya weaves.

I pull at a final branch, hoisting myself above the treetop. My whole body sinks unto the branch, every bone aching, protesting. My palms are scraped open, stinging.

I wipe tears away, and I hadn't even realized I was crying. Of course, my nose is stopped up too, and I catch my breath before blinking in surprise. The view is spectacular. Sweeping hills and woods, and the double moons. As if on instinct, I tip my head back, taking in the stars. The night sky is endless, the stars blinking brilliantly—. So much brighter, faster than I've ever seen before.

"They'll be here soon," The leprechaun whispers. "Hoyt got word to them just before Fagan's attack."

The view has taken my mind away from my throbbing hands. So many questions come to mind, but I ask the first one. I'm not sure I want to know who's going to show up.

I lick my chapped lips., "Who's Fagan?"

"A devilish leprechaun," My guide curses., "The Slaugh take him."

I'm taken aback both by his fierceness and his mention of the Slaugh. Another story from my childhood, wandering night riders, reaping the souls of men, I've heard of them. I didn't realize they also must be true. I'm beginning to wonder if everything I've ever heard is true. But I can't think too much about the Slaugh before venturing another question. "What did Fagan want?"

The leprechaun is quite a long moment. In the silence, I think I can still hear the battle. Or my mind is replaying the awful scene, forcing me to live through my murderous panic. A leprechaun is dead because of me. His body left abandoned, not far from the whispering trees, the birds singing below us. I rub the back of my hand on my lap, trying to rub off the sticky, dried blood. The dirt just smears, both my dress and skin stained.

"The Queen's son is missing," I almost jump at his words as they pull me from my horrible memories. I glance back at the leprechaun, another jolt of surprise as moonlight catches the glimmer of tears on his face., "The leprechaun clans are hunting for his captors. That's why

Hoyt was even above land before the summer solstice. Most of the leprechauns are gone, hunting Prince Edric." His words are etched with sorrow, and I don't need to ask what Anya would do. I reach for his hand, laying my aching palm atop his rough skin. He doesn't move, "I'm sorry. I know the Prince." My words feel so empty, but I try. "I know the prince means much to your people."

He moves his hand, pulling his fingers through his beard. "Fagan must think you know where our Prince is. Of course, he wants to be the one who finds him." I wait for more words, but he doesn't elaborate further. I'm left to guess why Fagan would attack his friends, and it dawns on me slowly how these clans are probably not friends. We're more alike in our loneliness, these leprechauns who live around each other but don't call each other friends. Anya is my only friend, just as much as she's now my only family.

A yawn fights me, and I feel my eyes growing heavier. I fight another yawn, thinking. I haven't slept in hours, my headaches. I need to see this Fae Queen, receive my gold, and get home to Anya. I'm close to putting together a question about when I can see the Queen, when the tree starts to sway wildly. I grab hold of my branch, holding it tighter.

"They're almost here," The leprechaun speaks above the wind, but I can barely hear him over the roar of my panic.

We're going to die.

Light flashes around me, and I nearly vomit. The light is blinding, my bones scream in protest. Claws dig into my shoulders; I want to fight them. But the light, it's so bright, so all-encompassing, I can't fight it.

And then, I'm hanging in the air. I am truly going to die. I scream for Anya, for the gods, for anything. Pain radiates in my shoulders as sharpness digs into my skin, and I twist, unable to break free. My eyes are still squeezed shut, but I can feel my body dangling. My lips move, begging for death, the prayers of my childhood pounding through my veins.

Death take me, grant me peace. Open the doors of heaven, may I find a seat at the feet of saints.

A shadow veils the light, hoarse commands. I can't understand the Fae language, the guttural sounds.

The light lessens, and then the claws release me. A scream rips from my throat, death coming to meet me. But I don't touch the ground. My scream dies as strong arms catch my waist, wrapping me close to cold armor. The wind pulls at my hair, and all of my fear and panic rises in me like a wave I've held back all night. My tears and sobs choke me, and I gasp for breath, trying to cling to my prayers. *Death take me, grant me peace.*

I'm still praying, my whole body shaking like leaves in the autumn when the air stills around me. The pain lessens around my shoulders, and I collapse to the ground, black dirt meeting my bleeding hands. I'm clawing at the dirt when a hand rests on my back. I pull away, trying not to scream as I grab at my waist.

The knife Hoyt gave me sits there like a promise.

"You don't need to be afraid," the creature's voice is smooth as freshly churned butter. I'm still on my knees, but I turn, glancing behind me. My vision is teary, but I'm staring into the eyes of this creature. I gulp again, looking over this strange face. Dark hair falls in a curtain around pointed ears and gleaming eyes. His feathery wings are a sharp contrast to his smooth skin, and I push back on my heels, glancing at his side. He's armed, of course—a picture straight from a childhood nightmare, one of the Fae soldiers.

"Apologies, little one.," The Fae speaks., "I fear you are frightened."

Frightened hardly begins to describe it. But I take in a shuddering breath, wanting to ask who he is, whether I've heard his name in a story before. As though he can read my thoughts, and perhaps he can, the creature speaks again., "I am Brendan, commander of my Queen's aerial squadrons."

Brendan, I breathe his name, sucking in another gasp of air. He stands up, and I shrink back. This man, this Fae, he is a giant. He turns, barking commands in a language I can't understand. And I stare at the wings. The silvery-white feathers stretched out behind him. Golden armor across his chest, ancient patterns swirled into the metal. Leather covers his slender hands, two swords strapped to his back.

His skin glows, patterns of light etching from him. He's dimmed now, but I realize, He can also shed light like the creature that nearly blinded me when they dragged me away from the treetop. My eyes drop to the Fae's hands, his feet—l. Long fingers, shimmering black boots, No claws. He is not the same creature that took me from the trees. My relief is short-lived. The ground shakes as another creature lands. I look over, a dark-winged creature—light shimmering from his skin.

My shoulders ache, and I glance down at his feet. Sure enough, talons peek out from his toes. My body begins to quiver in fear., I long for Anya's comforting singing. For my pallet, even for the sound of the ocean waves. This is no place for my kind. This is no place for any human.

The two exchange words, a harsh, short exchange in their own language.

I shrink back from the talons, whimpering. If I could form the words, I'd beg to be left alone. Fighting leprechauns, winged creatures, this isn't worth a pot of gold. If Anya knew I'd thrown away my life for a mere chance at the fabled gold, she'd be furious.

The Fae reaches for me, lifting me, bundling me into his arms. I don't have the strength to fight him or even ask questions. My bones ache with weariness.

But at least this time, when his wings beat and we are airborne, I'm not gripped by talons. No nails are threatening, just normal fingers—boots on his feet. Riding cocooned in this warrior's arms is a much better option. I look beyond the warrior's face, mesmerized by the stars. The sky is full of them, and I can hardly breathe as this warrior flies me so close to their blanket of black and silver. I should be sleeping now, resting before walking home to Anya. She'll be looking at these same stars tonight, thinking I'm safe.

My throat burns, knowing that Anya is walking the beaches in our village. She is probably praying for my safe return.

The stars can comfort both Anya and me. If the gods are real, I wish Anya could see a message from me in the skies. Some sort of sign, a shooting star or wandering planet. Anything to let her know I am thinking of her, hoping she stays safe. Even while my thoughts turn towards home, to my only family in the world, my eyes can't stay open much longer.

Chapter Four

Brendan

THE GIRL IS HEAVY in my arms, her head rolled back and hair tangled together in a knotted mess. Her dress is torn, her thin shoes ripped, the laces shredded. I take her up the flight of stairs to the guest rooms, relieved there's hardly any other Fae lingering in these dark hallways of the palace. I can't even remember the last time the Queen hosted guests, and the hallways are decorated with towering portraits of Fae warriors and legends. The portraits are supposed to impress strangers, but the human doesn't even stir in my arms. A fairy throws open a door, waving me in. I've probably seen her before, but she doesn't remind me of her name. She hovers around my arms, her wings batting as she exclaims over the human's appearance. I lay the girl down on the bed, her body folding into the thick blankets. She doesn't even open her eyes, and I'm almost jealous. If only I could fall into bed and instantly sleep. I just need to get back down the stairs and cross the courtyard to my quarters. It's long past midnight, so most of the Court is asleep. Despite my hopes, as soon take the last few steps down the stairs, I'm accosted. One of my father's men stops me. "Brendan." His voice is icy, echoing around the still hallway. I recognize him from nights spent drilling in the courtyards, his green-tinged skin, tattoos swirling around his neck beyond the collar of his tunic—one of my father's lieutenants. I think he married one of my cousins, just one of the dozens of distant relatives my father hires.

"Cousin.," I try to keep my tone casual., "It's a bit early to still be awake. How are you?"

He ignores my question., "Your father is asking for you. In his rooms."

Of course, my father won't wait until morning. I should have expected another useless conversation. I nod silently, stepping away. My father's apartments are at the opposite side of the Court, a long walk away from where I left the human girl.

The walk through the dark hallways gives me time to think of an excuse. I can tell my father that the leprechauns asked me to find the girl or that the Queen insisted I check on her. I walk swiftly down the winding stairs, passing the throne room, before taking the long hallway to my father's room. His men are stationed throughout, silhouetted in the flickering torchlight. They don't bother greeting me.

The hall is disturbing enough in the daylight, but at night, it is chilling. Skulls, spoils of war, hang along the stone walls. My father enjoys getting a touch drunk, then stumbling into the hallway long after dark to boast about the kills. I'm not sure how many stories are correct if he has actually fought in a dozen wars. Or if he has simply murdered tenants late on their rent and mounted their skulls outside his office.

When I was fifteen, my father doubled the rent, insisting that a half-century of good rain and sunshine meant that the tenants living on our land could afford to share more of their harvest. The goblins refused, insisting on calling a meeting with my father to negotiate his demands. My father dragged me along, but he never planned on negotiating. As soon as the goblins arrived, my father ordered me to attack. The goblins were hardly armed, unprepared for my father's fierce anger. I didn't train to kill goblins, and I'd spent years learning sword drills and spells to join the Queensguard. I slammed my sword around, trying just to scare the goblins. My father roared at me, pulling out his sword. I'd been whacked in the head too many times by that blade. Seeing him raise its hilt, I could nearly feel the slam of metal against my skull. I jumped forward, stabbing a goblin in the stomach. The goblin squealed, doubling over on top of the sword. I nearly fell forward, blood pooling around my sword, my hand wrapped around the hilt with the metal trapped inside this goblin's body. My father stomped over, swiftly arching his own sword through the air, slicing the metal through the goblin's neck. Blood sprayed, splashing my face with hot liquid. My father reached down, picking the goblin's head by the horns. He threw the skull at me. I presume he wanted me to hang it in the barracks. I stuffed it under my bed.

My father never visits the barracks. They're probably too far out of his way, and he'd have to leave his perch overlooking the entire Court. If he saw my room, he might be offended at my choice of décor.

I've only ever hung one item on the wall, the sword my mother gave me when I could barely walk. Now that I'm grown, the blade is more a knife in my hands than an actual weapon. I suppose I could still use my mother's gift, but I'd rather keep it on my wall.

I hear my father's voice before I even reach his door. Light spills out from under the wood door, and I wince. He's shouting, the sound echoing around the room, "Of course you knew what he was doing. Unless you also want me to believe you're a complete idiot." I shove the door open, taking in the sight. My father is standing in the center of the room, towering over Flavian. Flavian kneels on the floor, head bent over.

"I ordered Flavian to return.," I don't wait for my father to look at me., "He was obeying my commands."

My father turns in my direction., "The girl was under my watch. My men had her."

"We needed her to retain her sanity," I refuse to raise my voice., "Your creatures would have driven her mad."

His hands clench at his sides, eyes narrowing as he fumes., "You had no right. What were you even doing out of the Court?" Flavian looks at me now, moving for the first time since I came in and turning just enough to look at me. His eyes are a touch wide, and I can nearly read his thoughts. Surprise that my father didn't know.

My shoulders are tight., "I was under orders."

"What kind of answer is that?" My father snaps, taking a step., "I should finish what the Finn started and knock more sense into your skull." His comment makes me wince, his tone straight from my nightmares. He snarls again, "You are under my orders. I am your commander. I gave no such command for you to leave."

"The Queen," I answer quietly, though my words feel useless against his anger., "She gave me instructions. Keep the leprechauns from fighting."

His eyes flash, he turns towards Flavian., "You broke up the leprechaun's fight?" Flavian nods. "Ridiculous," My father grumbles., "You should have let the creatures devour each other." "Her majesty's orders,' I start, but he interrupts.

"We serve the country, not the queen," his breathing is heavier, and he glares at me, "I didn't raise you to chase squabbling leprechauns. Our family has worked all our lives for this position. Oona may have lost her senses, but we won't."

I worked my entire life to fight with the Queensguard. Yet every time I follow through with the

Queen's order, I'm met with my father's anger. I can almost quote his lectures about our family and his dedication to the Fae Court. He rants a few more minutes, throwing in his favorite lines about loyalty and all the sacrifices he made for me. Finally, he waves a hand, dismissing us., "Go find the Prince. We'll discuss this another day." He stomps farther into the room, slamming the door to his bedroom behind him. Flavian slumps forward, his eyes bloodshot., "Why did you do that?" "Do what?" I blink at him, too tired to guess at what he means.

He pulls himself to his feet, lifting his chin., "He's your Father. You might be able to live with his ranting, but that man commands the army. He decides what happens at Court." I don't answer, and he runs a hand through his shoulder-length hair., "Did you grab the girl on purpose, just to annoy him?"

"It was what was right," I stammer, taken aback by his question. Flavian rarely asks me questions, "The creatures were hurting the girl."

"The girl hurt Edric," He hisses, bangs falling into his eyes, "Whatever she did, he's now gone. Let the creatures devour her."

"Flavian.," I reach for him, but he brushes past me. "We don't know that the human girl had anything to do with Edric." "He disappeared, and then she appears. Humans haven't just shown up in a hundred years. Don't tell me the girl isn't involved." He shrugs me off, stepping towards the door. I follow him into the hall, knowing that he's going to believe whatever he wants about the girl. I speak to his back., "I don't know how long the girl will be here. But you should avoid her." I clear my throat before speaking to his back.,

"Seeing her will only upset you. I want you to stay away from her."

He snorts, looking back at me, lips twitching slightly., "I'm surprised your father hasn't already told you. He assigned me as her escort." I'm left gaping at him, trying to figure out what he's saying. There's an edge to his voice as he avoids my eyes, "He said that since you're so concerned for her, I could be your watchdog."

He turns, stomping away, boots echoing. I run a hand over my forehead, craving my bed. I can't think through everything that's happened. Not without sleep. And Flavian will be watching the girl in the morning, and I need to be around. Knowing the edge to his voice tonight, he'll be an absolute beast tomorrow.

Darcy

I blink awake the next day; at least, I think it's the next day. My hands reach for anything, and I touch the softest bed I've ever imagined. I lean my head back on the pillow, breathing a sigh. "Morning," a cheery voice interrupts, as someone draws the heave drapes around the bed open, light blinking in my eyes. I rub at my face, pulling myself up. That's when I catch my first sight of her. A small Fae woman. She looks more like a dream, and I glance down at my arm, pushing up the soft white cloth and pressing my nails harshly into my arm. A pinch of pain, just to make sure I'm not dreaming.

My skin reddens, and I look back up at the floating Fairy. Sparkling wings beat as she darts about the room, a cloud of golden dust billowing around her. Her skin is dark, the color of night. She looks at me, her eyes wide, a brilliant violet color.

"Where am I?" I blurt the question, pushing the blankets from my skin. Cold air meets my bare legs, goosebumps rising on the back of my neck. I'm definitely awake.

"Oh, sweet human," the fairy chirps, "you're in the Court of the Fae."

The Court of the Fae. I'm not sure the leprechauns called it that, but the name rings familiar. My mind flips through the legends I've heard, putting together remnants of the Fae Courts' stories. I must be in the Seelie Court. Even though I can't remember everything Isolt might have said, I think I wouldn't be alive if I were in the Unseelie Court. The courts supposedly dissolved long ago into one Fae Court led by the Queen, but the Unseelie went into hiding, feuding with Faes and humans. I probably remember something wrong, mixing up the names of the feuding Fae factions.

Hopefully, I've remembered enough to stay alive and get the gold for Anya and me.

I rub my eyes again, then glance at the nightstand. The knife with its golden hilt, it's sitting there. I reach for it, touching my fingertips to the gold medal. Next to the blade sits the pouch of salt. I look at my palms, but my skin isn't scrapped. I twist my fingers together, uncomfortable and not sure if I want to know what Fae magic can do. My knuckles were bloodied and bruised last night, and now they're smooth.

The Fae did something to me while I was sleeping.

"Did the leprechauns," I whisper, hoping Hoyt wasn't hurt in the fight last night. He was gruff, but he brought me to his home. His friends were fighting for me. He gave me my only source of protection. Well, actually, Hoyt gave me two gifts, both the salt and the dagger.

"Brendan and General Riordan have taken care of Fagan," the Fairy replies instantly., "Now, we need to get you bathed. Ready for your audience with Her Majesty."

An audience with the Fae Queen. My hands are already trembling. The Fairy doesn't seem to notice. She sweeps in beside me, urging me to my feet. I look away from her beating wings; they're going to make me sick. They move so quickly, so fast., hovering in mid-air beside me. Then she's clicking her tongue, "Such beautiful hair," she touches my greasy hair. It's come undone from my usual braid, falling in loose curls down my back.

I look at her hair, blue curls gathered into a braided crown. My eyes catch on the golden lettering swirling down her neck, and etchings stamped into her skin. Light gossamer clings to her skin before falling into a layered skirt around her waist. I've never seen anything like it, but I want to laugh the moment I think that.

Have I seen anything I'm familiar with this past day? There are truly leprechauns, floating fairies, winged warriors living in this place, living underneath our very feet. Under the mounds and hills, I've walked past my whole life. If Anya were here, she wouldn't be puzzling over the strangeness. Anya would be talking to this winged Fairy, asking her about her life and name if she enjoys helping lost humans. Anya would know what to say.

Anya should have found the leprechaun. Instead, I'm the one pushed into a tub, the Fairy pouring hot water on top of me. I hold back a yelp, wrapping my arms around my bare skin. The Fairy runs her small hands through my hair, pulling at the mess of tangles. She sings while she works, her voice light and clear. The song sounds familiar, like something Isolt might have sung back home. But the Fairy is singing in her language, and I've no idea what she's saying.

After the Fairy decides I'm free of dirt, she urges me out of the bathtub, draping me in a soft bundle of towels. I take the hairbrush she offers, running it through my dripping hair.

I'm still working on my hair when the Fairy holds out a dress. I take it from her, slipping the smooth fabric over my head. It falls in waves around me, a waterfall of green and gold thread. The Fairy pulls at the waist, cinching it tightly. My hair is still dripping. The fairy hums, her wings are beating as she touches my head. "Here, my dear, don't be alarmed." I don't know what she means, but then she blows on my hair, murmuring Fae words. I feel the warm air wrap around my hair, the water drying instantly. I yank away, my heart jumping.

"You," I'm sputtering, but I don't have the words to say. She just used magic on me, without my permission, without asking. I'm trembling. The Fairy doesn't seem to notice, dancing over to the bedside table. She darts back, holding out the holster and dagger. I push past my unease, taking the weapon. It easily slips around my waist, and I silently thank Hoyt. At least I know it works.

I pinch myself, trying not to stare at this dress. Gold stitching lines the bodice, pulling in at the waist.

The collar is low cut, and I touch my chest, flushing. I've never worn anything like this, and I can't even think of a word to describe it.

My hair lies in curls down my back, and a single green ribbon is woven into a loose braid. The dress is cut open in the back, but my hair covers my bare skin.

Then the Fairy hands me my pouch. I release a sigh of relief, rolling my fingers around the leather. I take a peek at the salt, where it sits safe and dry in the leather. I tuck the pouch into my bodice again, tying it to the elegant gold strings lacing the dress's front.

The Fairy flutters away from me, beckoning me to follow. I lift my skirts, jogging slightly behind her. I suppose if you fly, you never really realize how must faster you are. But then, most of the Fae I've met so far don't seem to realize how pitifully human I am. How much slower I simply am.

The hallways are dim, the floor embedded with polished dark wood. I glance at the portraits hanging on the wall, my eyes widening—swirls of glittering colors, hues of sparkling blue and golden green accented by crimson shadows. I crane my neck, but the tops of the painting slip into the dark arches of the hallway. I can't even see the entire picture, though I study it for several moments.

The Fairy pauses, waiting for me to catch up. "Do you like the art?" the fairy talks as I come next to her. She hovers next to me, and I look away from her ever-beating wings. "I've never seen anything like it."

The Fairy's face falls, her lips pinching into a frown., "How dull the world must be now. I remember when humans and fairies painted together." she lets out a wistful sigh. "Those were glorious days."

She darts ahead, and I hurry to follow, catching up as she stops at the door. A Fae male stands there, his body rigid. "Gwen." He nods at the Fairy, and I flush, my bare neck reddening as I realize I forgot to ask her name. I wondered how Anya would chat with her and somehow, still didn't ask the right question. The Fae turned to me, and compared to the blue-haired Gwen, I now feel incredibly small. He towers over me, his blonde hair tied back into a long ponytail.

A sword hangs at his side, black leather boots rising to his knees.

"I'm here to take you to the Queen." He's not asking. I nod at Gwen, "Thank you for your help." I touch the knife at my waist, "You've been very kind."

Gwen laughs, the sound echoing in the empty hall. The guard glares at her, his dark brown eyes narrowing, "Pixies think everything is funny."

She titters before zipping away. I watch her wings fluttering, the shimmering golden dust trailing behind her. I'd much rather the cheerful pixie take me to the Queen, instead of this glowering Fae male.

"Come along," The Fae growls., "I don't like wasting my time."

His comment makes me drawback., "Sorry to interrupt your packed schedule."

His lips curl slightly., "If I have my way, this should be a short interruption."

"Believe me.," I follow him through the doorway., "I hope this is a short interruption, too." He pauses, turning my way., "Do you know what you're asking for?"

We're standing on a massive staircase, the loop of the steps downward, I glance away from his face., "To see the Queen? Hopefully, I'll take home a pot of gold."

He takes a step on the stairs., "So it's true then. Humans lie as easily as they breathe."

"I'm not lying.," My cheeks flush., "I'm just here because I caught a leprechaun." He shrugs, beckoning me forward.,

"You can tell me more about the leprechaun later. The Queen is waiting."

This place, it's beyond anything I could have dreamed of. Glistening walls, they remind me of a clear spring day, the ocean dappling around our village for miles. Like the sea, these walls hem me in. Root me to the earth. My mouth falls open as the elegant Fae guard begins our descent. The stairs slope, going deeper, deeper into the ground. Patterns etch on the palace walls, and I stop, wanting to run my hand over the glittering stones. I want to feel the glimmering edges. Anya would smile at the etchings, chatter about using the elegant pattern in her weaving.

"Did you hear me?" the Fae calls back at me., "I said the Queen is waiting. On you, specifically."

I jump back from the wall, clamoring down the steps. As we walk, there are even more Fae. They pass us, staring at me. The hair on my neck stands on end. I cross my arms, trying to avoid their gazes. Some are tall, elegant. Their clothes shimmer, their skin flushed with colors. Elegant dresses drag on the marble steps, bells tinkling from their sleeves. One reaches out to touch me, and I nearly jump away. His clear nails are so long, longer than my pinkie fingers. I shrink from his touch, and my Fae guide snaps a command.

I can't tell what he says, and the language is guttural, ancient. But the Fae backs away, smirking at me. He's a threat without touching me.

I stumble after my guide's heels, trying to thank him. He pulls short, hesitating at a step. He looks down at me, "I don't need your thanks, human. It seems everyone is trying to find ways to waste my time."

My teeth grit together, and I want to roll my eyes. If he has so much to do, I don't understand why he's leading me around this palace. The Fae glides down the next step, not bothering to wait for my reply. As finely dressed as he is, his pale hair neat, clothes finely trimmed, his toned muscles, the Fae male is simply an elegant snob. Fiercely rude. Others are not so elegant, though they are even more fierce. I avert my eyes from the bark-like skin, the scales covering one female's bald head, the twitching tails of a set of males. They sharpen their claws, running their elongated fingers together. One nibbles on his hand, and I gape at his teeth, long visors that reach past his chin.

I look away from a naked Fae. Her skin is inked, deep blue patterns swirl across her back. Rings cover her face, silver and gold piercings dangle from her lips.

These creatures used to rule Ireland. I remember the tales Isolt told. Of fairy festivals, of nights when the Fae and humans danced till dawn. The leprechauns used to make special shoes, shoes that let you dance for weeks without growing weary.

But no one has seen the Fae for generations. And what I see now, an entire people living below us.

"Why," I stumble next to my guard, "Why do you live here?"

The Fae doesn't bother looking at me, "When the Saxons came," When he isn't peeved, his voice is lyrical, rich, and musical, "Our people chose to live underground. The Saxons are numerous and fierce. Even our magic could not fight their armies forever."

Saxons armies. The Saxon lords have bows, arrows of iron. And even a child knows a Fae's weakness – iron. But after seeing these people, the winged guards, their magic light, I can't imagine anything weakening these creatures. This guard, this giant of a man, is also a warrior. His muscles ripple with his every step, a sword strapped to his back. And a bandolier on his waist, I look over, he must have at least a half-dozen knives strapped at his side.

"Iron weapons can truly kill Fae?" I finally venture the question, hoping I don't accidentally offend him.

He looks down at me, red lips curling, "It wasn't our lives we feared for. But yours."

I blink, and he continues, "The Saxons brought new gods. New lives. You humans would have to choose between the seen and the unseen."

I think of the priests I've seen on the Saxon estates. The crosses and foreign prayers. Long robes, shaved heads, short days, and sacraments. The seen and the unseen., "But you can't see the Saxon gods."

The Fae doesn't reply. He just keeps walking, long, perfect steps. His feet barely brush the ground. I stumble, trying to keep at pace with him. He didn't answer, I think suddenly. And Fae can't lie. They don't trust me; I pinch my hands together. A reminder that I should not trust them. I touch my neck, the pouch of salt riding in my bodice. It's small protection, but the bit of salt is all I have.

The stairs taper into a courtyard, and I lean my neck back, looking up at the ceiling. I can't tell, is the ceiling open to the sky, or is the domed ceiling painted? Clouds float across, the skies the lightest shade of blue I've ever seen. "Come along, human," The Fae snaps at me. I want to scowl at this Fae's annoying need to always hurry. The Fae Queen isn't going anywhere. I'm certainly not going anywhere.

I scamper closer to him. The Fae has paused in front of a large door. The wooden paneling is etched with Fae words; my eyes trail over the elegant script. If I could read, I'd study the lettering longer. But even if I could read, I suspect it would be useless, and the words are in a different language. The doors swing open, and I follow the Fae. But the moment my feet cross the wide threshold, my chest squeezes.

Tightness fills my stomach, my fingers throb.

I want to close my eyes; my head is beginning to pound. But I force my eyes to stay open, my breathing heavy as I traipse behind my guide. If the pain weren't so intense, I'd look around this throne room. A balcony runs along the wall, Fae line along the arches, peering down at me. Plants grow on the wall, blossoming around the faces of the Fae audience. But I can't look at them. My hands clench against my stomach, I'm desperately trying not to throw up as my stomach twists in pain.

I don't notice when my Fae guard stops, and I stumble into him. He snarls at me, pushing back with a snarl. He spits out a string of frustrated words, but my head is spinning, and I can't hear a single word he says. I grab at his arm, and my knees are shaking while my throat burns. The Fae stares down at me, his face too blurry for me to read. I try to take in a breath, desperate to clear my eyes and head, but the air stabs my chest. I can feel the magic in the same way, I felt it when the leprechaun took my hand. His spell was cold. This magic is hot and slicing into my body in lashes of pain.

The Fae grabs my shoulders, holding on as I try to walk. We make it a few feet into the room before I start to fall again. I can't breathe. Tears course down my face, and I breathe in a sob. The pain radiates down my spine, and my ribs press against my lungs. It feels like dozens of knives are stabbing into my chest.

"The girl is suffering," a voice speaks lightly, and the pressure eases from in my neck. I shudder as a cool breeze caresses my cheeks., "She feels the magic."

"Indeed, Majesty," the Fae continues., "The leprechauns insist she saw them unaided. No rainbow."

Heels click on the marble steps of the throne room. The cool breeze on my cheeks is insistent. I raise my chin, grimacing at the sharp pain lacing my bones. Tears are streaming from my eyes, but I keep my head up, taking in the legendary Fae Queen.

She is beautiful. Blonde hair cascades to her feet, splashing around her on the moonstone floor. Her cheeks are sharp, her lips red as spring flowers. My eyes burn when I look at her pale face. Her crystal blue eyes are piercing as she gazes at me. She tilts her head, the silver points on her crown shimmering. The legends all said the Queen was too beautiful, that humans were overwhelmed and unable to speak because of her blinding beauty. I want to talk now, but I'm frozen, cold air holding my skin in an icy grasp.

I'm still holding my head up when the Queen speaks, "She knows nothing of my son." I don't know if her words are a question or a statement. Either way, I don't know anything about her son. The words are still hanging in the air when the coolness retreats and a spasm etches down my back. I cry out, falling against the cold floor. My whole body trembles, my head is pounding fiercely in harsh, sharp stabs of searing pain.

"The human knows nothing," Fae finally repeats the Queen's words. I feel as though talons of magic shred my heart.

"Take her away," the Queen's voice rings clearly., "Keep her tonight, entertain the human. I will see her again." I can't stand up because my legs simply refuse to move. The Fae grabs my arm, pulling me up. I fall against him, gasping another sob. He heaves me across the throne room, dragging me in his iron grip. I fall into a heap outside the throne room, my dress soaked by sweat, snot caked on the sleeves. My tear ruined the delicate green cloth. A shudder passes through me, my hands shaking. The magic, the Fae Queen, I look up at the Fae.

"That's why I can't speak to her," my words are hoarse, and I clear my throat. "The magic, the pain."

The Fae sniffs, waving a hand at my soiled dress., "You're disgusting."

His words are a sour reminder of the Fae's prejudice against humans. I just experienced the worst pain I've ever felt in my entire life, and he can't even muster up an ounce of compassion. I rise to my knees, my bones quivering, "And you're a beast." I spit the words, fighting to stand. My back screams in protest, "You drag me before your Queen. Your magic nearly kills me. And you stand by and do nothing while I writhe on the ground."

The Fae doesn't even blink, his lips curling as he snarls at me, "We didn't feed you, human. Be thankful you had nothing to vomit."

I open my mouth, and I'm so angry. I'm angry at these proud Fae and all their magic. My hands are still quivering; it still hurts to breathe. I suck in another breath, but the Fae grabs my shoulder.

He shakes me, "I am no beast," His breath is hot on my face, "Your kind kills, you've no grace for any beauty." Then he drops me, and I crumple to the floor. I press my sweaty palms into the cool marble as he peers down at me, his dark eyebrows furrowed, "If my Queen did not command me, I would have nothing to do with you."

I could have guessed that. I pull myself to my feet, trembling, my knees shaking. He waves a hand, inclining his head toward the stairs., "Gwen will be waiting to clean you up. Her Majesty expects you at the feast tonight."

He stalks towards the stairs, but I can barely follow. My legs still feel weak; my stomach roils with each step. He's three steps up the never-ending staircase, and I can't do this. I simply can't.

I grab the banister, holding it tightly in my hands. I lean against the wall, and the Fae pauses, looking down at me. I can almost hear his snarl, but I don't care that I'm human. Magic is painful. I simply can't be as strong as these Fae. The Fae scoops me up into his arm, the leather straps on his arms digging into my back. He jerks his chin up, but I don't care. He doesn't have to talk to me.

I expect he'll drop me on the floor at the guest apartment's entrance, but he keeps walking. His long strides cover the short distance. The hallway is dark, but my room is bright as he opens the door.

He lays me on the bed, barking at Gwen while she hovers next to him.

While his barking makes my nerves taught, the winged Fairy is peeved. She lets out a shrill whistle before a torrent of words. I don't understand any of it, but I love watching the angry sparks in her violet eyes. She darts around the tall Fae's head, spitting and flashing at him.

I think the Fae male will lash out at her, but his shoulders droop slightly. He doesn't look at me but speaks quietly to Gwen. I wonder if he's apologizing because Gwen simply nods, dismissing the Fae. I'm sure he will walk out. I close my eyes, hissing at my throbbing head.

"Dear child.,"The Fairy bumbles over to me, sinking unto the bed next to me. She touches my forehead., "Humans aren't supposed to feel magic." She breathes through her teeth., "But you certainly felt the magic."

"She felt the Queen's magic." I hear the Fae's voice, "It's impossible."

"Stop talking, Flavian," the fairy grumbles, "The girl's suffering enough without your voice."

"She'll suffer more," He speaks again, and I do wince at his voice. Perhaps I hope the Fairy will notice and force him to leave. But either she doesn't see or doesn't think he'll go. Either way, he continues, "If I had known she would feel the magic, I wouldn't have dragged her in front of the Queen."

"Tell her, not me," the Fairy scolds again, "Otherwise, your you're talking will give the poor girl another headache."

I almost smile. She definitely noticed me wincing. I crack open my eyes, just enough to see the Fae standing over the bed, "I did not know you would feel the magic." He drags in a breath, "I'm sorry." He steps away, and I hear the door shuts softly behind him.

"He can't lie," the Fairy speaks softly., "He may not have any manners, but he's not heartless." I don't know what to say as she presses her cool hands against my forehead., "You must be starving."

At least I can answer that., "I was hungry until I saw the Queen."

"You'll be feeling better soon, child." The Fairy gently massages my shoulders. Her fingers are so cool, so refreshing against my flushed skin.

She takes another breath. "Flavian misses the Prince. He doesn't intend to take it out on you."

Flavian. I want to spit his name, call a curse of the gods down on him—his utter disregard for humans, his disgust. Gwen lets out a sigh. "Flavian is not himself." She taps the top of my hand., "The Prince, they mean much to each other. Flavian will not be the same without Edric."

Gwen is such a pleasant fairy, her golden tattoos, her soft violet eyes, and I can't imagine her being mean to anyone. She hums as she massages my neck, her fingers light, relaxing.

I lean into Gwen's fingers, closing my eyes at her cool touch. Her words, compassion for Flavian, wrecks with my feelings about the tall, blonde Fae. Flavian is, I don't know the word to describe him. His snarling disgust, he clearly can't stand the sight of me. But he has deep feelings for the Fae Prince and resents everyone as long as the Prince is missing.

His apology, my head spins as I try to work out his words.

Fae can't lie, though I don't know if an apology can count as a lie. And my head is whirling, my stomach burning, I can't keep thinking about Flavian.

Gwen pulls back from me while she keeps humming a soft tune. My eyes close. I'm so incredibly weary. I lean back into the soft sheets of the bed, running my hands idly on top of the covers.

"Child," the Fairy speaks, touching my shoulder., "You need to drink this."

I open my eyes, raising my head slightly. She presses a silver glass into my hand., "You need your strength back."

Gwen helps me pull the pouch of slat out, pinching out a bit. The white salt fades into the purple drink, disappearing. I start sipping gingerly at the liquid, warmth tickling my lips. But the drink, it's soft honey, incredible. I gulp the drink eagerly, feeling the fine drink run through my veins. My blood picks up speed, my heart beating quicker. The salt may block enchantment, but the drink is still fiery—a Fairy drink.

I drain the glass, holding it back out to the Fairy. Gwen takes the silver cup, hovering in front of me.,

"May I ask you something, child?"

I blink at her nervous tone., "Of course."

Gwen runs her tongue over her dark lips, "What is your name?"

My cheeks flush, and I almost laugh., "I'm Darcy." I brush a strand of my hair away from my sticky face., "I never asked yours. I'm so sorry."

The Fairy tilts her head, still smiling., "Darcy. Such a fine name." She floats away from the bed, setting the silver glass on a mahogany table. "Some keep their names secret." She looks back at me, and I marvel at the swirling liquid depths of her violet eyes, "There is power in names."

I let out a nervous laugh; now that I've drunk the honey liquid, I feel on edge. Jittery., "There's no power in my name. I'm just a human." Gwen hums softly at my answer, "You humans have lived too long without Fae wisdom." She darts back over to me, her wings fluttering, "You have no more imagination."

I want to argue. Isolt has plenty of imagination, though her Fae and the Queen's stories aren't nearly as fantastic or terrifying as this strange country. I didn't know I could feel magic in waves of cold and heat. I didn't know the Queen's beauty could wrap itself in painful lashes around your skin. Gwen lays a hand on my forehead, her thin hand cool, "You still have a fever, Darcy." She twitters to the bedside table, picking up a brush.

My shoulders ease as she uncoils my sweaty hair, "You should sleep now. I'll wake you when it's time for tonight's festivities."

I wince at her words. I just have a few hours to sleep and try to feel better. I don't know if I can handle seeing the Queen again. Gwen lays a hand on my shoulder, urging me to lay back. I want to close my eyes and sleep forever. But I can't. If I don't face the Queen and her searing magic again, my entire journey here will be a waste. Anya and I need the gold.

Chapter Five

Brendan

For the second time in a week, a messenger rushes into our barracks, his hooved feet stamping on the cobbled floor, the golden embroidery on his coat flashing. I take the glittering envelope, breaking the seal.

The entire squadron of men all leans forward as I read the message. "The Queen wants Brendan again.," one of my men whistles low., "I swear, there's something tricky in the air." I hand back the envelope, and the messenger scampers off. The men look at each other as I mumble a protest. They can think whatever they want. I'm just following orders. Messages directly from the Queen always stir up gossip, though the human girl has already sent waves of gossip through the entire Court.

I still haven't decided whether I want to lay eyes on the mortal again. I know Flavian has been dragging her around.

She probably doesn't need me. I was useful the other night in the forest, even if it did cause problems with my Father. I don't debate interfering with my Father's men or feeling pity for the girl. Right now, showing up anywhere near the girl will only make my life messier. My Father and Flavian might disagree, but I don't try to make either of them angry on purpose. Even though my Father has ignored me since our argument, I know he's still furious with me. At least my Father's range doesn't extend to my men. They don't need to worry about my dealings with the mortal. So I answer as curtly as possible, "It doesn't matter what I want. I'm here at our Court to obey orders."

I don't need to look to see they're all rolling their eyes at me. Muttering about knowing I'd say that. I might have dismissed court gossip with this game answer a hundred different times, but at least now, my constant excuse protects me from having to talk about the mortal. Or how I freed her from my Father's creature. I snap my cloak around my shoulders, my feet stamping across the open courtyard. Behind every pillar, standing in every door, clusters of courtiers whispering.

The mortal has us all in turmoil. I can almost hear my Father snarling about it, a mortal making Fae ears twitch and turning his son into a rash fool. I'm not sure which my Father is more upset about, the Court's infatuation with the mortal or my insubordinate attitude. My actions surprised him, which explained his immediate anger. Hopefully, the disturbed Court will keep him distracted until he calms down.

Anything that makes a Fae's ears twitch riles my Father. The whispers are more humorous than infuriating, a fuss over a mortal girl. I'm not sure the girl is much more than a child. She was nothing but skin and bones; I could feel her shoulder blade poking through her dress. She's simply a girl who wants help. Whatever happened in her own family, she needs the gold to escape. I'm sure she's heard stories about leprechauns and gold and accidentally stumbled into our world.

It's unseemly. But mortals aren't known for being seemly. And from the state of her dress, the thinness of her bones, a starving mortal. Willing to do anything for food. Eagerness for gold and plenty blinding her good sense.

Sometimes humans are confusing. With their finite lives, finite understanding, it's strange that humans remain such puzzles. I think of our Fae scholars hidden deep beneath our Valorah Temple. Years of books and spells and mortals are still elusive mysteries. Why they even exist, how they feel so deeply, their ability to create falsehood so easily. Lives without consequence. If a scholar with decades of research can't grasp the human heart, then I cannot. I don't think this girl is hard to understand, and she's probably just hungry. I don't think her human heart played a role in landing her in our Court.

I weave my way through clumps of Fae courtiers. Sometimes, the courtiers will chat about romance or family arguments, or upcoming tournaments. Not today. Every Fae I walk by is whispering about

Darcy, the human. I'm surprised any of these empty-headed courtiers know Darcy's name. Most Fae would just refer to her as a mortal and nothing else. I think this morning's audience with the human and our Queen impressed most everyone. I'm still glad I didn't see it. My Queen's magic isn't limited.

Though what the human feels is supposed to be limited.

Darcy shouldn't have suffered. The magic seared her: a rare thing, any human who can truly feel Fae magic. Most Fae magic will hardly bother a human. Humans might smell something, a tangy flavor, or static in the air. They know leprechauns can spin wheat into gold and that Fae can walk through their world into our own.

The magic tortured Darcy. Fae whispers repeat the story, how she crumpled with agony before the Queen. I didn't need to see the torture to know what it must have been like. A ghastly sight. Magical pain is not a sight the Court likes to see. Magic and pain belong on the battlefield for Fae like my Father and our family. The Court thinks this torture was a spectacle. I'm relieved I didn't witness the girl's pain. Watching my men suffer is hard enough, and I imagine human suffering is nightmarish.

When I was younger, I saw a Fae tortured with sheer magic. The first time I'd followed my Father to the frontiers. It wouldn't be the last time I'd join him. Sleeping in the mud was hard. Drilling with the men, eating weeks old food. Skirmishes with rebellious pixies and hunting goblins.

Nothing prepared me for the punishment. I can't even remember how old I was, maybe twelve or thirteen. I'd seen a whipping, but it was with a whip. Nothing magical about it. I was expecting that when my Father bound the sentry. He put us all at risk when he fell asleep. The sentry vomited, writhing in pain as my Father tore at his organs, blood pooling through his skin. His bones splintered like aged wood. My Father forced all of us to watch, though I couldn't tear my eyes from the sight. I'd never seen my Father so furious and powerful. Of course, I wasn't blind to his power. But on the battlefield, it was so much different from the restraint of Court. It was raw, untamed, blinding. A fury I vowed never to cross.

I still shudder at the memory, my Father forcing the sentry to his knees, his skin hanging in shreds, bones crushed. My Father touched the Fae's ears and burned the pointed tips off as the Fae screamed. Losing his ears was infinitely worse than the horrible pain of my Father's torture. A Fae without ears is eternally shamed as unfit to serve. I swallow back the memory, focusing on the elaborate swirls decorating the marble floors—torchlight flickering off the emerald patterns.

As always, two Fae guards stand before the Queen's hall. "I received Her Majesty's summons." "Sir.," they each bow their heads, greeting me before they swing the doors open. The darkness hits me. The Queen must be disturbed; the hallway is so dark, the Queen's light hidden. Despite my disbelief of the rumors, the Queen's mood is sour for it to be so dark. I quickly dim my light, my skin losing its soft glow. Not all Fae have natural light, but my mother's blood allows me to shine. I won't let myself shine when the Queen's light is dim. It would be inappropriate, dishonoring. My mother would laugh at me, telling me not to hide just for someone else's comfort. My mother had never cared much about comforting the Fae Queen.

My senses are on high alert as I tread the quiet hallway, my eyes narrowing. At least this hallway is empty. Not groups of courtiers whispering Darcy's name. I pull up short at the Queen's door, gently knocking on wood.

A moment passes before I hear her voice., "Come in, Brendan." I push open the wood, bowing in the doorway. I drop one knee on the stone floor, my sword skimming against the ground., "My majesty."

I barely see the light move as my Queen turns from her balcony. Despite what I heard about her pale face in the Court, her voice is lucid. No tremble to her greeting, as she begins without preamble, "You were not present in the throne room this morning."

"As you say, majesty." I look up as my Queen steps forward, her skirt glimmering. She raises her palms, light flickering from her fingertips, "You missed a sight worth a thousand years."

Again, I repeat my previous words, "As you say, majesty." I don't hope to live a thousand years, but my Queen has seen years beyond most, thousands of years into the past. I trust her judgment.

"What are they saying among the guards, Brendan. What did you hear?"

"Rumors, majesty. Rumors of a mortal who could taste true magic. A mortal who suffers magic acutely." My words hang in the air, and I glance at my Queen's face. Her eyes narrow, but she's not looking at me. I hold my breath, hoping the answer is sufficient. I can't imagine she wants me to repeat what the entire Court says, the story I heard. Darcy the human, a heap of tears and vomit in front of the throne. The Queen ran from her throne, turning away from the girl's pain. I'm sure the Queen didn't run. The story is gossip, exaggerated. Fae Queens don't run from humans. "Brendan," the Queen releases my name softly. "You are no fool. You know my son is missing." I don't say anything, lowering my head. The Queen steps again, her shoes clicking on the stone floor., "I must speak to the mortal alone.

She is the key to reaching the Finn."

Reaching the Finn, I almost jolt at her words. The Finn envoy teased me five weeks ago when I collected the annual taxes. Everyone knows the Finn King Murtagh despises the Queen, only swearing loyalty to the Seelie Court because a war would decimate his own kingdom. The Finn are ferocious and cruel. If they touched Prince Edric, the Court would clamor for war. It's a monstrous idea, and I'm sure they wouldn't dare touch the Prince.

"Brendan.," The Queen's tone is sharp,., "You will speak of this to no one. These are my theories. Mine alone." "Yes, majesty," I can barely breathe my assurance., "I stand to serve." My Queen's harrowed face lightens, the lines around her eyes smoothing., "I have always counted on your family. What I ask of you must remain secret. Not even your Father can know."

Lines in my back tense at her words, my shoulders straightening. This conversation will be another reason for my Father to rage at me. I bow my head before taking leave of the Queen. She didn't give me any specific answers. Wait around until I'm needed. I've done that my whole life, and since I don't plan on dying anytime soon, I should just get used to waiting. I should also get accustomed to my Father's anger. My mother would laugh at me and tell me to give up trying. Perhaps if Edric hadn't disappeared, I might have abandoned the Court for my mother's estate in the North.

It's isolated and quiet, but they're no cryptic queens or angry orders. But if I left, Flavian would still need me.

My thoughts must have summoned him because Flavian rushes around the dark hallway, nearly colliding into me.

He's panting, and sweat clings to his forehead. He must have rushed to the barracks before finding out I went to the Queen's rooms. He looks around, searching for one of the Queen's guards before demanding to know what I've been doing. I easily evade his question. "You're supposed to be with Darcy."

"The girl's sleeping." His words come fast., "She's not human," he sputters, "She's not just here because of gold and leprechauns. She's not human."

"Of course, she's human.," I knock my fist into his shoulder, "I thought you had more sense than to accost me with random theories."

"She felt the Queen's magic."

"And nearly died from it," I interject. "Only a human would have felt that level of pain. Any other creature can handle magic. That's why humans aren't supposed to feel magic at all."

He lets out a shaking breath., "She's more than human, then." I shrug. "You're probably right. Just keep watching her, obeying my Father." I can't entirely hide the edge from my voice, "You both have everything under control, I'm sure."

His chin jerks up, eyes glittering. "I'm not conspiring with your father."

"Then what are you doing?" I try to shoulder past him, but he grabs my elbow.

"Brendan.," His breath hits my face., "Your father disdains me, and I'd never trust him with Edric or anyone." "I didn't ask if you trusted him.," I shake his hands from me, beginning to step away., "You're working with him to spy on Darcy. You don't need to trust him to go behind my back."

"That's unfair, Brendan." I look over my shoulder, raising my hands, "The girl might be awake. Better get back to spying."

Darcy

Gwen wakes me as promised, pulling me out of bed. I'm dreading tonight's dinner; my chest is still sore from earlier. I can't imagine living through that pain again. But Gwen is so happy, so I can't glower at her enthusiasm. She prattles on about the dress she picked out for me—a deep royal blue, a gold thread woven into the collar. Hundreds of buttons line the back, and I slip the pouch of salt into the front. Gwen pulls my hair into an elegant twist. She divided my long dark hair into three sections, braiding little white flowers into the strands before fastening the braids into a crown. Then Gwen turns me around by the shoulder, flitting to a long cloth hanging on the wall.

She raises the cloth, and I gasp at the crystal mirror hidden underneath. The fabric falls to the floor; the entire wall is a mirror. I step close, holding out my hand, touching the glass. I've only seen my reflection a few times. In a well-polished copper plate or a bowl of clean water. I hate going to the ocean, though I know Anya claims she can see her reddish hair in the water. I'd rather not know what I look like than fight my fear of the water to catch a glimpse.

But this mirror, I can see more than a reflection. My very face looks back at me. I turn slowly, lifting the heavy skirt of the elegant dress. The golden threads twinkle back at me, and I'm laughing. It's so strange, seeing yourself like this.

"Ah, Darcy," Gwen sighs., "How much humans miss now." I give her a sad smile before looking back at my reflection. I grin, my teeth flashing. I reach out my fingers, touching my nose on the mirror, then I'm giggling. I could live here, just to have this mirror.

Just as I'm thinking how pleasant living here would be, someone's pounding on the door. I jump while Gwen darts over, opening the wooden door. Of course, it's Flavian. "You're not letting her admire herself," Flavian mutters to

Gwen, loud enough for me to hear., "Humans are already vain enough."

With all the hundreds of Fae I've seen standing around this palace, you'd think they could afford to spare a more hospitable guide.

I swirl, the skirt swishing against the floor., "It's just like you Fae to hoard all the mirrors to yourself." I snap the words., "Since humans are beneath your very notice."

Gwen gasps, and I feel my cheeks flush. She doesn't deserve the accusation; I want to apologize to her. She's been nothing but kind.

"If we hadn't noticed you, you wouldn't be here," Flavian replies smoothly. He jerks his chin at me, "But unless you plan on being late to dinner, I suggest you hurry up."

"You could arrive earlier," I retort. Gwen touches my arm, and I look at her. Her face is screwed together, concern edging in her eyes. I touch her thin hand; she's so small compared to Flavian, "Thank you, Gwen." She licks her lips, slipping my knife into the belt around my waist., "Your shoes.," She inclines her head, and I glance at the pair of dark heels sitting in front of the mirror.

I've never worn heels, and I don't want another reason for Flavian to sneer at me. "Can I go without them?" Her eyes widen, dark eyelashes batting. "Without shoes?"

"Of course not," Flavian answers., "That's nonsense."

So much for trying. I step gingerly into the heels. My feet rarely feel any pain, but my pinched toes are almost too much. I can't stand it. And I've barely put them on. Flavian stalks to the door, swinging it open. I look back at Gwen, wanting to thank her, apologize for spitting at Flavian.

But I'll see her later tonight. I'll thank her properly then when Flavian isn't listening.

Flavian leads me the same path from earlier today. Except, I simply can't keep up. My ankles fight the heels, I keep my skirt bunched in my fists, cursing at the stupid shoes. I want to leave them behind. Especially the third time one of the shoes falls off. I trip down several steps before darting back to pick the shoe up. The worst part, there's even more Fae standing on the stair landings, watching me. They don't bother hiding their laughter.

As we descend, my stomach grows tighter, my breathing more rapid. Sweat breaks out, and my palms are clammy.

The pain from earlier, I don't think I can stomach it again.

We step off the final step, or I should say, I step off the last step. Flavian is pacing in circles, waiting for me. He grabs my elbow; my feet skitter on the stone floor. If this is what condemnation feels like, I think I can imagine an execution. My breathing is sharper, but there's no time to prepare. The doors to the throne room are open, two Fae guards standing armed on each side. I try to drag my feet, willing myself not to step over that threshold. But Flavian's hold is insistent. Against every ounce of my will, I must go in that throne room.

I take in a breath as my heels shoes clamber over the threshold. I clench my fists; my eyes squeezed tightly shut.

There is nothing. Not an ounce of magic. No pressure. No pain.

Instead, I hear music, the beat of drums and trill of flutes. I slowly open my eyes, my breath releasing in a slow sigh of relief. I didn't take in the throne room earlier, notice the elegant vines carved into the pillars or the tapestries hanging from the ceilings. When you're trying not to vomit from pain, you don't take that the time to enjoy the Fae Court. Now, the throne room is lit brilliantly with thousands of candles. I turn my head, still slightly nervous. Anya would know what to do, how to curtsy or smile, or even how to dance. Clusters of Fae Courtiers nod to me, a few bowing slightly as Flavian and I walk past them. I don't know if I'm supposed to speak to any of them or courtesy at their greetings. Anya would have found a way home by now, charmed these creatures into giving her gold without even making a foolish bargain. I finally look back towards my escort. Flavian is smirking; I pause at the amusement written on his delicate features. Lovely to know that my obvious discomfort is amusing someone. "You know, I can smell your fear," he chuckles, laying a hand against my shoulder. "Humans have no way to control their emotions."

My blood boils, thoughts of Anya and her charm slipping away, "And Fae have no way to control their pride." He roughly pulls his hand away, and I nearly trip in the ridiculous heels, losing my balance. The heel of these stupid shoes wobble, and I gather my skirt into my hands. Flavian is feet ahead, taking quick steps past more of the Fae onlookers. He leads away from the throne I saw earlier, walking between pillars to a long alcove.

Rows weave between tables, wooden chairs filled with groups of Fae eating and chatting. Musicians stand in the corner of the alcove, playing stringed instruments and flutes. The music is at times lighthearted, cheerful. Then the notes shift, the tones growing dark and brooding.

Flavian must be a well-known figure. Several Fae turn from their chairs, standing up to speak to him.

One claps him on the shoulder before looking me over, not bothering to keep his voice low., "She doesn't look strong enough to last much longer." My skin flushes, my fingers bunched tight around my dress.

Flavian spares a glance at me, his eyes narrowing. But the blasted Fae answers in their language, and I'm left ignorant, watching them talk about me without knowing a word they're saying.

Finally, Flavian leads me to an empty table with Platters of food lined up on a silver tablecloth. Flavian pulls out a chair, motioning for me to sit. I do, kicking my heels off immediately. Flavian pulls out another chair, sinking into the seat. He reaches for a platter of meat, serving himself the food. I watch him as he gathers vegetables and pours sauce over the pudding. His plate is so full; the food begins to pile up. He looks at me., "We're not poisoning you. Eat something."

I reach for the meat, picking up the golden serving tongs. I should be hungry, though the drink Gwen gave me was certainly magical, that was hours ago. Usually, I'd be starving, my mouth watering at the sight of this food. But worry, my fear of magical pain, it keeps my stomach tight. The Queen may not be here now, but I still don't know if I'm completely safe.

I feel Flavian's eyes on me. I reach into the front of my dress, pulling out my pouch and sprinkling salt across my plate. I take a small bite and nearly groan. The flavors are enticing. I don't bother with more seasoning or adding the sauce. Flavian watches me, commenting almost to himself, "Protecting yourself from enchantment."

I swallow before tucking the pouch back into my bodice. Flavian's eyes follow my hand, and I resist yanking the collar back up. No sense in keeping his eyes on my chest. "I don't intend on being bound to your court for seven years.," I stab at a piece of meat. "I'm only here for the promise of gold."

Flavian flicks his bangs away from his eyes. "As though we'd need a weakling like you for seven years." My cheeks heat, but I don't bother replying. The Fae don't need humans, but they still use their enchantments to bind my kind to service. A golden taste of food for a lifetime of slavery. I'm sure I've heard that story a dozen times, though I haven't seen any humans in this Court.

"I meant to ask," Flavian's elegant voice throws me off guard., "Why did you catch the leprechaun?" I glance up at the Fae's face, my mouth full of something delicious. A quick swallow., "Why does anyone catch a leprechaun?." I raise the golden fork in my hand.

Flavian eyes me coolly., "You seem stronger than gold."

I open my lips, but I'm not sure what to say. The Fae, I think he's just trying to get under my skin. He leans toward me, resting his elbows on the table., "Humans can't live under magic. It should have broken you." The magic practically broke me; the thought comes quick. My fists clench., "I nearly died meeting your queen.," I'm seething, his calm infuriating me., "I don't want to live through that again." "Then why did you come?" "You think I knew I'd feel that?" I drop my fork, the metal clanging against the plate.

"You can see leprechauns." Flavian waves his hand at me., "You know humans can't speak to the

Queen. Of course, any rational creature realizes you're sensitive to magic."

Well, I'm not sensible, I think irritably. I was stupid to try to move away from the sea, silly to catch Hoyt. I push the plate away. I should be eating dinner with Anya, something hearty and warm she made for us both. I'm stupid to be sitting here, talking to a Fae. A pretentious, snobbish Fae who despises me. But Flavian isn't done. He leans even closer., "You are either incredibly stupid or deviously cunning."

I gape at him. He's insane, "And you're either incredibly pompous or downright rude."

A muscle tightens in his jaw, his long fingers curling. His nostrils flare. "When my Queen is done with you.," He breathes in a rush., "When our Prince returns, whatever you've done to him, you'll suffer for it."

He jumps to his feet so quickly; I don't have a moment to react. The chair falls to the floor, crashing. But the music is loud enough, and no-one looks our way. I'm left alone at the table, Flavian's fierce words and anger unsettling.

I know nothing about the Fae prince. But Flavian thinks I do. The Queen, my knees tremble. She'll torture me again if she thinks I touched her son. The extreme pain from earlier was only meeting her. I'm suddenly nauseous, my hands quivering. Actual Fae torture would be so much worse than simply feeling magic. My heart pounds into my throat as my eyes burn. I need to get out of here.

Chapter Six

Darcy

THE ONLY PROBLEM – I don't have a clue how to leave. The way Hoyt led me to the leprechauns, that was long ago. In daylight. But the winged warriors, the dark forest. I've no clue how to get back. I push back my chair, my knees shaking. I can at least return to my room, beg Gwen for help. She's been kind, perhaps. I shake my head, stepping around the table.

The room is full of Fae. I wipe my sweaty hands on the silk dress before taking several quick steps.

It's hard to avoid looking up, staring at the Fae seated around the large room. But I can't. I simply can't attract their attention. All I have is the pouch of salt, the dagger at my waist. The Leprechaun promised me safety, but I don't know if Hoyt's promise will even begin to hold here.

I walk away from the central aisle, skirting under the balcony. Torch-light reflects off the stone walls, and I dart along the pillars, pausing in their shadows. No-one moves to stop me. No curses are flying toward my head. No Fae gazes are turning my way or whispered glamor. I'm still my own person. Their whispers cannot touch me, not now. I need to leave this court and leave this twisted palace before any protection I've promised wears thin.

I take several breaths before scurrying to the next pillar. My palms are sweaty again, and I fist my fingers into the skirt.

"Little mortal," the voice echoes behind me, and I jerk. I turn around, grabbing ahold of the pillar. His voice is familiar, caressing me as though I've been dreaming.

I press my back against the pillar, my hand dropping to my dagger. The metal is snug in the grasp of the gilded belt at my waist, offering me some small comfort. I took down that beastly Leprechaun. I try to force my breathing to slow down. The Fae is looking at me, his dark eyes sweeping over me. I pull my arms together, digging my fingers into my ribs. I notice his wings, alert, pearl feathers glistening in the damp light.

"My queen would see you," the Fae speaks again, his voice brisk., "Flavian informed me you were at the table." *Flavian*, his name is bitter on my tongue., "He was misinformed." I spit at the Fae warrior., "He makes too many assumptions."

The Fae's lips curve., "Then you already know Flavian well." He holds out a hand, leather guards on his wrist. "Come, follow me."

I hesitate, trying to remember him. His voice is so familiar. But I didn't see him earlier, and I'm sure I would have seen those flashing dark eyes, his sharp cheeks. I press my fingers into the pillar., "You're taking me to your Queen?"

He dips his head slightly, torchlight reflecting off his dark curling hair. But he doesn't answer. His silence bolsters me., "I can't see her. She practically killed me last time."

"Ah.," The Fae raises both hands. "Darcy," He peers at me., "May I use your name?"

I swallow, briefly wondering how he knows. I still can't place his face and voice. The Fae continues, "My Queen does not need to bind you with magic or glamor you from pain. She has no desire to see you suffer." He holds out a ring, "This will protect you."

The ring glitters, dark blue stones set in a golden circle, "What is it?"

"It doesn't break the curse," The Fae replies steadily, "It just dulls the pain."

"The curse," I step forward, studying his tan hand, "What curse?"

The Fae's black eyebrows furrow at my question, "The curse that prevents humans from talking to my Queen. You mortals often call it by something else. The magic of Oona's beauty."

In the stories I've heard, Queen Oona is so beautiful that mortals are left speechless just by looking at her. "We're forced into silence." I sputter sputter, my frustration with the pain, the Fae, everything rushing forward., "Her beauty is a curse on us?"

"Mortals use simple words to explain the extraordinary." The Fae shrugs, a dark curl nearly falling into his eyes., "You can't be troubled with the truth."

"Truth?" I take a step, wrenching the ring from his fingers. "Or do you just not bother to explain things? It suits your purposes to keep us all in the dark?"

The Fae's lips curl again as he grins. "Remember, mortal. We're the ones who live below ground in perpetual darkness. We know a thing or two about being kept in the dark."

I scowl at him before looking down at the ring. It slips easily onto my finger, but I'm still nervous.

The Queen didn't expect me to feel the magic earlier, and yet I did. Does she even know how to protect me? The Fae touches my shoulder, and I startle, stiffening. I hadn't even realized he had moved. Fae stealth, I grit my teeth at him.

"Remember, Darcy," he speaks softly, leaning down to my ear., "If you think to break the curse, you'll need to take the ring off."

"I'm not breaking any curses.," I run my finger over the ring, "I'm only here because I caught a leprechaun." The Fae snorts, pushing me forward as he begins to walk, "And do you know how many leprechauns' you mortals have caught in the last thousand years?"

I look up at him, and he's still grinning. He pats my head, and I scowl at the pampering way he treats me.

As if I don't know anything. Though it's practically true, at the moment, I seem to know nothing.

"I know you want to flaunt your way home, a reward of gold for catching one of the Queen's spies." He turns me down a corridor, "But that's not how the Fae Court works, little mortal. When something strange happens, we investigate." "And I'm something strange."

He barely nods. "One of many strange things that have happened lately."

"The queen's son?"

His fingers tighten around my shoulders, digging into my shoulder blades., "For your sake, Darcy, I hope it is but a coincidence that you arrive so soon after Edric's disappearance. You do not want the Fae as your enemy."

His voice has gone lower, colder. My heart is pounding in my chest again, my palms sweating. If his hands weren't so tight on my shoulders, I'd bolt. But this Fae Warrior, he's not letting go. "How long?" I choke out the words., "How long has the prince been gone?"

The warrior doesn't answer, and I risk a glance up at his face. My next breath nearly burns my lungs. The Fae's eyes, a vibrant blue, have darkened to almost glittering black.

His lips curl, elongated teeth showing., "Five weeks," he snarls. "Five gods-cursed weeks."

Over a month, my thoughts whirl. The Fae magic, they can see beyond their world, I've heard that before. But if they could see any-where, wouldn't the Fae Queen know where her son was? And what did *the beyond* even mean? If I weren't so nervous, I'd laugh. My cheeks flush, and my fingers tighten, my stomach tightening. The stories I've heard are mostly rubbish.

Leprechauns don't hand out gold to mortals. The Fae are nothing like sweet pixies. Magic forced on my people, disguised as beauty. My feet skid on the marble floors, and the Fae warrior practically lifts me, taking it on himself to keep me up to pace. The hall here is quieter, the lights dimmer. Shadows lengthen on the floor, and the stones glisten in the semi-darkness; I can practically see my reflection in the marble.

I almost catapult forward, the Fae dropping my shoulders. Stum-bling, and then I'm on the floor. My hands scrape on the stone cut floor, my knees bumping painfully.

I hiss at my grazed palms. A door in front of me, the wood so dark, black as shadows, nearly night.

Guards are standing on each side, smirking, glancing at each other.

"Stand up.," The Fae leans down, whispering, catching my shoulders between his grip. "Don't grovel at anyone's feet."

"It wasn't intentional," I hiss back, trying to shake out of his grip. He loosens his fingers slightly, the cloth rubbing against my shoulder. "Just keep standing," he breathes into my ear again, "and keep the ring close."

At his words, I touch the ring, pushing it further, it bites into my joints. Then I twist the metal; it turns stiffly, tight on my forefinger. The doors open slowly, silently. But it's just as dark, open or shut. "Get on," the warrior urges just behind me, and I take a soft step.

The floor is still the same as I step over the threshold. Instantly, my hand throbs, and I grasp at the ring, pressing my open palm into the metal.

"I'm truly sorry about that," a faint voice speaks in the still room. I turn, and my eyes blink. A hazy gaze steps towards me, the tall Fae Queen wreathed in sparkling light. Her long blonde hair falls around her, fluttering in waves around her waist. Her dress, it's nearly translucent, wisps of silvery air moving around her as the Fae Queen walks towards me. "I can do only so much to contain the magic.," The Fae Queen gestures towards me., "I have not had the chance to meet many Halflings such as yourself."

Halfling, I don't look down at the ring. I twist my hands together, my thoughts quick, a dozen questions I don't want to ask. But my brain seems to have a mind of its own, thoughts tumbling forward. The words want to come, but even as I open my mouth, the sound is trapped. I can't speak, though my entire body lounges forward, my throat fighting to say something, anything.

"I cannot say with certainty what you are," the Queen speaks quietly, and I close my mouth, ragged breathing fighting forward. I gasp, then try to catch my breath again. "I can still see your thoughts," The Queen continues, "Murky, but not hidden." She lifts her head, "Only fools would bind humans to silence if they could not read minds."

I almost smile at the dry tone of the Queen's voice. Of course, she can see mortal thoughts. My fingers are trembling, as pain still buries its way into my palms. "But mortals." She steps to me, and I nearly fall back. She is so tall, looming over me, her pale face glowing. Her crystal eyes blink, and she raises a hand touching my chin.

My flinch is automatic, but the Queen remains composed. I look away from her intense eyes, studying the flowers braided into her hair. They aren't shining but reflecting the light from the Queen. And as I watch, a petal falls loose, drifting to the ground. My eyes follow the single petal, and the Queen lets go of my chin. She snaps her finger, the petal curling into a flame.

My eyes widen, my breath catching again, and the Queen tilts her head, smiling softly. She touches a petal close to her ear. "Can you count the petals?" I look at the flowers twisted into her loose hair and weakly shake my head. A few dozen, perhaps, I'm not sure. "I stopped counting long ago," the queen murmurs., "Back when I first took the crown, the petals were never-ending. An eternal wreath." She lets out a sigh, touching one of the flowers.,

"Now, the time grows shorter. Fewer petals, fewer years."

Her hand falls away from her hair, letting go of the flower. Whatever the flowers do, I've still no idea. "Darcy," the Queen murmurs my name, drawing my thoughts away from the petals., "You love, not as a mother, but as a sister." I don't have a sister. But my cousin, Anya. I think she may be closer to me than most sisters. The Queen continues, raising her hands. Light shimmers at the ends of her fingers, I turn away, my eyes burning, "I love as a mother.," she places her hands together., "And I know when my child suffers."

The Fae Prince. I want to say something, offer my condolences. But the Queen doesn't wait to read my thoughts as she continues speaking, "I knew the Finn Folk took him. The gods gave me that much knowledge. But until you came, I did not know why."

My fingers are tight around the ring. The Finn are barely familiar. I need to close my eyes and sort through stories I've heard to remember something more about them. There's no time for my brain to catch up. Queen Oona lays her hand on my head, running a finger over my hair. She pulls at my braid, pinching a strand.

"You feel what you should not. And you lack what you should know." I go rigid, goosebumps climbing up my arm, down my neck. I want to step away from this Queen, but her loose touch on my head has tightened.

"The Finn folk don't want my son; they want to use him for something else." She forces my head up, "After you came, I forced myself to look to the Finns again. You mortals, you think so simply of my powers. You assume I can see anything."

Of all the stories I've heard, I can barely remember what I've heard about the Fae Queen's power. I knew she was beautiful, but I can't seem to clear my head. To remember what Isolt might have mentioned. I'm still trying to remember who the Finn are. I think they live in the ocean.

Her pale lips curl. "It takes so much of my strength to invade the Finn kingdom. I can barely hold the vision together. But it was enough."

She lets go of my head, and my chin falls, my temple aching. I again touch the ring, wanting some reassurance. The magic bites my palm, but that is better than nothing.

"Look.," A pure command, laced with power. I look up. The Queen holds something in her hand, dark against the light.

My toes inch forward, the darkness ripples. A mirage.

The rippling image, Finn Folk flit about, their faces fierce. As soon as I see them, the stories rush back. They look just like the Fae, except their hands and feet are webbed. Their teeth are sharper, their ears ending in harsh lines. They hate humans, and they gut stray fishermen merely because they can. My eyes drift over the mirage, my throat burning at the glimpse of their long, knifelike nails. The armor clasped around their waist, swords strapped to their backs as they dart about in murky waters.

Then I see her. Anya. My breath catches at the vision of my cousin. My knees give, and I fall forward, clasping for the image. Anya. Her name rings through my mind, Anya; her name sits on my tongue, an aching silent cry.

Her skin is pale with red curling hair floating around her. Dress billowing in the water. Held in a cage, the Finn Guards are pressing the tips of spears to her skin. Anya, tears prick my eyes as I drag in another breath. Anya, my Anya. Sweat is pouring down my neck, I blubber, but the sound is void. I can't say anything as sheer panic grasps me. "You are not ignorant of the Finn," the Queen speaks, and the mirage disappears. I blink at the light, tears running down my cheeks. My eyes ache to see the mirage again, to see Anya. They have Anya, and my mind beats with questions., *how did they take my cousin, whatever for, why?*

"They have something we both love," The Queen says quietly, "I don't pretend to know the mind of the Finn king. He would never let me take a glimpse into his soul."

I look up. If the Queen could see Anya, why not the king? She must read my thoughts as she holds out her palm. Flat, I see the jagged black marks cut across her porcelain skin. My stomach flips.

"Visions have a price." The Queen peers down at me., "The Finn wanted me to see your cousin, or else they would have never allowed me to see into their kingdom."

I still don't understand. Anya, the prince, what could these Finn want? "I was not looking for your cousin.," The Queen steps away, the wisps of light trailing behind her, "But your arrival prompted me to search. You are so different. I had to wonder. Few kingdoms dare touch a Fae. The Finn Folk are one of those."

I've heard a few Finn stories, but the tales I've heard are horrible. The Finn are the sort of stories told around embers at a Samhain fires. I'm trying to fight back my panic, searching for one of the stories. The details are vague, I think I've heard someone mention that the Finn and Fae don't get along.

Of course, it's just my luck to stumble into an ancient quarrels between two magical kingdoms. If only I hadn't seen the Leprechaun, tears pour over my cheeks. I left Anya, and I wasn't home. I should have been there for her. Anya should be home safe, not caught up in this mess I made.

I fidget with the ring, twisting it back and forth. I just want to leave this cursed palace and find the Finn. The leprechaun could take me back to the ocean. I've heard the mermaids and Finn visit the ocean surface before the sun rises, maybe if I waded out knee deep before dawn, the Finn would see me. I can speak to them, I think, I'd find a way to beg them to trade me for Anya's life.

"Mortal," the queen sighs, interrupting my runaway thoughts., "Always conjuring useless plans. The Finn avoid the ocean surface at all costs as the sun is poison to their skin."

She shakes her head, hair swaying side to side., "Instead of suffering through useless guilt," the Queen is still talking as my thoughts tumble. "Work with me. You want your cousin; I want my son. The Finn don't want me, but perhaps, you could journey to them."

Journey to the Finn? I blink at her suggestion. I've never heard of a mortal wanting to see the Finn. There are no stories of Finns letting humans go—only stories of tortured souls, broken minds. Again, I see the vision of Anya bound in a cage, chains around her thin wrists.

The Queen's voice is sharper., "The Finn want our Fae vision. They wanted to see something. Whatever the Finn want to see, they need your mind."

But wouldn't any Fae work? I think quickly, and the Queen is apparently reading my mind as she catches my thoughts. Her eyes narrow, shoulders hunching, she glares at me., "You think any Fae can read minds? Only those of royal blood, ignorant mortals." She sputters, turning away from me before she speaks again, "I can't help you without a bargain. I don't trust anyone without sealing my trust with a bargain. Only magical bargains." Silence, and then,

"Normally, I would seal a bargain with a vow, but you cannot speak."

The Queen's back is to me. I don't know how I can bargain with her. "You will need to bargain wisely." I haven't made a wise decision since I met that Leprechaun. My last bargain was truly, truly stupid. But to save Anya, I'll do this. Face the Finn, the ocean, and their entire deadly kingdom.

The Queen speaks firmly, as though we've already decided what to do, "Here is our bargain, I will provide you passage to the Finn Passage. In return, you swear on your life to return my son, Prince Edric, to me."

"I will bargain with your mortal life.," She turns and takes a steps closer to me again, and I can almost swear that she's grown taller. She steps over to desk, brushing aside a bottle of ink and pulling out a leaf of parchment ., "You mortals think too highly of your own lives; you never think beyond your own existence."

She pronounces each word on the parchment as she writes them, "In return for my assistance guiding you to the Finn Folk, you swear on your mortal life that you will do all in your power to return my son, Prince Edric, to me. If you break this vow, your mortal blood with turn to poison in your veins and your heart will shrivel into stones."

I'm doing this for Anya, throwing all caution away and nodding along to the Queen's words. The Queen gestures for me to step forward, holding out the pen. But I don't know how to write my name, there's no needs for pens or parchments back in my village. I think this dawns on the Queen as I stare at the parchment, the swirling scrawl of words.

The Queen hisses through her teeth, muttering about ignorant humans. She swirls behind her, her hand clattering on the desk again. The she grabs at me, yanking me forward. I don't have time to pull back before she's slashing at my fingers with a knife.

Pain shoots up my arm, and if I could speak, I would yell a string of curse words. My entire hand is throbbing, an instant pain stabbing through me. I double over, gasping, before the Queen yanks me up and shoves the parchment under my hand. My hand is shaking, blood spitting on the contract, a landscape of dark blots under the Queen's penmanship.

Chapter Seven

Darcy

I GRIT MY TEETH, looking away from my own blood. The Queen pulls the parchment back, her grip steely around my wrist while she peruses my blood. She mutters a satisfied grunt, before dropping my wrist, and I stumble back, the pain intense.

"Very well," the Queen is muttering while I try to hold back tears. My hand is in agony, four of my five fingers sliced jaggedly. You'd think since my blood was part of her magical bargain, the Queen could take the time to practice her own magic and heal me. That's giving the Fae and their magic too much credit. The Queen rolls up the parchment before leaving her study. She's still talking, but I don't think she is actually speaking to me. She switched to her own Fae language, and I'm in too much pain to try and figure out what she's saying.

Her door slams behind her and I slump forward, reaching for the bottom of my dress. The fabric tears easily, and I take a strip and wrap it around my hand. The pain has settled into a dull throb.

I glance around, noticing the walls lined with wood paneling, etched with delicate flowers and shamrocks. The lines of the flowers glisten, dusted with golden flecks. The paneling ends with a large window, curtains blowing gently in the night breeze. Stars twinkle beyond the balcony while my heart leaps into my throat, the story the Queen has told me roaring in my ears. Anya, my cousin who loves the waves and craves the sound of ocean spray beating against the rocks. She can't see the stars wherever the Finn have taken her and trapped my kind, gentle cousin beneath those waves.

Every time the ocean beats viciously, I'd look to the stars. Even when the clouds darkened the sky, I knew they were there. If I closed my eyes, I could see them.

But I don't need to close my eyes now. The stars are so close to the Queen's window; I can almost touch them. Still, I don't reach my hand out. I take several steps towards the balcony, the cool air drifting through the window a whisper against my cheeks.

I hear the door open, and turn expecting the Queen. She's been replaced by my blonde, grouchy guard. "Where's the Queen?" I look past Flavian, the door stands open, but the Queen's luminous dress is gone.

"Her Majesty summoned me.," Flavian sounds pained, as though even the thought of having to stick with me longer is personally painful to him. "Honestly, I don't see the point of keeping you here."

I shrug, looking away from Flavian's hostile gaze., "She didn't tell me what to do."

"No," he snarls in reply., "That's my job." He takes a quick step towards me., "We don't have time. We need to go now."

I stumble away from him, sliding across the stone floor. There must be other Fae guards who can take me to the Finn. Flavian has made it abundantly clear that he doesn't trust me and doesn't want to follow me around the palace.

"It's my job, Darcy.," He gestures at me., "Despite your objections, I'll take you to the Finn. We need to leave." I'm scrambling for an excuse, a reason to wait. "I haven't said goodbye to Gwen." Maybe I'll run into the Queen again, beg wordlessly for another guide. Someone who doesn't hate leading me around and complains about my constant human weaknesses. Though apparently, they're only half-human weaknesses.

"The Queen's orders.," He quickly reaches for my shoulder, grabbing at the dress. I stiffen, and he lets the fabric go. "Don't touch me," I sidestep away from him, cradling my throbbing hand., "I don't know why you have to be the one to help me. You're not very helpful at all."

His jaw twitches., "We don't have time for this. This is serious."

"I am taking you seriously," I bite back, and he starts to shake his head at my words., "You're the one rushing me around."

Flavian takes in a breath, "Edric, my prince is gone." He stumbles over the Fae Prince's name, and my stomach tightens. He's so angry, but his anger is fiercer. As though the Prince belonged to him and not an entire Court. "It's a long journey to the Finn." He holds out his hand, his voice tinged with impatience, "And I'm not wasting a moment more for you to whine."

Flavian stifles as someone chuckles behind us., "No, Flavian. You're wasting your time scaring the lass to distraction." The voice is softer, and I release a breath as Flavian drops me, spinning towards the the gentle voice of my guide from earlier.

"And you wonder why her Majesty won't let you venture out alone."

"Shut it, Brendan," Flavian snarls at the other Fae.

Brendan, I swallow. The name is familiar. My mind wracks, trying to remember where I've heard it.

"I don't need your help," Flavian is speaking, his words biting at Brendan. "I could handle Darcy myself." I've never heard Flavian say my name. He keeps calling me "the mortal" so much that I almost thought he was refusing to learn my name. The two of them are arguing, quick words that mix in their own Fae language.

Flavian tosses his long blonde hair, his nostrils flaring as his fists clench at his side. I shift my weight from foot to foot, glancing out the window. The longer these two argue, the longer it will take for me to get to Anya.

Brendan takes a step, his heels clicking on the marble floor., "Only an idiot would be blind not to see your feeling. You're supposed to be a soldier. You can't fight for our Prince and rage about Edric at the same time. He belongs to the kingdom, not just you."

I wince at his harsh tone. Flavian may be rude, but Brendan's words aren't just rude; he's stripping away at Flavian's feelings. I've never felt more than a slight crush, but I've seen Anya fall in love. I know she'd pull out her own heart to save her man from drowning. If Flavian is anything like Anya, he probably feels as though he belongs to Edric just as much as he cares for Edric.

Flavian's hands clench into fists, his wings tight against his stiff shoulders. Brendan leans in closer, his words barely loud enough for me to hear, "Edric chose to walk away, you and I both know; he's too powerful just to let the Finn take him. He left you." Flavian lunges, and I let out a sequel as he throws a punch. My dress is too long, I stumble backward, tripping on the hem. Brendan steps out of Flavian's throw, blocking it quickly.

Flavian spits, his wings trembling. He twirls, throwing another punch. Brendan side steps, landing a blow to Flavian's gut. Then he rams a fist into Flavian, knocking him back. The two grapple, falling into the balcony, punching at each other. Their wings unfold, fists smacking against leather and bare arms. I don't want to look, but curiosity drives me forward. I peek around the corner. Brendan kicks, sweeping Flavian off his feet, and Flavian falls forward into the curtain. He lands on his knees, his breathing heavy.

Brendan grabs him, deftly lifts him, and then throws him over the balcony's railing.

I let out a scream, unbelieving what just happened. Brendan is standing on the balcony, the wind rustling in his hair. I gasp, stumbling towards the railway. I'm shaking, and I grab hold of the stone ledge, my eyes adjusting to the darkness surrounding the palace. I peer over, my hands tight around the railing.

Darkness stretches below me, small flickering lights the only sign of the ground below the palace walls.

Moments ago, I might have called Brendan the nicer one. But he just tossed Flavian from the palace. I can hear Brendan behind me, his shoes clicking on the balcony stones. I'm barely holding back another frustrated scream as I stare into the darkness, looking for the glint of Flavian's white hair. I jerk away as

Brendan's fingers brush the top of my head., "You killed him."

He chuckles., "He has wings. He'll use them."

I look up at him. The wind off the balcony is ruffling his feathers. "I never saw them."

His eyes dart above my head., "Prince Edric doesn't have wings." He clears his throat. "Flavian prefers not to remind him." Then Brendan turns on his heels, stepping out of the window. I stare at his back, his profile against the midnight sky. I wipe at my face, dragging in another breath. And I turn, looking around the room.

I hadn't seen it earlier. So spacious. Wooden furniture, patterned carpet, a wide desk. And directly behind me, a portrait. It must be the Prince, just as I'd expect a Fae Prince. Tall, but of course, he's in a painting. Anyone can be tall in a painting. Dark, curling hair surrounds an angular face and piercing blue eyes. His face is sharp, with harsh angles, but his hair defies the sharpness. Pointy ears and bony shoulders match his cutting face. Peeking out from his dark cape, pale long fingers, rings covering several of his knuckles. And just as Brendan said, no wings. The Queen doesn't have wings. I suppose the royal Fae are too elegant for them. There's something animal-like about Brendan's feathers, as though he's more beast than Fae. My mind flits through the myriad of Fae I've passed in the hallways. Scaly skin, purple hair, horns. If I had to choose anything Fae, I'd pick a set of wings because at least you could fly. Horns, strange colored hair, they might mark you as anything but human, yet they're not ugly. Even though the Fae Court is full of strange creatures, I don't think any of them are anything less than stunning. The only magical creature I ever thought might be ugly would be the Finn. They don't have tails like mermaids and sirens. Instead, their hands and feet are webbed. Thinking about the Finn makes me shudder, we have to leave, the sooner we can save Anya.

Brendan speaks behind me., "He's flying back." His boots come closer., "We'll be on our way then."

I turn. "But what about food? Traveling things?"

Brendan cocks his head, his bangs falling close to his eyes, "Are mortals not kind?" The question doesn't make a bit of sense. Brendan stares at me, and I simply shrug. He brushes his loose hair back, tying into a ponytail, "We may be more animal than mortal, but the Fae provide for each other. Wherever we travel, every creature in this kingdom is hospitable. If anything, we'll get more food than we could ever eat."

He must sense my doubt because he grins., "The leprechauns fed you, didn't they?

I scowl at him, annoyed at his easy manners. Grinning right after he practically threw Flavian out of the window., "The leprechauns offered you food. Our court fed you. You should worry about other things other than food." "Of course," I answer quickly. I touch my loose hair, fingering one of the golden pins, "But you have armor, your weapons. I'm in a dinner dress."

"You can't have weapons.," Brendan shrugs, his mouth pinching into a thin line, "The Finn will feel threatened. You're going to them as an envoy, not an enemy."

That's absurd. "They stole my cousin," I snap at him., "I'm not their friend."

He holds up his palms., "You can't argue about this. You must appear fine, lovely to the Finn. They only take pretty things."

Pretty things, my face heats, jaw clenching. The nerve. "Anya wasn't just a pretty thing, and they took her." I can see my cousin, her dress tattered, hands calloused. She's not just a pretty thing. "We're not just toys for them."

Brendan lets out a sigh., "I don't know why my Queen thinks you can bargain with the Finn. But I'm under orders. Her majesty makes choices for reasons. The way you are is the way we take you."

Before I can reply, there's a loud thump and banging on the balcony. I jump, looking past Brendan. Flavian. Brendan turns, and the two speak gruffly to each other in Fae. I watch as Flavian touches his wings, dissolving them in a haze of glittering magic. Light glows at his fingertips, the feathers hiding beneath his hands.

Brendan's face darkens, and he barks another string of words at Flavian. I'm not sure whether Flavian is vain or stupid or both. If I had wings, I'd make sure the whole world could see them. The two stare a moment more at each other before Flavian snorts and turns away. Brendan's gaze flits to me. "Since Flavian is averse to flying, we'll meet him at the base of the crags." His lips twitch as he rolls his shoulders. "Unless you'd rather walk with him." "She doesn't need my help," Flavian speaks at the same time as I rush to say no.

Brendan's eyes glitter. "Very well.," He holds out a hand., "You'll ride with me."

"We're going to fly?"

"No, we're going to swim," Flavian mutters, snapping his fingers. I choke out a nervous laugh, and Brendan releases a sigh of his own. "If you'd like to swim, Flavian, I won't stop you." "Sorry," I sputter, my cheeks hot., "That was a stupid question."

Brendan shrugs., "Only a matter of opinion." He slowly cracks his knuckles, "Other things weigh on your mind. We're throwing a lot at you."

"It was a stupid question," Flavian interrupts, walking to the door., "Brendan barely avoided lying."

I want to laugh, but instead, I find a weak smile, turning back to Brendan., "It has been a long night. But for Anya, I would do anything." The air is still for a moment before Flavian clears his throat, "You would do anything for your cousin. I would do anything for Edric. Brendan would do anything for the Queen," he shrugs, opening the door, his voice sharpening., "I don't know why, since the Queen wouldn't do anything for him."

The door slams behind him, leaving Brendan and me alone. Standing at the edge of the open doors to the balcony. Brendan looks away from me., "I might feel for your cousin." The wind rustles my hair in the silence, "But I do this for my Queen and prince," he finally speaks., "For your sake, I hope you can save both of them."

"You don't have to justify yourself for what Flavian said," I answer quietly., "I don't care if you're just doing this because it's the queen's orders."

The last time I flew, I was so exhausted, I fell asleep. This feeling is so familiar, the muscled arms around my shoulders. I jerk my head back, looking up into the Fae's chiseled face. Brendan must notice the recognition on my face because he speaks., "I'm surprised you remember that night."

My memory from that night is hazy, just blurred shapes of leprechauns and dark wings. My panic tinges every thought. I was so exhausted; it's a struggle to remember the details. Brendan steps towards the edge, the wind a cold bite on our faces.

There's no exhaustion to fall into, and I can sense my fear building in my stomach. My back pressed against his leather chest, cradled in his arms, I can see the ground below us. The hills are branching out beyond this balcony—the endless dark skies beyond all sight.

I'm almost grateful to my aching hand, the pain a near distraction from this terror. I must have tensed because

Brendan squeezes my shoulders. "Look at the stars, Darcy. Keep looking at the lights. You're safe."

I tilt my chin up, holding my breath. Then Brendan takes a step, and we're falling into nothing. The scream rips from me, a bubble of absolute terror, my throat raw as tears sting my eyes. Wind biting at my face, we're falling and falling, tumbling like a dish about to smash into a thousand pieces of broken glass.

There's no breath left in my body, my stomach seizes, and my fear grips my throat. "Open your eyes, Darcy," Brendan murmurs, just above my head, his voice the only warmth in this cold sky. "Look back at the stars."

Hesitantly, I open my eyes. Light sparkles closer than I've ever seen before. So close, I swear you could touch the starlight. Brendan said we'd meet at the crags. And even in the darkness, I can see the jutted mountain peaks. I peer over Brendan's arm, staring down at the flickering village lights. Below us sits a circle of houses nestled into the mountain pass. I've never climbed mountains before, but I think if I pictured a journey into the mountains of a fantasy fae land, this is what I would have imagined.

Brendan wings are still beating, but the sound is slower now as he circles slowly over the handful of small huts. He stretches his wings out wider as we drift towards the center of a small cluster of stone cottages. I swivel my neck around, taking in the houses. They remind me of the leprechauns' homes, with rock walls and thick wooden beams holding up thatched roofs. Brendan lands heavily, and I dig my fingers into his arms, biting back a squeak. If he notices, he doesn't say a word, holding my arms as I stumble back from unto my feet. The ground wavers, the buildings, and lights spinning. I grab Brendan's arm, shaking my head. The earth settles back into solid shapes and still, cozy cottages, so I turn slowly, pulling away from Brendan. The mountains loom, the moon almost dipping behind a craggy peak. I turn back towards Brendan, "Where's Flavian?"

Brendan chuckles, "It's a long walk from the palace. I don't expect him till midday."

I look at the two mountain peaks, hiding the stars. "Do we have to wait for Flavian?" I know I'm probably talking too much, but I don't understand why we need to stay here, so the questions tumble out in a rush., "If the Finn trade me for Edric, does he really need to travel with us all the way? Edric will be back whether he comes or not."

Brendan lets go of my shoulder, cracking his knuckles., "We gave him our word. We wait here." I don't think Brendan would appreciate me pointing out that I never gave my word. And I don't have time to speak as a door flies open, a silvery Fae darting out from a cottage.

"My lord.," The Fae darts forward, and I stare at his feet. Well, they aren't feet at all but a set of hooves. He prances towards us., "The Queen didn't send word, and we weren't expecting a Guardsman."

"Well met.," Brendan holds his hand forward, palm up., "Peace to you, Roland."

"Peace, sir." Roland tips his head, ears twitching. I notice a set of horns behind his long ears, "We're glad you're here peacefully. Unexpected guardsman is always a cause for nerves."

"But you've got the best set of nerves of any Faun, Roland," Brendan answers while I'm still studying the Fae. Though, he's a Faun. I'm trying to remember if Fauns are also considered Fae. I bite my lip, frustration making my head spin. The Finn have kidnapped Anya, and Flavian isn't here.

Brendan insists on waiting for him, for gods know how long. "Brendan, when will I meet the Finn folk?" The words come tumbling, "My cousin is out there." I gesture towards the sky, and I don't even know where to begin looking., "I need to find her."

"The Finn folk.," The Faun's hooves crunch on the ground., "You go to seek the Unseelie Court?"

Brendan flinches., "They are the Finn, Roland. Nothing more."

The Faun's ears twitch, his hooves stamping., "Of course, sir. Forgive me. I have lived through both courts." Brendan speaks, murmuring something. But I don't hear him. My heart is pounding, the Faun's words settling like a cloud of bad news. My heart twists in fear, and I had nearly forgotten about the idea of the Unseelie. The cruel, unfeeling Fae. Of course, the Finn must be Unseelie. Anya is in their grasp. They will delight in hurting my gentle cousin, crowing over her tears, her pain. All of the Unseelie stories talk about their cruelty, their lack of feelings or emotion. I rub my fists against my eyes., "I can't waste time."

"You're not wasting time.," Brendan touches the top of my head. "Take a breath, Darcy." I choke on the damp air, and Brendan tips my head up., "Another breath." Air tumbles back into my lungs, as Brendan commands softly., "Hold your breath for a moment." I suck in another gasp of night air and try to steady my breathing. Brendan's dark eyes meet my gaze. "Look at me.," He grips my chin between his fingers., "Your cousin will be fine."

I can see her, the monstrous Finn swirling around her. They've probably thrown her into a cell, left her crumpled behind a set of bars. Chained her in their sea castles, feeding her scraps of food and laughing at her pain. "The Unseelie," I gasp the word.

"The Unseelie and Seelie have been one for half a century," Brendan answers quietly., "The Finn are cruel, but they bear no allegiance to an Unseelie Court."

I fight for another breath, and Brendan murmurs, encouraging me to breathe softly., "My Queen believes the Finn still follow our orders. My Queen's lieges. We are not declaring war on the Finn."

I let out a breath, sucking in another. "But why?"

"The Finn want something." Brendan lets go of my chin, long fingers brushing the tears hovering on my cheeks,

"They have the right to fight for answers. An answer you may have."

His words are useless. My shoulders slump. "I don't know anything about the Finn." I barely know anything, apparently. I only followed a leprechaun, and now my cousin is gone, and the Fae insist I'm not even human.

Brendan's eyes flicker away from my face., "It may be something the Finn know about you."

His fingers drop away from my skin, the cold evening air biting me again. I cross my arms, shivering. "Why won't the Queen tell me? Why make me bargain with her, hike to the Finn when I know nothing?"

Brendan isn't looking at me., "We can only guess. And half knowledge is more dangerous than ignorance. And if the Finn want you, think that you have something, we should lead you there."

His words are a tangle of half-truths and confusing, and he might as well be a spider weaving a trap. I grasp for something more solid, some hope in his web of words, "But how do you even know the Finn want me?" Brendan sighs, "We take you to the conjunction. If they want you, they will come." Another one of Brendan's half-hearted answers, true enough that he can at least speak the words. I barely listen as he speaks to the Faun, asking about supper and resting for the night.

The Faun is babbling to us, starting to step away. Brendan touches my shoulder, pushing me along as we follow. I turn my neck, looking around the dark village. A still water fountain, moonlight reflecting in the pool of water. Our feet brush the cobblestones, and a wave of frustration washes over me. I can't sleep here for an entire night. Waiting for Flavian to decide to show up. Anya needs me now.

I hesitate at the threshold; Brendan urges me forward. The room is smoky, a fire roaring in the center. The warmth is an embrace, comforting touch from the night chill. Several Fauns look up at me as we step into the room. They're all talking at once, and Brendan clears his throat, introducing himself. A chorus of hellos, huzzah, and harrumphs follow.

I'm almost dizzy, the smoke, the noise, the warmth. Brendan leads me to a chair, and I sink into it. A female Faun steps over to me, spooning broth into a bowl.

"My, my," she speaks lights, "it's been decades since I've seen a human girl." She sets the bowl in my lap., "And generations since I laid eyes on a Halfling."

My fingers clench the edge of the bowl., "I'm human."

"And something more," the Faun murmurs, reaching for my head. I want to duck away, but there's nowhere to move. Her fingers rest on my hair—more words about the blessing of my visit. I want to push her away, tell her this visit is no blessing. The Finn have stolen Anya. I'm not here just to visit with these Faun or Fae or any of these magical creatures. I just want Anya, safely curled up next to me, her breathing heavy and hair neatly tucked into thick braids. The smell of food jerks me back. I need to eat. I reach for my salt, but one of the Fauns shows me their supply. I dust the porridge with the white powder. I pick up the spoon, dipping it into the broth. I take a sip, the warm, beefy flavor intoxicating. The Faun is still talking to me, mentioning a place to sleep. I don't answer as I take another bite. Brendan might insist on waiting, but I don't want to sleep.

I want to leave. Get to Anya. The Faun comments about how tired we must be, and I hate that she's right. But while exhaustion colors my vision, I still want to argue, remind Brendan that my cousin's life matters more than a night of sleep. Whatever answer I might have said is blown away as the door slams open. I jolt back in my seat, the soup sloshing over the edge of my bowl.

A Fae woman stands in the doorway. Her green eyes sweep over the room, landing on Brendan.

"Where is he?" Her words hang over the room, the fauns shuffling. I clutch my bowl, staring over the woman's appearance. I've not seen such a fierce woman, not even the scale-skinned Fae I saw back at the court.

Blond hair wound in braids around her head, long braids falling down her back. Golden hoops dangle from her pointy ears. Her clothes are dark leather; a coat buttoned up to her chin. The buttons sparkle as she takes a step over the threshold. My eyes drift to her hand, and I hold back a gasp, staring at the gilded sword resting on her hip.

"Your brother is not yet here," Brendan speaks quietly, barely moving., "He will be here tomorrow."

"He volunteered, didn't he?" The woman snaps, stepping into the center of the room. Her heeled boots crunch on the wooden floor., "Tell me the truth."

Brendan shrugs., "You know him better than most.," He picks up his spoon, taking another bite of soup before he speaks. "he's sworn this task to the Queen."

"Fool," she spits the word, slamming her hand into the table. Dishes rattle, and her voice cuts through the air, "He's risking everything for that boy."

The fans aren't quiet, murmuring among themselves. I look down at my soup as Brendan and the Fae woman exchange harsh, quick words. I don't have to listen hard to gather that she's Flavian sister, and she thinks his feelings for Edric are a useless distraction. Flavian can be petty and cutting, but his feelings for Edric are as plain as a cloudless sky.

"He'll be here tomorrow," Brendan repeats the sentence for the fourth or fifth time., "But we have to leave as soon as he arrives."

"And I'll be going with you.," The woman shoves past Brendan, walking around the room. She turns her head, glancing over the circle of Fauns. She snorts, turning again, and I can see her back. The wings folded underneath her cloak, silver feathers peeking out, shimmering in the firelight.

"I'll have some soup," she speaks to a Faun, reaching for a bowl. I glance down at my bowl. I only have a few bites left. But the female Fae crosses over to me, her boots stomping. She stops directly over me; I feel the heat of her breath. She clinks her spoon on the bowl. I keep my head lowered as she takes several loud slurps. My eyes rest on her pointy boots, black etchings swirling in a pattern across the shoes.

"So, Halfling.," She swallows loudly., "My brother is dragging you to the Finn."

"Yes," I mumble, wondering why she thinks I'm half-human. Everyone keeps calling me a Halfling as though they know more me better than myself. I'm just a human girl who wanted gold, followed a leprechaun, and is now stuck trying to save my cousin. Any other human would do what I've done.

"The Queen tricked you into her dirty work," she sputters, her spoon clanking loudly., "And you were too much of a human fool to agree." I finally look up from my soup, the Fae's piercing eyes narrow at me. She rolls her neck., "For a supposed Halfling, you let yourself be entrapped in Oona's magic far too easily."

"My cousin," I start, but the Fae interrupts. She taps her spoon loudly on the side of the bowl.

"Yes, family loyalty," she sneers, her face looking so much like Flavian, the way her lips curl and eyes narrow. She leans back on her heels, head inclined towards Brendan., "Something my brother could use to learn."

"Flavian is loyal to the Queen," Brendan says quietly. "As we all are."

"He's only loyal to Edric," she guffaws, rolling her eyes. Another roll of her neck, and she catches sight of a Faun staring at her. "Are any of you more loyal to the Queen than your own family?"

The Fauns glance at one another, a few stamping their feet. Their hooves are loud on the wooden floor. "Brigit," Brendan starts, but the Fae chokes him off., "I hate being the evening entertainment." She kicks at the wooden floor. "I'll speak to you outside." I glance up at her fierce eyes., "To me?"

"Who else? I know everything these creatures might say to me." She snorts again, and I stand up. A faun reaches for my bowl, taking it from my hands. Brigit tips her bowl back, slurping down the rest of the soup. She runs a hand over her mouth before beckoning me to follow. I follow her, glancing at Brendan. He crosses his arm, barely shaking his head.

"What are you waiting for?" She stops at the door, and I stumble forward, catching up with her.

I'm shivering as soon as I set foot outside. The moon has dipped below the craggy mountains; I fold my arms, my teeth shattering. The Fae must notice me shivering because she slips off her cloak, holding it out to me. I take the thick fabric, pulling it over my shoulders. My body is much smaller, the cloth drapes against the ground, and I bunch the soft cloth between my fingers, pulling my arms across my chest.

"You heard Brendan." She starts chatting, her wings flaring out behind her.

"You look intelligent, even if you think you're human. I'm sure you gathered that Flavian's my brother."

I can't tell if she's insulting me, so I just nod as she continues, "He's desperate to find Edric, risking his life to take you to the Finn. Fool," she mutters, "But love turns anyone into a fool."

I cross my arms, tucking my hands into the leather. If I pick apart her words, she might think I'm a fool for wanting to save Anya. She's not human, and she wouldn't understand that humans don't have magic. We have our families. Anya is everything, and I'd do anything foolish to save her. But I don't want to spend my time arguing about why I'm here, so I turn my focus to Brigit's comments about her brother.,

"You don't want Flavian to loved Edric."

Brigit shrugs, tossing one of her loose braids., "My brother is my brother. I don't interfere with his feelings. Unless he tries to throw his life away." I barely can think of what she means when she speaks again. "If the Finn want you, they'll be agreeable. And they'll let Brendan and Flavian be." She pulls out her sword, holding it out before me., "But if the Queen is wrong, they'll take pleasure in slaughtering all of you."

"Don't frighten her.," I jolt at the sound of Brendan's voice., "She's wary enough."

"Let her be ignorant then.," Brigit twirls her sword., "But I figure the Halfling should know the kind of danger she's walking into."

"Flavian and I can protect her well enough."

"You truly think Flavian is here to protect her?" Brigit laughs harshly, "He intends to save Edric and leave the Halfling to her fate."

She slips her sword back into her holster., "And I'm here to keep my brother alive."

"I can keep an eye on Flavian," Brendan starts, but Brigit snarls at him. "He is my brother." Her nostrils flare., "And no warrior or prince or Queen will keep me from him."

Her words hang in the air. I look back at Brendan. His face is blank, but he curls his hands into fists. "Your brother is not only sworn to the Queen; he is my Second." He turns away from Brigit, glancing down at me., "Come inside, Darcy. You need to rest." Brendan beckons to the door, and I step back towards the cottage. I barely remember to take off the cloak, holding it out for Brigid.

She steps forward, taking it from me. "Thank you," I murmur, dipping my head.

"At least she knows manners.," I hear Brigit talking behind me as Brendan closes the door. I'm not sure where the Fauns have gone. I suppose there's another door at the back of the cottage because the room is mostly empty.

The kind Faun from earlier steps to me., "There's a bed for you in the loft." She walks me to a ladder. "all the gods' blessing on your sleep." I murmur a goodnight, gathering my skirt in my hand as I climb up the ladder. I pull myself into the loft, sighing in relief at the soft pallet. The shoes fall off, and I rub my feet, wiggling my toes. I should have left the shoes at the palace. I can't stand wearing them; my feet ache.

I want to take off the dress, but I've nothing else to wear. Instead, I lay back on the downy pallet, sighing. The bed is so comfortable, I stretch my aching muscles, massaging my hands. I'm still sore from the confrontation with the Queen earlier today.

My eyes drift close. So much in one day. And Anya, the vision of the Finn guards, their ragged sharp teeth, I push away the thought. I can't do anything now. Not until I reach the Finn.

I pray she is safe. Sleep is fighting at the edges of my mind, but I force myself to stay awake to pray.

"Keep Anya safe.," The words jumble together, and I turn my head into the pillow. Tears burn my eyes, my voice trembling. "Gods and saints protect her." A yawn forces itself from my throat, and my weary mind flits over Brigit's words., "And show us what the Finn want."

Voices stir me awake. I buried my head into the soft pallet last night, my nose snuggled into the covers. I keep the blanket pulled around my chin; the air is frigid.

"If this were the first time, or even the second, Brendan," Brigit's voice hisses below me. I still under the covers, my breathing ebbing., "I might understand. But this is our life. Your life. Flavian's life. My entire family. I won't lose everything."

"You're speaking treason," Brendan's low voice interrupts., "Letting your emotions dictate your thoughts will lead to war."

"Maybe we need a war."

I wait for Brendan's reply but only hear the door banging open. Along with the familiar, arrogant tone., "The fauns told me you were here."

Flavian. Cold air rushes into the loft, and I reach for the blankets, clinging to the wool. At least, he is as harsh to his sister as he ever was to me.

"The fans are far more polite than you." Brigit is snapping at her brother. "Never a word. You'd go off to the Finn without so much as a goodbye to your sister?"

Chapter Eight

Brendan

I HOLD BACK A chuckle as Brigit's nostrils flare. Her brother stops, turning to me, spitting out the question, "Why is she here?"

"I could ask you the same question," Brigit steps closer to us., "Why you've even started on this foolish journey."

Flavian's eyes narrow, his fists clenching., "I don't answer to you."

"I'm the only one you should answer to," Brigit snaps back, "These people," Her voice is dripping with hatred., "They don't deserve us."

Flavian stamps his feet, his hands smoothing back his cape., "And it's your mouth that keeps ruining my name at court." His lips twitch. "I'd thank you to keep your poison to yourself."

Brigit's lips twitch, a mirror to her brother's face. The way her fingers curl, she's going to rant. We don't have time for them to argue this out. I stand, taking a step towards the loft., "Darcy, you awake?"

Brigit levels a glare at me, obviously annoyed that I interrupted. But the sun has already risen. We need to be on our way.

Darcy's voice floats down., "Who could sleep through their yelling?"

Behind me, Flavian snorts. I keep my voice steady., "Come on down. We'll be leaving directly."

Flavian starts speaking to his sister before I can even finish., "You can't come."

"Of course, I can."

"We're under orders from the Queen. This is a secret mission. Gods know how you even learned where we were."

"Secrets," Brigit tosses her hair, sending me a glare. "What good has ever come from the court keeping secrets?" That's not an answer to Flavian's question, one I've wondered as well. Brigit may avoid court, but there's no doubt she has contacts. Someone who tells her too much information.

She won't let that slip; she's too careful to give away her leads. Right now, we need to finish this journey, then I can worry about Brigit's spies.

I hold up a hand., "We don't need a history lesson, Brigit. I can't order you to stay. However, if you come with us, you'll be under my orders."

"She can't come," Flavian immediately protests.

I open my mouth, but Darcy loudly creaks down the stairs, her auburn hair a tangled mess. Her eyes flit between the three of us, cheeks flushing., "Can't you two stop arguing?"

Brigit barks a laugh, while Flavian just glowers. He shoves his arms together, feet tapping impatiently.

"We're discussing things, not arguing." I smile tightly, hoping the answer is enough. A knot of hair falls into Darcy's eyes; I almost reach out to push the hair away from her face.

She shakes her head, blowing the hair from her face., "Well.," She looks at me., "Is Brigit coming?"

"Of course, I am," Brigit starts, stepping toward her brother, practically spitting in his face. His shoulders straighten as he turns deliberately away from her, grumbling, "You can't come. You've lost your sense of sanity."

"Brigit doesn't live at Court.," I ignore them, explaining the situation to Darcy, "She doesn't have to obey Court orders if they don't apply to the entire kingdom."

"You don't live at Court." Darcy's gaze jumps to Brigit, her eyes widening.

Brigit grins., "I was exiled. All the better."

"Our father's exiled," Flavian jumps to explain., "Not her fault. Or mine."

A grin breaks out on Darcy's face, and she smiles towards Flavian., "I can't imagine why anyone would want to exile such a friendly Fae."

Brigit guffaws, and Flavian's face reddens. I step towards him as he bares his teeth. "Flavian.," My voice stays calm., "Calm down."

Brigit is still laughing, shaking her braids. Darcy bounces on her toes. "I'm glad you're coming." She bunches her skirt in her hands, crossing the small room towards Brigit., "You don't answer to the Queen."

With her skirt lifted, I can see she's not wearing shoes. I would say something, but Brigit is already talking, "You don't trust my brother?"

Darcy glances at Flavian, looking away from his fierce glare, and Brigit continues, "You don't trust Brendan?"

The girl's shoulder stiffens, her voice quiet and hesitant. She doesn't look back at me. "I'm not sure."

Suddenly, I want her to look my way. To see her green eyes, just so I can nod at her, make her understand, she can trust me. I want the best for her, to help her reach her cousin. Negotiate with the Finn.

Brigit's face breaks into a full grin, her teeth sharp on her lower lips., "Good.," She pats Darcy on the shoulder., "My brothers a fool, but Brendan.," Her eyes narrow at me, words coming in a hiss., "He's a snake." Darcy's eyelashes flutter, a fast look between Brigit and me I. Beside me, Flavian snorts, "If you come with us, mind your tongue."

Brigit stomps to the door., "Another thing the Court tries to teach you." She yanks at the wooden door, ushering Darcy before her., "Hiding lies behind a veil of truth."

Flavian lunges, snarling, but I grab his arm. His ears twitch as I pull him back., "Leave her be."

"Don't you hear her?" My second's ears are red. "I haven't seen her in months, yet she greets me like this, as though

I'm betraying her."

"I know." I pat his shoulder. "Don't provoke her."

"Provoke her," Flavian splutters., "She wants to gut you, Brendan. And the things she says about Edric." I roll my shoulders back, stepping past Flavian, reaching for my baldric, slipping the metal over my shoulder., "We aren't here to defend his Highness." I speak before he can interrupt me again, "Our orders are to deliver Darcy to the Finn Court."

"If they have Edric," Flavian mutters, "I'm going to be doing more than delivering."

His stupid, stubborn ideas, my jaw clenches, "You will obey orders, Flavian." I won't repeat his full title, knowing it will do nothing but irk him. I can't speak his father's name, the shame of exile forbidding me to say his family's name. Flavian's eyes narrow, and he stomps towards the door, "Some days." His hands still on the wooden frame., "Some days, I wish I'd never taken your oath. You know, I could have stayed home and been free of you."

He looks back at me, blonde bangs falling into his eyes. I tighten my baldric., "You don't wish that, Flavian." My voice is quiet, but I won't let him say things he doesn't truly mean., "Where would you be today without your position?"

He huffs, tapping his nails on the wood., "Alone."

"And under Brigit's command." I force the issue., "Either way, you'd be under someone's orders."

His shoulders stiffen at my words., "She wouldn't touch me."

I don't answer, just looking at my second. Flavian flushes under my gaze, enough acknowledgment that he knows I'm speaking the truth. His father would have placed him under Brigit's command, manning their family estates. Cut off from any chance at court, at redeeming their family name. Cut off from his dreams.

"You have a chance here, Flavian.," I step to the door, a half span taller than my second. His eyes flicker away from me, but my breath still hits his face., "You won't always be under my command. You'll earn your own place, without your sister. Without me."

Our eyes meet, his ringed with lines and worry. Another night without sleep. He blows air through his lips., "I won't be anything without Edric."

As he speaks, he shoves against the wood, stumbling out the door. His dark green cloak flaps behind him, and he yanks a hand through his blonde hair.

My stomach rolls at the tense set of his shoulders, his fingers still fisting in his hair. I should tell him he is enough by himself, that he doesn't need our Prince or me. He is Flavian, my second, rising military leader.

But the words fail me. I watch Flavian plow across the village square, his wings glittering in the morning sun. I don't have the heart to call him back.

Darcy

I thought Brigit might talk to me when we left the cottage. But she doesn't say a word as she paces around the Faun village. Light touches the eastern sky, but the mountains still shroud the town in darkness. I sit on the edge of the village well, the chilly stone biting my bones. My hair is such a hopeless tangle, but I run my fingers through it before twisting it into a braid. At least, there won't be any loose strands in my eyes.

The door slams open, Flavian stomping out. He doesn't glance at me as he marches away from the house. Brigit jumps to attention, hurrying after him. I almost laugh; from the little bit I heard them argue, I know this fight will be useless. Neither one will be happy with the other.

Brendan walks a bit slower, adjusting the cape around his shoulders. He spots me, taking a few long steps to my seat., "Apologies.," He runs a hand through his brown hair., "I'm sorry our words woke you."

I wasn't expecting an apology, I flush., "Don't worry.," I push myself from the edge of the well., "I was almost awake anyway."

Brendan's eyebrows knit, confusion in his eyes. "How can one be almost awake?" Instead of laughing, I shrug., "I had enough sleep. And it's not that early."

Understanding crosses his face., "I hope you're ready. We should be at the Hollow by midday."

The Hollow, my eyes skitter to the mountains. The Fae haven't explained much, but I was expecting to head towards the ocean. I haven't seen any water since we left the palace, and I mention this to Brendan.

Brendan nods at my question., "The Hollow is neutral ground.," He clasps his hand around the hilt of his sword., "The ocean is far too dangerous. We must be on equal footing with the Finn."

As much as I've heard of the fierceness of the Finn, it's hard to grasp that the Fae are nervous about them. I think of Brendan's blinding light, the way Flavian's holds his brutal sword, the magical pain I've felt. Even with all that power, to still be worried about the Finn. Their power can't hide the whispers I've heard about the Unseelie, their uneasiness with the Finn. Flavian and Brigit storm back over, a Faun on their heels. The kind female from last night carries a basket on her arm, holding out the food as an offering.

I reach for the bundle she holds out to me, thick warm bread. The Faun hands me the small jar of salt, which I sprinkle across the basket. I notice Brendan look away, and I almost smile. Unable to look at the salt, strange things that weaken the Fae. She baked honey into the crust; my mouth begins to water. Brendan thanks her, taking some bread as well. He runs his hands along the edge, wiping off any loose salt.

I bite into the crust, savoring the warm flavor. The scent is rich, incredible. For a moment, I feel at home. Anya handing me a fresh slice of bread, just baked, slightly sweet and warm. The memory is so brutal, my eyes burn. I swallow the bread, taking another rabid bite. I should be with the Finn by noon, close to Anya. I don't know what the Finn want, but I know I can find a way to free her. The Fae Queen didn't explain much, but I've made it this far, I'll figure something out to save Anya.

We finish the bread, and Brendan is ready to start. The Faun touches my arm, squeezing gently., "The gods' blessings on you, Halfling." I meet her intense gaze., "Thank you."

"You've made bargains.," The Faun's fingers are tight around my arm., "To do what you must."

I don't acknowledge the truth of what she says. Brendan is pacing, Flavian at his heels. Brigit waits beside me, pulling out a dagger. The Faun pauses, then continues when she realizes I won't answer., "Use them carefully, or they will use you." She lets go of my sleeve, and I scramble away. Brigit keeps pace beside me, grinding a stone against her dagger. I glance at her nimble hands, the scrape of metal grinding.

Around us, the village is just beginning to stir. Fauns stand in their doorways, wishing us good luck. I can't help waving at them. The younger Fauns are simply adorable with their tiny horns poking up past their thick curling hair. Brendan leads us through the village, past the short wall and gate. The road before us slopes downward into the mountain. The dawn isn't touching these crags, and darkness shrouds the road. As I pass through the moss-covered gate, I look back at the village. Close cottages, fern-covered chimneys, heads watching through windows. Of all the places I've visited in the Fae Court, I wish I could stay with the Fauns. Kinder then the leprechauns, less threatening than the court. It feels like home should feel, a village wanting you and helping you, treating you as though you belong. If I could save Anya and bring her anywhere to these magical lands, we'd visit the Fauns together. She would enjoy the younger Fauns and converse easily with our kind host. Anya would enjoy the village. The path is rocky, boulders jutting out from the mountains. Brendan and Flavian lead the way with quick, sure steps. I clamber over rocks and tree roots. Brigit's wings flare as she marches in front of me. "Did the Queen tell you much," she speaks over her shoulder, "or did you actually let yourself get trapped this easily?"

Cold air nips at my cheeks, "The Finn have my cousin." I can't see Brigit's face, but I hear her snort,

"So now your life doesn't matter."

Her words are biting, and I stop, gasping, "She'd do the same for me." Brigit stops on the gravel road, looking at me.

Flavian and Brendan pause as well, a glance back at us. "I used to think that too,"

Brigit speaks quietly, her eyes lowered., "But you see my family now."

I know Brigit wants me to understand, but I don't., "You're not held captive by the Finn." my voice is shaking., "You don't need your brother. Anya needs me." Brigit kicks at the gravel with the edge of her boot. "Human.," She sighs the word., "I forget how little you see." Then she turns back, stalking past Brendan and Flavian.

We walk in silence for some time, Brigit ahead of all of us. Brendan's jaw is clamped shut, the lines on his face tight.

"Where are we going exactly," I finally venture a question, "What is the Hollow?"

Brendan looks down at me., "The Hollow." He gestures down the path., "The Finn can't stand sunlight, and we are not friendly with water."

The path descends lower and lower, and when I look up, the mountains seem to press around us. Brigit stomps back to me, placing a hand on my shoulder., "I know you do this for your cousin," she speaks quietly., "But I urge you to think through your decision."

I finger the sleeves of my dress., "I don't know what else to do."

"The Finn have stolen a human," Brigit replies in the same quiet tone., "We should bring this to the council, unprovoked attacks on mortals. It's cause enough for war."

I look at her., "But the Fae steal from us all the time?" I think of the bowls of cream we leave out at the change of seasons, the mills left unguarded at night. All my life, I've been told these offerings are gifts for the Fae. We can barely afford to give up the cream and bundles of wheat, but everyone knows if you don't share with the Fae, they'll find ways to steal from you instead.

"Taking what we need is not the same as stealing souls," Brigit answers fiercely., "Those acts were forbidden when we crushed the Unseelie Court." I mull over her words, wondering if she knows how hard it is to leave out our food for her Fae friends. I wonder if Brigit saw our homes and small meals if she'd still think the offerings are needed. Now that I've seen the Fae Court, our small offerings don't make sense. Brigit interrupts my thoughts, repeating her earlier words, asking me to change my mind again.

"I've already made a bargain.," I look up at Brigit's pale face., "I have to go to the Finn."

"Gods," Brigit breathes., "You are stupider than I even thought. You made a bargain with the Queen?"

At my nod, Brigit curses again, "First bit of advice." she shakes her braids., "Don't make another bargain. Whatever you hear, bargains are never worth their price."

"I just want to save my cousin.," The words come in a rush., "And leave all of this. Believe me, I never wanted to start making bargains with my childhood nightmares."

Brigit snorts, lips quirking just a bit. "I'm not sure I can believe you." We stay in step as the road dips again, Flavian and Brendan passing into a massive cave. Darkness stretches out in front of me.

"Come on.," Brigit pressed a hand against my back., "We're almost to the Hollow. It's at the center of the mountain." I look up, the rocks black, jutting out from the arched path of the cave. We're walking into a mountain.

I shiver, pulling my arms tight across my chest. My mind runs through a list, marking down what I need to do. First, reach the Hollow. Meet with the Finn. Trade myself to them. Find a way to save Anya.

Brendan

I knew the Queen sent word ahead of us and attempted to communicate with the Finn king. It is still unnerving to see the Finn guards waiting for us. A circle of light around the ancient stones, their legs covered in shimmering purple scales, black tattoos thread across their smooth faces and chests. Twisted corded hair, braids held back by razor-sharp pins along with double rows of long teeth, their pincers reach past their lips. They outnumber and outman us.

Behind me, Darcy lets out a small gasp, her feet coming to a stop. The Finn are a horrifying sight to my own eyes, and I knew what to expect. The mortal can't have imagined these monsters even in her dreams. Their leader steps forward, flat webbed feet sliding on the stone floor of the cave, "You have come, Brendan, son of Riordan." His voice hisses at me, and I keep my gaze away from his sharp teeth. His nails glitter, they're nearly as long as his hands. He raises them now, razor-sharp talons. I've heard about the Finn's nails, how they easily gut their enemies with their knife-like sharpens. The talons are as much a weapon as any of my daggers.

I hear Darcy's breath catch, my ears listening as her breathing stills.

"You are no fool, Brendan," the Finn hisses again, his forked tongue slipping between his teeth.,

"We do not come to the Hollow fruitlessly."

Brigit snorts, but I don't bother glancing at her. Flavian shuffles beside her. I meet the Finn's eyes., "I come only at my

Queen's commands.," I don't motion to Darcy, still nervous at bringing her into this. To these merciless creatures., "Our queen," I emphasize this, "our Queen is hopeful of your loyalty and wisdom. That you will return what you have stolen."

The Finn grins, gesturing wildly., "We return what we have stolen.," He points to Darcy., "For her."

My fingers still around the pommel of my sword. My Queen's commands, sending Darcy with us. I knew this was the choice we were walking into.

Darcy steps forward. "I'm here." Her voice trembles, "I want my cousin. Her safety and I will go with you."

The Finn's mouth opens wide, rows of teeth-baring., "The Fae brought you. We bargain only with them."

Darcy reels back, shock etched on her face. Brigit grabs her arm, whispering, "Don't do this." She glares at me., "She's a mortal, Brendan. In their hands."

The Queen's commands, my fingers are trembling. I turn away from Brigit's fierce green eyes and catch Darcy's wide-eyed expression., "Please.," She wrestles forward from Brigit's touch., "For my cousin." Flavian touches my shoulder., "This is for Edric," His fingers dig into my leather., "Our prince."

I can't let myself think of what the Finn might want with Darcy. Their nails are touching her human skin. It takes all of my training, every mental shred of steel I possess, to look away from Darcy. I force myself to meet the cold, inky eyes of the Finn.

"We give you Darcy for what you have stolen," I barely manage the words., "Return him for her."

The Finn takes a step forward, webbed toes slapping. He holds out his hand., "We take her to return what was stolen."

I hold out my hand, and our hands hover over each other. My breath shudders, goosebumps lining my neck., "We give the mortal for what was stolen."

Magic crackles between us, and I meet the Finn's black eyes. He steps back and raises both hands.

"The girl." He inclines his head, and Flavian walks over to Briget, pulling at Darcy. He shoves her forward, closer to the Finn. Brigit howls at him before howling at me, raging at our bargain. I block out her voice, but the Finn screech angrily. They're hissing at her protests, stamping their spears against the ancient stones.

Magic sears my fingertips, and I hold up my hand, glamoring Brigit. She stamps her feet, pulling at the gag of wind pressed to her face.

I turn my eyes, watching Darcy fall at the Finn's feet. She's not fighting, still clinging to the hope she can do something for her cousin. My heart twinges, feeling her pitiful pain. Whatever the Finn have done with her cousin, I don't know how the Queen thinks Darcy can help her.

"Now.," I shoulder past my feelings, my voice a touch loud., "Return what was stolen."

The Finn nods, turning back into the darkness of the Hollow. He walks past the ancient stones, stepping on the dark bridge that connects the Finn's borders to our own.

I glance at Brigit, and she's still fighting the glamor, stamping her feet and clawing at the wind around her face. Darcy sits crumpled at the feet of the Finn, eyes looking wildly, fearfully around her.

The Finn walks back into the light, carrying a bundle. Flavian and I both step forward, but my second's shocked gasp checks me.

"What was stolen?" The Finn dumps the bundle on the ground; human legs pale against the black floor.

Darcy lets out a cry, crawling toward the bundle., "Anya," she gasps, reaching for the bundle. But the Finn's grab her arms, holding her back. She screams, fighting against their scaled hands.

"This isn't." I fight for words, keeping my eyes focused on the Finn. "Our bargain," I can barely breathe the protest.

"What was stolen?" The Finn laughs maniacally, teeth clattering together., "We returned what we stole."

"My prince," Flavian screams, lounging for the Finn. The Finn knocks him back with a harsh blow to the chest. Flavian falls back, and I look between him and the bundle on the floor.

Darcy is still fighting in the Finn's arms, and I lose focus enough for Brigit to wrench the glamor away. She rounds on her brother, grabbing his hands and yanking his arms behind his back.

I'm suddenly relieved Brigit is here; otherwise, Flavian might kill someone.

I turn back to the Finn, my voice hardly louder than Darcy's frantic screams, "What do we need to do?" I can barely think through the words., "For our Prince."

The Finn holds up his hand, "Did it ever occur to you," he hisses slightly, the words snaking through his jagged, sharp teeth. "Your Prince may have come to my king of his own free will?"

I don't need to listen to any more of these words, and my chest feels caved in like his words are shoveling out my heart. "There's nothing your Queen or Court can do for him. His words hold him bound to our court." The Finn is gloating, his teeth glinting at my misery.

The Finn snaps his hands together, barking commands at his men. They pull Darcy away, dragging her to the bridge between our worlds.

"Brendan," she fights to shout at me, her voice scraped raw., "Take her, keep her safe." The Finn yank her toward the bridge, toward the magic of the Finn kingdom. Water will block out all sound. I hang unto her last words.

"Keep Anya safe," she screams one last time before the Finn submerge into the black waters.

Silence.

I look for Brigit and Flavian. Flavian is running toward the bridge. Brigit on his heels. It is hopeless.

Magic binds the Finn kingdom against guests. Nothing can pass without the Finn king's permission.

My knees shake, and I step toward the bundle. The girl's face is hooded, only her pale legs, her curling mass of hair tumbling unto the stone floor.

I kneel beside the girl, touching her shoulder. She doesn't stir, and I pull the hood back.

My stomach clenches at what I see. Purple bruises cover her otherwise pale face. The bones are taut, eyes sunk in deep shadow. Gently, I lift the mortal into my arms. Her breathing is shallow, her heart a faint flutter.

Darcy

Water presses in around my face, clouding my vision. Webbed hands hold my arms, and I pull against them. I kick, scrambling against the weight of water, of Finn bodies too close to my skin.

Anya, her body tossed on the stone floor, makes me clench my teeth. The Finn don't have her anymore, and I shudder before trying to wrestle away. Anya still isn't safe. She's not home. My brain screams for me to take her and run, run back to our cottage, our village, our home.

"Stop," a voice hisses at me, commands my thoughts. A hand lifts my face, and I'm looking at the horrible face of the Finn. The one who threw my cousin to the ground.

Anger fills my veins; I lash at him, trying to slap him. More hands hold me back; I don't notice their nails digging into my skin, my arms bruising. I'm so angry, furious with their trickery, their brutality.

"Calm yourself," the Finn hisses softly, mouth just above my ear. "Or I will calm you."

Words rise to my mouth, but the Finn covers my face before I can say anything, finger pressing against my teeth, "I don't want to cross my king, so I won't let you say what you're thinking."

I struggle, my teeth running against his skin. He laughs, his body shaking. His skin is so hard, my attempts at biting him are a miserable failure.

"Reminds you of him, doesn't she?" Voices filter around me., "Has his temper."

The words float away, the speaker's voice dull. I look around, I can see them speaking, but I can't hear them. The Finn's hands cover my mouth still, fingers pressing into my cheeks. I blink in surprise; his long nails are gone. He must have retracted them back into his skin.

Hands lift me, and the hand over my face drops away. Gold chains are tied to my wrist, pulling me along. My body stumbles, but only water meets me. It feels as though I'm floating. The Finn begin to swim. I look around, awe and terror curling in my stomach, my throat burning. I can't throw up, not here.

I've been too angry to ask questions, but the wonder of this sight weighs on me. I'm underwater but still breathing and dry. The Finn have surrounded me with a cocoon of air. Outside this small bubble of air, I can barely hear anything. I can see the Finn talking to each other, but their voices are filtered and distant.

They swim rapidly, pulling me along with them. I look closer at them, their scales shimmering. Though the scales only cover their legs, their chests are bare, except for armor. Long hair, tied into elaborate braids. All of them have green hair, along with a slight purple tint to their skin. Or that could be just the water, filtering my view.

I look at my own hands, still pale without a hint of purple.

We pass tangled green vines, stone arches reaching upwards into the oceanic sky. As we swim past these stones, I see other Finn. I crane my neck around, looking at the strange creatures. Any of them that notice me bare their teeth.

I can imagine them hissing; though, of course, I cannot hear them.

A thought passes so quickly, and I reach for my neck feeling for the bag of salt. The Finn guard looks back as I move the chain. I don't meet his gaze, fumbling for the pouch.

The salt, it's dissolved. Gone. My breathing quickens, my stomach curling. I can't be enchanted. I shake at the gold chains. I can't live here forever. These creatures will bind me to them, a slave underwater away from Anya forever. Fear fills my veins, and I yank harder on the chains, pulling away. The ocean has swallowed me whole, condemned me. I'm going to die.

The Finn are pulling at me, pushing me, and telling me to keep going. But I curl into myself, salty tears falling. I shove the water away, kicking at the airlessness. My breathing is too fast. I jerk on the chain, trying to get it off.

The gold digs harder into my skin. A Finn's hand touches my head, harsh commands in my ear.

But I can't hear him. I'm trying to shove him away, and I know my words don't make sense. I can barely string together a thought; my mind tangles with Anya and salt and curses. Then, the Finn drops me back, releasing me so quickly that I'm afraid of his anger. I cringe, prepared for his fierce grip, his harsh blows.

"Don't touch her.," The command rings around me, and I blink as a shadow falls across me.

"Darcy.," A face emerges in front of me, and his armor glints. He is flanked by more guards, a golden chain around his neck, with his hair long and golden. My eyes are darting, looking between the green hair of the other Finn and this warrior. His skin is dark, and I know I haven't seen things. The other Finn does have nearly purple skin. The Finn lifts his head, speaking at the guards, but I can't hear him. The fingers digging into my arm let go, the guards holding me falling back, offering salutes.

He comes closer to me. Sharp, dark eyes narrowing, his webbed hands touch my cheeks. I feel his golden rings, the metal cold against my skin. He speaks softly, "Daughter of my heart."

I can't be hearing him correctly. I flinch, trying to pull back. But the Finn doesn't let go, his fingers press into my chin, "I had thought you dead for so long.," his fingers trace my hair, pinching a strand., "You are finally found. Returned to the Sea of your blood."

His words make no sense. Yet, what he says sinks into my foggy brain., "I'm not Finn." I gasp at him,

"I don't know what you're talking about."

He smiles, his teeth hidden, "You don't know what you are." His smile is making me feel nauseous again, and I shake my head wildly. I clamor for words., "I don't belong here."

His fingers are cold on my face., "Your heart is wrought from the sea.," He suddenly grabs my arms., "Let's take her before the High King." I almost don't hear the rest of his words, but somehow they float down around me., "By the Gods' blessings, what has been stolen is returned."

I'm too dizzy and overwrought to keep my head straight for the next few minutes. I tense when the Finn reaches for my arms, but his webbed fingers barely graze my arms. The chains around my wrists drop, and he gathers the links close to his chest before darting forward, his powerful webbed feet gliding through the water.

My eyes fall closed, I don't see the winding spirals of the Finn court. The gates of coral, the road of pearl stretched out before me. The words repeat in my mind, making me shiver—daughter *of the Sea.*

Daughter. A Finn's Daughter.

The thought makes my stomach curl, the wave of nausea building in my throat again. I don't want this man's hands around me, but I'm too weak and confused to fight away from his grip. The Queen called me a Halfling, but the idea of me being half Finn, it's unthinkable.

The swimming stops, and I gasp as fresh air enters my lungs in a rush. The man is walking, footsteps echoing. It is strange to hear, but I open my eyes, blinking at the sight. The Ocean is gone. I take in a breath looking around me. He sets me on the ground, and I shakily stand to my feet. My blue gown falls in waves around me, but the cloth is dry. It's as if the water never touched my skin. I glance at the Finn. His hands are damp while his hair drips with water.

He doesn't give me much longer to collect myself before we're walking into a throne room—the throne room of the Finn king. Pearls glisten on the walls, massive coral columns holding up the pitched roof. Finn guards stand in place around the circular room.

My gaze turns to the center: the throne, seven steps rising to the seat. The Finn on this seat is stone-faced, hands resting delicately on the arms of his chair. Long nails are touching the pearl surface of the throne.

"Dewain," the King speaks, his voice carrying around the room., "You have the treasure we have long sought."

"Eminence," the Finn's voice rumbles behind me as he sets me to my feet. I wobble, my knees shaking., "My Daughter of the Sea."

The King leans forward slightly., "As the Slaugh took her, so she is returned."

My brows knit in confusion. The Slaugh only come for the dead. Everyone knows that. The King smiles, lips curving over his sharp teeth., "Only they left her alive." He chuckles, and the guards around the room laugh. The King waves his hand., "Darcy, daughter of Dewain. You have returned to your birthplace."

I'm shaking my head, horrified at his words. "I don't belong here," the words come before I can think through what I'm even saying, "I'm only here because of my cousin, a bargain with the Fae Queen."

The King holds up his hand, releasing a sigh, "Dewain, she's as stubborn as you."

Behind me, the Finn speaks, "Both a blessing and curse, Eminence."

I turn slightly, just enough to look at the Finn named Dewain. The Finn looks from the King back to me, his eyebrows twitching. He's watching me, and I shiver at the expression in his eyes, the intensity of his gaze.

"Darcy, Daughter of Dewain.," The King's voice makes my skin crawl, how he uses that title, *Daughter of Dewain.*

I turn back to the King, and he raises an eyebrow., "Do you know who I am?"

"You're the Finn King." He gestures wildly at my answers, "Yes, yes, of course. Anything else?" I shake my head, lost to find an answer. He retracts his black nails, tapping his fingertips together., "I am

High King Murtagh, Protector of the Sea, servant of the Unseelie Court." "But the Unseelie," I begin, remembering all I heard from the Fae.

"Yes.," the King, Murtagh, waves his hand carelessly., "Yes, the Unseelie court is crushed." His eyes narrow at me, "Not dead, as the Seelie want to think."

I don't think I'm even breathing as the King continues, "How do you kill Winter? How do you kill Darkness," the King hisses, baring his teeth., "The fools of the Seelie Court can no more destroy the Unseelie Court than life can destroy death itself."

The guards stamp their spears in approval, the room reverberating with the sound. I shiver, tucking my trembling fingers into the folds of my dress. Perhaps there is no official Unseelie Court, no band of evil Fae wreaking havoc on humans. But there are the Finn, this Court. This High King Murtagh.

He's one of the evil Unseelie, and he holds my life in his hands.

"What do you want from me," I whisper the words. "What am I supposed to do?"

Murtagh licks his blood-red lips., "Wise question," his green eyes flicker behind me, "You belong to Dewain. Halfling daughter."

When the Queen called me Halfling, she stated the word plainly. Perhaps, even curiously. The King speaks the word with a veiled sneer, and my cheeks flush. I run my sweating hand over my skirt, hating everything this King is saying. That I belong to the Finn standing stiffly behind me, that I belong to his Unseelie Court, his shifting, evil ways. King Murtagh continues, "If you had been left here as a baby, we could have simply changed you. Shed your humanity." His lips curl into a full sneer, tone dripping with distaste, "But your human heart has grown too much. Only magic and bargains can turn your skin into true Finn blood."

I don't want to lose what he calls my humanity; my stomach tightens at the thought. Murtagh chuckles, "Since only the magic of bargains can change you, you must choose to become Finn."

"I don't want that," I spit., "I want to return to my cousin. My home."

Murtagh shrugs., "You heard her, Dewain," he speaks past me, reaching for a glass of wine. He raises the glass, the red liquid staining his lips, "Simply refuses."

Sharp fingers curl around my shoulder., "I will speak to her, Eminence." Dewain's voice too close to me. "She will choose her own blood."

Murtagh flicks his thin wrist, and Dewain pulls me away from the throne. I stumble beside him, my teeth chattering.

They should have known I don't want to become Finn. I don't want to live in the Ocean, obeying the whims of an Unseelie Court. I'm just supposed to be helping the Fae queen, getting gold, and going home. They took Anya. That's the only reason I'm here.

I stumble down the steps that lead outside the throne room before catching a glimpse of a solitary figure. He steps out of shadows, a green cloak falling in waves around his shoulders. His skin is so pale that it's nearly translucent. Thin, dark hair sweeps over his violet eyes and pointed Fae ears. The same face from the portrait in Queen Oona's rooms.

"Prince Edric," I gasp, pulling up short and trying to tug myself away from Dewain, "It's you."

Dewain lets go of my shoulder but leaves his hand on my back., "Highness," he speaks gruffly., "My daughter, Darcy."

Edric steps closer, eyes flickering over me., "She is truly your human daughter, Lord Dewain."

"For now," Dewain growls., "Her human desires are still too strong. Her natural Finn blood will win out eventually." Edric meets my gaze., "A pity for her." He looks past me at Dewain, nodding his head, hair falling into his eyes, "She will make a beautiful Finn, my lord."

A grunt., "It is her blood." I shiver at his words, trying to take another step away from Dewain. He catches my back, laying his webbed hand against my shoulder blades.

"Perhaps, Lord," Edric speaks softly, taking a delicate step closer to Dewain. He looks down at me, a head taller than me, "I can introduce her to the Finn Court. Help her adjust."

Dewain shuffles behind me., "This is my home."

"Of course.," Edric drops his head forward, his tone conciliatory., "But I know the experience of seeing this place for the first time. It can be quite shocking. Even overwhelming."

Dewain touches my head, fingers digging through my hair, "Do not touch her, frighten her, or betray me." "I will protect her with my very life.," Edric smiles, sharp teeth betraying his soft look.

Dewain leans down to my ear, whispering to me, "I will see you at our meal, Daughter," he tips my head back, long fingers brushing under my chin. I barely hold back a screech, my breath frozen. His dark eyes study my face, "You have been absent from my table for too long."

His fingers pull back before he brushes past Edric, growling threats at him. I watch, open-mouthed, as he takes a few long steps on the pearl walkway before diving into oceanic water—the water ripples around him before he disappears into the dark depths.

Brendan

Brigit keeps Flavian alive. I don't envy her. He runs again and again at the barrier, knocking himself bloody. The wall doesn't give, the invisible strength barring his entry.

While Brigit struggles with Flavian, I assess Anya. The Finn broke her ribs, possibly all of them. I ease back her dress; her arm is fractured below the elbow. The Finn must have stomped their spears on her hands, her fingers are crooked, and several nails are torn out.

I take the bundle of cloth, tearing it into strips. I wrap Anya's hands then take larger straps and gingerly wrap them around her chest. Her breath catches, a painful rattle in her lungs.

I'm not a healer. I was trained to destroy life and tear apart our enemies.

All I know is that we need to get her back to the village, send for a healer. How the girl is managing to hold onto life is beyond me. I've seen men on the battlefield, bones broken like this. If her ribs pierce her lungs, I force myself to stop thinking.

Flavian is screaming, raging. I lift my gaze toward him, my voice firm, as I resort to sheer magic., "I command you to silence."

He whirls on me, face breaking into a snarl. But his silence holds, the intensity of our relationship, upheld by the bonds of magic. He must obey me until I release him from my service; he has no other choice.

My eyes turn to Brigit. "Help me." My voice breaks., "I don't know anything about mortals." Brigit crosses the floor quickly, coming to kneel beside Anya.

She touches the girl's hair, "In the mortal lands, she'd be dead." Her chin lifts, and she meets my eyes.

"It's all Darcy wanted," My tongue is heavy, and I fight to think through what I'm feeling, "And after what we did, giving her to them."

"It was evil," Brigit snaps at me., "Besides stupid." she cups Anya's face in her hand, lowering her lips to the girl's pale mouth. She breathes into her before pulling her head back., "She'll stay alive until we reach a healer." I start to reach for Anya, but Brigit slaps my hands away. She urges me to my feet, and I hobble on my toes, watching.

Brigit carefully gathers Anya, cradling her neck. She scowls at me. "You want to carry her."

It's something for me to do, some way to help. Brigit still glares at me., "You're utterly useless; you know that?" I nod, and Brigit stands slowly, then hands me Anya. The girl weighs nothing. I cup my loose fingers around her cheek, the skin cold. She's still breathing; I take a step, praying to the gods, keep her breathing.

We walk out of the Hollow, our steps echoing in the emptiness. Flavian is breathing heavily, but he is silent, his face practically purple with rage.

Brigit alternates between glaring at her brother and me. She falls into step beside me, "You heard that Finn. He said Edric choose to go to their Court."

I don't reply. There's nothing to say. Brigit huffs, "Unless nature has reversed itself, he can't have lied."

"I never said I didn't believe him."

Brigit looks at me from the corner of her eyes. "What are you going to tell the Queen?"

I look down at Anya's bruised face., "As you just reminded me, I can't lie."

"Hasn't stopped you before," Brigit bites back, her lips curling into a snarl. The look reminds me so much of Flavian, the same narrowing of her eyebrows, eyes flashing.

Her irritation is amusing, but I keep my mouth pressed closed. "Brigit," I tread softly, I've only seen Flavian's sister once or twice since I met my second. She barely ever speaks to me.

"I don't have the faintest idea why you detest me, except for the fact that I'm from the Court. Though I will remind you I wasn't even born when your family was exiled. I've never advocated the continued exile, and I treat your brother fairly. You know, I certainly cannot lie."

Brigit lets out a breath, the air a hiss., "You promised my brother redemption. A place at Court."

I nod at her statement, and she continues, "You've enslaved him to your will."

My chin jerks up., "Flavian chose to be my second."

"Are all seconds chained to always obey, even against their will?" Her eyes flash, and she jerks her shoulder towards her brother. Following several meters behind us, his feet dragging, breath ragged. I don't need to look at his clenched fists to know he wants to speak, to fight my command to silence.

I know the answer. Only a rare set of men in our history have ever enforced the chain of command through magic.

The stories are legends, traitors sworn to their enemies, bound to their every whim.

Flavian might be the only second in our history magically bound to his commander's orders. A commander he neither disobeyed nor shamed. Still, from the moment he showed interest in being my second, it was the only way to accept his service. A bond I rarely exercise, but the entire Court knows of the bargain. A bargain my father himself suggested, insisted upon.

"You don't regret chaining him to your will?" Brigit snarls at me., "Keeping him like a leashed dog?"

I stare straight ahead., "Your brother wanted a place at Court. A position of respect and honor. There were few options for granting him his desires."

"Few options," Brigit spits., "And when will you release him? Or is he your dog forever?" I look down at Anya's face, pasty white in the gloomy darkness. "Until the favor of the Court is assured for Flavian, he remains under my protection. Without our bargain, Flavian would never have been allowed in the Queen's household service." "A man of honor wouldn't have offered him the bargain," Brigit answers sharply., "Trapped him to you, with a bare promise of escape." She storms past me, the sword strapped to her side glinting. Brigit and Flavian's family cherish their freedom more than most Fae. Their ideals have landed them in exile, banished from the presence of the Queen and Court.

I can understand Flavian's desperate longings to find his place at Court, his willingness to bargain with me no matter the consequences. But Brigit's ideals of freedom, her flippancy about our way of life, it boggles my mind. I simply can't understand Brigit's disregard for the Court, our Queen.

Anya moans, her head shifting. My fingers rest against the base of her skull, barely holding her neck. Her eyelids flutter but don't open.

I glance ahead, seeing the bare traces of light flickering. We're almost to the cave mouth, and I can fly her to the village from there.

Flavian steps into pace beside me, his face white with fury. I look at him., "Are you angry with me?" A pause before he shakes his head. "The girl is fragile.," I clear my throat., "If I release you from silence, you can't disturb her." Another nod, quicker this time. I speak the required words, "I release you from my command." The magic eases its hold on him, his shoulders slumping as he lets out a gasp. "Brendan, that was beastly."

"Really?" I quirk my eyebrow., "I should have just let you keep ranting, screaming at empty air?"

"They have Edric," he snarls, his sister's twin in ferocity, if not in tone., "They tricked us." We're close to the mouth of the mountain., "I know, Flavian." I step around some loose rock, "They played us all for fools."

Chapter Nine

Darcy

EDRIC LEADS ME ALONG the pearl steps of the terrace. I look beyond the walkway, staring at the wall of water around us. "You don't need to worry," Edric comments, turning back to me. He stops still., "The water never breaches the palace."

"Why not?" I reach out, stepping close to the terrace. I lean over the railing, touching the salty seawater. My fingers pierce through the wall of water, but the water doesn't run down my arm. Instead, it stays, held back from the palace. "Ancient magic." Edric leans against the railing, draping his arms against the elegant white balustrade., "And it's inconvenient to host guests who can't hear and speak."

I smile a little at that. It is nice to speak; it was suffocating the way the Finn dragged me through the water. I'm not sure it's very different from drowning, surrounded by water, and unable to speak or hear a sound. If the Finn left me in the water, alive but alone, I think that would be a living death. Goosebumps rush up my spine, and I take a quick breath, looking back at the Fae Prince. "Are you a guest?"

Edric shrugs lightly, pushing back from the railing. I follow his long steps, watching the back of his cloak. The golden shamrocks are sewn into the green velvet, the symbol of his mother's court.

"The long-lost girl." Edric looks back at me, speaking as he leads me along the edge of the terrace., "As average as you appeared."

I look at the Fae prince, his sharp nose, long dark eyelashes hooding his eyes. "How do you know they've been looking for me?"

He smiles lazily, again shrugging his thin shoulders., "It's why I'm here."

"You chose to be here," I repeat the words I heard earlier., "They didn't steal you."

Edric eyes me., "You are very ignorant." He speaks matter of fact, no humor, no gloating—a simple statement.

"Yes," I breathe, nearly amused by his flat tone., "I suppose I am."

He nods slowly, words quiet, as though he thinks through each syllable before speaking, "If the Finn king stole me, it would have been an act of war. I was always free to choose to leave."

My question is quicker., "Why did you choose to leave now?"

"Ah.," Edric's eyes flicker towards me with a touch of surprise, the long dark lashes widening around his crystal blue eyes. "Now, that is an interesting question!" He stops, turning to look at me. He is entirely still, unmoving only as the Fae can be. Not blinking, not breaking, still as stone. I wait, almost holding my breath. Edric's lips curve slowly, and I finally speak, a touch breathlessly, "Well?"

Edric raises his thin hand., "Your room.," he gestures behind me., "I trust you'll approve." I turn enough to see the elegant open doorway, though I don't peer beyond the threshold. Edric lays a hand on my shoulder, urging me forward. I take small steps, my skirt brushing against the floor as we step over the threshold.

"Until you're one of the Finn, you stay here," Edric comments, motioning with a flick of his wrist around the room.,

"You are the King's subject, Lord Dewain's daughter. They will treat you well."

I can hardly take in the elegant coral walls, the bright bed with soft billowing curtains. Instead, images press in on me, and it's all I can see, Anya, surrounded by Finn guards, caged.

I round on the Fae Prince., "My cousin, they hurt her, kept her caged," I snap at him. "Why wasn't she given a guest room?"

Edric releases a breath, "My mother showed you a vision."

I breathe heavily, but Edric takes my silence as confirmation. He runs both hands through his hair, "The Finn went for you, reaching the coast to take you. They were not pleased to find you gone."

"So they took Anya." I can barely think through her horror, my body is shaking, and I squeeze my eyes shut. If I had stayed, hadn't caught that leprechaun, Anya would be safe. Untouched.

Edric lays his fingers against my arm, leading me to a chair. He pushes me into the cushioned fabric, speaking softly, "It took all of my mental powers to locate you." he brushed a hand over my hair., "I did what I could to help your cousin, Darcy. I regret her pain immensely. Yet, she was still a prisoner."

My eyes flicker open, taking in his body leaning over me., "You sent them to her, and they took her because of you."

He stiffens, stepping back., "They were searching for you. It is not wise to disappoint the Finn."

My fingers clench around the edge of the chair., "My life wasn't any of your business," I seethe at him, barely able to speak through my teeth, "I didn't want them, or you, or anyone."

Edric blinks., "Yet you caught a leprechaun."

My breath catches, and I lean forward., "I didn't know the legends were truly horrors waiting to tear apart my family.,"

Tears choke on my voice, my eyes burning., "I just wanted a better life for Anya, for me, for us both."

"You will have a better life here.," Edric holds up his hand, his words rapid and fierce. "Trust me. You were not born to live with mortals. Your blood craves magic, demands magic. Without magic, your existence is misery."

"I don't want a better life.," My answer comes just as quick., "I want my life. My life, the life I chose. Not one destined by gods or magic. The life I made for myself."

Edric is shaking his head as I speak, blue eyes flashing. He raises his fingers, pointing them at me. "Darcy, Daughter of Dewain, this is a life you can choose. But, it is a life you must choose."

"Don't call me that," I snap back at him instantly., "I will never choose this life."

Edric huffs at my answer, his lips quirking into a ghost of a smile. His eyes sweep over the room, and I follow his gaze, glancing around the room. As large as our cottage is back on the shore, the bed doesn't even take up half the floor in this spacious room. A crystal mirror hangs from the ceiling, the wide-open windows, greenery climbing through the window panes.

"I find," Edric calls my attention back to him, his voice soft, "I find we are often surprised by our own choices." I don't want to be surprised by anything else. Edric bows, his cape sweeping over his shoulder, gold embroidery glistening, "I will return before dark to escort you." He stands straight, turning on his heels. His black boots click on the floor as he leaves, shutting the door behind him.

It is late afternoon when Edric leaves me fuming in the center of this spacious room. I pace the space and then lunge at the door. But the metal handle doesn't budge, and I am locked inside.

I fall back from the wood, clawing at my face. Hot tears course down my cheeks, and I collapse on the soft rug. I can't close my eyes, not without seeing Anya, thrown to the ground, a mere bundle of bones.

The King's voice rings in my mind; he's sneering, "Halfling mortal." My shoulders shudder, and I gasp for air. He sneered at me, and I am at least half-blooded, a child of the Finn how they must despise Anya, completely, utterly mortal as she is. Nothing more than a prisoner to them, a doll to be tortured, her pain an experiment.

Fear clouds my thoughts. Anya must be safe. I clutch my hands together, whispering every prayer I've ever known: the new prayers the Saxons bring, chants to saints and virgins. My chest aches, and I beg harder, prayers to the gods of my childhood—the gods of Fae and Finn alike.

My tears soak past my hands, and I press my nose into the blue velvet of my gown, Brendan, he must have promised to protect her. Tears soak into my dress, but I can't remember his face.

All I can see is Anya, a heap on the black stones. Flavian's shock and fury, the Finn hands holding me back. "Please.," My lips form the words, but the sound chokes in my throat., "Don't let her suffer for my choices anymore.," I can barely form thoughts., "Give her her life back. Her own life, without fear of Finn and Fae. Free her from them all; gods, please keep her safe."

I'm still curled up on the floor, my breathing calmer. I'm not crying anymore, but my face is still hot, my eyes crusty.

Then, finally, the door rattles open, and I barely raise my head.

"Dewain's daughter," the Finn speaks, looking down at me., "Please, stand up. It is almost dark."

I uncurl my legs, shuffling to my knees. The Finn looks mainly like the guards who brought me here, braided green hair, purple-tinted skin. She wears a gossamer dress; slits cut past her knees, the scales on her legs shimmer as she steps toward me.

I can't help but glancing down, noting her webbed feet. "Your name is Darcy?" she asks; her voice isn't rough, almost plain. Not frightening.

"My name is Darcy.," I yank at my dress, pulling myself to my feet. Even standing, the Finn towers over me. "May I know your name?"

"Mara.," She widens her lips, showing off her rows of teeth., "I will be attending you."

I nod, and she steps closer., "You have been crying.," I look back at her face, the slight surprise in her voice. She reached her long fingers toward me, running her nail along my cheek. I wince; her nails sharp enough to cut if she presses just a little bit., "You know," Mara speaks quietly, "the Finn cannot shed tears."

I shake my head, I didn't know. Mara runs her forked tongue across her lips. "Tears are for the weak." Her eyes narrow., "Even the Fae weep."

I don't think Mara wants a reply, so I nod. She clicks her teeth together before stepping past me. Walking to one of the wardrobes, opening the cabinets. "It is unfortunate you are so small.," She talks while she rummages., "Your legs are too short.," She turns to me, holding out a crimson gown., "When you accept your Finn heritage, you will look much better in your gowns."

My teeth clench, but I don't answer. I can't let myself talk back, annoy these creatures. This isn't Gwen, with pixie laughter and gentleness.

Brendan

I was nervous about flying with Anya, but walking out of the valley was a risk. It is difficult to climb down into the mountain, with the multitude of boulders crowding the path. Hiking back up is all climbing uphill, fighting crumbling boulders and your own ragged breathing. Now we have to take the hike with a dying human. Flying was the only option. Brigit scrambled ahead, her feet quick on the slick rocks until she made it out of the mountain cave, and then spread her wings, jumping into the skies to speed off and search for a healer. I focused on keeping Anya still in my arms, watching the path to making sure I didn't slip or jolt her body harshly.

Flavian followed me until we were clear of the overhanging mountain, and then we spread our wings. Anya moaned occasionally, but her eyes stayed closed. I risked looking down at her face, my wings catching in the wind. Even with all the training I've ever received, there's nothing I can do. I know nothing about keeping hearts beating, only where to cut off a heartbeat forever.

Brigit has already landed in the Faun village, and when I land, a cluster of Fauns is immediately on me. The mothering Faun from last night, the one who baked us bread this morning, I see her first. She offers me her home, and I walk to her cottage.

They lay out a pallet for Anya, and I gently lay her body down. Her head brushes on the feather pillow, and for the first time, her eyes open.

They're soft gray, confusion mixed with fear. Her mouth parts open, and she yelps, trying to sit up. I lay my hand against her shoulder. "Anya, it's alright."

She shakes her head, still trying to sit up., "You're hurt.," I rest on my knees., "You need a healer, and we're going to help you."

"Darcy," she speaks the name brokenly, gasping., "Where's Darcy?"

"Anya.," I can't answer her question; sure, it will only frighten her more., "Anya, lay back down, please." She shakes her head, tears streaming down her face, repeating Darcy's name.

The healer must have come in; Brigit pulls me back, letting the healer reach Anya's side. Anya is crying louder now, panic and fear mixed with her questions about Darcy.

I turn on Brigit, whispering, "How are we supposed to tell her?"

Anya cries out again, and I wince., "She can't return to her home, not without Darcy."

Brigit looks at me, her face scrunched in confusion. "She's a mortal, Brendan. She needs to return to her home." The healer must have put Anya back to sleep, and I look past Brigit. Anya's eyes are closed, her breathing steady. "She can't return to her home.," My temples ache, and I massage the bridge of my nose. "I promised Darcy I would keep her safe. She's not safe on land."

"Not safe.," Brigit grabs my arm, yanking me back from the pallet. We stumble out of the cottage., "Of all places on earth, the Court might be the most unsafe for a mortal like her."

"The Finn might try to use her again." I stare into Brigit's passionate eyes, hoping she'll understand. "I don't know why they wanted Darcy, but they could use Anya to get Darcy to do anything. If we take her back to her home, the Finn will return for her."

Brigit's fingers ease on my arm, and she drops me, comprehension dawning in her eyes. "Then what are you going to do?"

I shake my head, still unsure. Flavian lands, as I'm thinking, his feathers rustling. He stalks over to us, a question in his stormy eyes. "We won't return to Court tonight," I speak to both of them., "We rest here; allow Anya to recover." "The Finn," Flavian starts, his words harsh and angry.

I hold up a hand, "Let me think about it, Flavian." I look to the mountain peaks, the dust approaching, coating the village in the evening darkness, "The Finn won't speak to the Queen. Perhaps," I look my second in the eyes, "Perhaps, we need to find a way to speak to the Finn ourselves."

Darcy

Mara braids my hair into an elaborate twist, holding the braids into place with sharp pins. She pulls my hair so tightly back from my head, my eyes water. I don't look in the mirror while dressing, partly because I simply hate the fact that this is happening.

But after she inserts the last pin, I turn around. The crimson dress falls in elegant waves around my hips, slits running to my knees. I've never worn red, and the color makes my skin flush, my hair even redder.

I turn at the sound of knuckles on wood, the door opening to reveal Edric standing on the threshold. "Are you ready?" His eyes sweep over my dress, and I touch my warm cheeks as he turns to Mara, "Do you have to highlight her mortality?"

Mara straightens, hissing, "I don't have mortal clothes." She clicks her nails together., "If she wanted to dress like a mortal, she should have brought her gowns."

She sweeps past Edric, grumbling and giving him a nasty look. Edric ignores her. "Well, I suppose there's nothing you can do."

He jerks his chin, "We don't want to be late."

I don't have any shoes on and look around the room, wondering. But, of course, my feet are more comfortable bare, but not wearing shoes feels strange.

"You need something?" Edric questions, still standing by the door.

"Shoes.," I bunch my fingers around the skirt, lifting it just enough to highlight my bare feet, "Mara didn't give me any."

"Of course not.," Edric holds out his hand., "The Finn don't wear shoes."

I flush again, remembering all the webbed toes I've seen. Shoes and webbed feet don't work well together. I let the skirt fall, crossing the carpet to stand by Edric. "Anything else I should know before dinner?"

"First.," Edric touches my elbow, walking me out the door., "It's not dinner." He inclines his head to the dark waters surrounding the walkway, the dimmed lighting., "The Finn are creatures of the night. They don't eat in daylight. This is their first meal today."

"There's no sunshine down here," I protest. "How can they even know when it's day or night?"

Edric nearly smiles, amusement in his eyes. "You can't ignore time, Darcy. The Finn light their territories just as sunshine might light our Fae lands."

Of course, I twist my hands together, thinking about the double moons in the Fae court, the sunlight's light hanging over the mountains. The Fae had skies with stars, though they live underground. The Finn might not have sunlight, but they still have something that resembles daytime and nighttime.

We walk past the throne room, Edric's boots clicking. I look down at his feet, noting the dark gleam of his shoes that he still wears his elegant boots. Edric looks down, following my gaze before he speaks, "I brought my footwear," I look back at his face, the amused glint in his eyes, "Unfortunate, you were not so prepared."

I yank away from the touch of his hand, crossing my arms together. Whatever reason Edric has to be here, it's his fault that I'm here, that Anya is hurt. Edric told the Finn my location, helped them find me.

"Take a breath, Darcy," Edric murmurs., "You will need all your wits tonight."

We step away from the terrace, walking down a set of stairs. He leads me down a long hall, Finn guards standing on each side of the wide path. Greenery grows here as well, twirling vines along shell-covered walls. In between the vinery, hang mirrors and paintings. I gape at the paintings, the life-size rendering of Finn warriors. Kings, and even Queens.

I don't look in the mirrors; I don't want to see the elegant dress I'm wearing, the careful braids. I can't get the picture of Anya and her clothing torn to rags out of my head, comparing how the Finn discarded her while draping me in the fanciest clothes.

We walk in silence, passing under an arched doorway into a long room. The gloominess clouds my eyes, and I blink, adjusting to the darkness. A few candles flicker on a long table, but the space is murky dark.

"Darcy," I startle at the sound of Dewain's voice. He steps towards me, draped in a dark cape, his armor glinting. I have no idea what I'm supposed to do, but I bow my head, bending my knees into something of a curtsy.

His hands touch my shoulders, pulling me straight, "Don't bow to me." He frowns, brushing his sharp nails against my hair while I try not to cringe.

"You are my daughter," Dewain murmurs., "My heir. I will not have you serving anyone."

I can barely process his words, looking at his strange, stone face. *His heir*, I'm holding my breath, pinching my fingers together. I *can't be this man's only child.*

He reaches for my arm, walking me towards the table. As we step closer, I catch sight of the seats crowded with Finn. Most have green hair, and a few have red-tinged hair; others like Dewain have golden hair. Dewain keeps walking further down the table, past Finn, who raise their glasses to him.

Some speak in their language, but most call out in the common tongue., "She bears your bearing, Dewain. It is well she is found."

My skin is hot, my hands slick with sweat. Their words make my head spin, the way they talk about me. As though I were a lost possession, a weapon to be given back. You belong to Dewain; the King's words from earlier roll through my mind.

Belong to Dewain, as though I weren't a person. *Belong*, as though I have no choice. My breathing quickens, but Dewain is still walking, pulling me along with him.

I want to stop. I want to sleep, to escape this nightmare. Instead, my feet catch on the too-long gown, and I stumble.

If it weren't for Dewain's hold, I would have landed on my knees.

Dewain pulls me closer, his other hands curling around the back of my neck. He leans down, speaking just into my ears., "Don't fight me, Darcy. I have no desire to see you suffer."

His fingers urge me forward into a chair. Then, hands-on my shoulder, I sit stiffly on the hardwood. I'm far too small, my feet several inches from the ground, the table too high. Everything here is just so much larger.

Dewain sits in the chair next to me, immediately pouring a glass of wine. My stomach growls, and I suddenly realize how thirsty I am. I haven't eaten or drunk anything in hours, almost for a whole day.

Dewain holds the glass towards me, and I reluctantly reach forward. My mind screams in protest, and my fingers are shaking. In my hand, the wine shivers, and I stare into the silver goblet, holding it above my plate.

"Are you not thirsty?" Dewain questions, pouring himself a glass.

I lick my lips, and my mouth is parched. "Yes.," Even if I can lie, it would be stupid to try. I am thirsty., "But I am mortal."

I look away from the darkness that passes over his face; he sets his glass down, "You do not need salt."

He reaches for a platter of food and roasted meats arranged elaborately, clusters of grapes hanging from the edges of the silver. Then, spearing the beef, he sets it on my plate, repeating, "You do not need salt."

Hearing the words a second time does nothing to reassure me. Instead, he pulls his lips back, teeth glimmering,

"Even if your blood allowed enchantment, no one would dare enchant you."

I still must look doubtful, as Dewain releases a sigh, "Do you know who I am?"

My fingers are still around my wine glass, the metal clammy on my sweaty palms., "You're Dewain."

He raises his eyebrows., "Yes, anything else?"

I shake my head, and Dewain picks up his glass, taking a long sip. "King Murtagh married my sister," he speaks quietly., "I command the Finn armies." His eyes flash, lips pulling back, the edges of his teeth sharp., "There's not a soul in the ocean who would dare cross me."

I look back down, my fingers still shaking. The deep red wine trembles while Dewain speaks again, "Perhaps the only one who has ever dared cross me is you." I don't look up at his words, my heart rate doubling., "Though I blame the Slaugh and know you will eventually obey me."

"Obey you?" The question squeaks from my throat.

Dewain's hand closes over mine, steadying my jittering fingers and the wine glass., "Drink.," I raise my head just enough to meet his dark eyes, "Take a drink."

The metal touches my lips, every fiber in my bones revolting, my heart strumming with fear. The wine passes over my tongue, and I swallow, gasping. Dewain presses the glass to my teeth again, and I take another mouthful. One more swallow and Dewain pulls the wine back., "I have your interests at heart, Darcy." He pats my hand, "I am not upset you did not let Murtagh turn you immediately, it was expected," My eyes widen at his words, and he smiles, though his teeth remain hidden., "I will be patient with you, Darcy. But you will obey."

The wine is not enchanted; I don't feel dizzy or giddy. But I am exhausted. The meal drags on and on, and during the fifth course, Edric takes a seat several chairs down. Then, finally, he raises his wine glass in my direction, and I give him a shallow nod.

Seeing him, watching him, reminds me of his mother, Queen Oona. Her words and my promise to return Edric. But if Edric chose to come here, does my vow count?

Dewain pours another glass of wine, but I barely touch it. I've never drunk such strong wine; the rum our village breaks out at Samhain is nowhere near this strong. I'm feeling lightheaded, and I've only taken a sip from the second glass.

As the servants clear away the plates, bringing out yet another course, the King appears. The table rises for him, and I jolt from my seat, nearly falling forward. Dewain touches my back, steadying me. The King raises his wine glass, and the company reaches for their goblets, taking a drink.

I touch the cold glass to my lips but don't take a sip. I don't think I can handle any more of the wine.

Then we're all sitting down, the servants filling more pitchers of wine. My head tips forward, my eyes heavy, and I rest my forehead on my palms.

"Dewain.," The King's voice breaks through my heavy thoughts., "Have you told the girl her story?"

Dewain murmurs an answer, and I look up, rubbing weariness from my eyes. I lean forward, just enough to meet the King's dark eyes. "I would tell her tonight.," King Murtagh smiles at me, his rows of teeth flashing., "But she appears ready to collapse."

Dewain looks down at me, his eyebrows creasing., "Are you tired?"

I yawn again., "I tend to sleep with the moon, my lord."

"Don't call me that.," Dewain pushes his chair back., "I'm your father, not your master."

Father and master feel very synonymous right now. Dewain stands, holding out his hand. I take it, rising shakily to my feet.

"A child of the light," King Murtagh calls out, and several other Finn laugh. Dewain is glowering., "She will adjust, Eminence," he speaks to the King., "It is, after all, her first night in our court."

"Of course.," Murtagh waves his hand at us, rings flashing. "But don't leave, Dewain. I want to talk to you more. Have someone escort her to bed."

Dewain looks ready to protest when Edric stands up., "I can take her, my lord." Before turning to Murtagh, he speaks to my father, "Unless your Eminence needs me."

"No.," Murtagh shakes his head, "You've given us all we need for now."

"I don't want him," I barely whisper, but Dewain's ears pick up on my words. He looks down at me., "What is it, daughter?"

Calling me daughter makes me cringe, but I want to ask this, "I said," I speak just a little louder, "I don't want Edric to escort me."

Dewain inclines his head, his voice sharper., "Did he hurt you?"

In a million little ways, whatever he did, it hurt Anya and brought me here. "He's the reason Anya was hurt.," I fight for the right words, my brain cloudy, but I hope this Finn will understand, "I don't like him."

"Sir," Edric speaks behind me, and I nearly jump., "Your daughter has had too much wine. What she says is true, I did give her cousin to the men sent for her. But that was as much my fault as her own."

I glare at Edric, hating that he knows my feelings. That he blames me for Anya, whatever these beasts did to her. Dewain squeezes my shoulder., "Edric serves King Murtagh." I turn to look at him. "What happened to your human cousin was unfortunate, but no one's fault. Don't blame the prince for it."

I want to protest, to argue, but my tongue is heavy. Dewain pulls my hand away, setting my palm on Edric's arm., "Edric knows more about mortals than me; the Fae live closer to the mortal lands and interact with mortals far more often."

I don't know why he's saying this until he continues, "Edric will help you adjust, prepare you to shed your humanity." My face must be pale; my heart is beating so hard, Edric must be able to hear it. I shake my head., "I don't want to shed anything.," the words tumble in a rush., "I want to go home."

Dewain is shaking his head, and Edric pulls me back, talking in my ear, hushing me. I scramble away from his touch, raising my hand to slap him. But, instead, his fingers close around my wrist, and he pulls my arms to my side.

I'm shaking all over, dizzy, nauseous. Dewain is talking, and Edric replies. But I don't understand what they're saying.

I can't breathe, I can't think, not with these beasts talking all around me.

"Darcy.," Edric pulls me away, and my feet trip over the gown., "Darcy," my name again., "Darcy, don't you dare pass out on me."

My eyes are wide; the room is too small., "I don't know.," I can't breathe., "I don't know what to do," Somehow, I'm crying again, and I can't stop. I can't breathe in here; it's too small, too crowded.

"Darcy.," Edric gathers me closer, and I scramble, trying to get away. My nails claw at his face, but I can't breathe, can't think. Everything is dark, darkening. Edric is holding my face, telling me to keep breathing when I pass out.

Chapter Ten

Darcy

WATER SPLASHES ON MY face, and I jerk away, spluttering. I rub my eyes, sending a glare at the dark-haired Fae. "You aren't drunk.," Edric pulls a wet curl back from my eyes, "You don't have an excuse to pass out."

"Leave me alone," I just want to sleep, I curl my legs, but the cold hits my bare skin. "As friendly as you look.," Edric helps pull me to a sitting position., "You don't need to be scared of Dewain or me."

I stare at him, images from the banquet hall flooding my mind., "You helped them hurt Anya."

Edric frowns. "Dewain didn't touch Anya, and I certainly had no part in what they did."

"You led them to her," The words come in a rush of my frustration, pictures of Anya and her bruised body some of my only thoughts., "They hurt her because of you."

Edric touches my hands, "Listen, I was trying to find where you live, the barest trace of your presence." He swallows.,

"I thought it was because of the quality of Dewain's memories, and it never occurred to me you could be at the Fae Court."

"Never occurred to you?"

His eyes narrow., "You thought you were mortal; visiting the Fae isn't an average mortal pastime."

I let out a huff., "Why were you even helping them?'

"Part of a bargain," Edric answers shortly, "and as always, it was more trouble than it was worth." I sit up straighter, looking past Edric. We're sitting on the edge of a stone bench, candlelight twinkling on the wall. Perhaps it's the darkness or my still foggy head, but I don't see anything in the room. It appears completely bare.

Edric helped Dewain and Murtagh, and as much as I hate what I did, I need to know., "How did Dewain know to find me?"

He lets out a breath, rubbing his hand on his knees., "A fisherman died recently, your uncle."

I jerk at the mention of my uncle., "What does he have to do with this?"

"Wait." Edric holds up his hand. "Dewain recognized him when the sirens brought him."

The sirens, I'm confused. Edric sighs, "The sirens capture sailors as payment to the King." Edric looks at me, shifting uncomfortably. "Dewain knew you were still alive." A sick feeling fills my stomach., "Your uncle wouldn't give away your location." his voice is soft., "He died protecting it."

I'm shaking again, angry and horrified. Edric is still speaking., "Dewain needed me to search the memories, find where you were."

I jump away; I can't stand sitting next to him. Everything that's happened, Uncle Kian's death, Anya's suffering, even my being here, it's his fault. "Darcy," Edric starts, standing. But I whirl, my fists clenching. "Don't say my name, don't talk to me." The words come in torrents., "You are my enemy, and I curse you by all the gods."

Edric's face is downfallen, his eyes wide., "Darcy, please, I never intended."

I don't care what he intended. "That's doesn't matter," I spit at him. "Anya could be dead because of you. You stole my uncle's memories. You ruined my life."

Silence follows my words. Edric drops his head, barely audible., "You may never forgive me." his fingers twist together, touching the dark ring on one of his slender knuckles, "But I hope one day you understand."

We stand there for a long moment, my breathing heavy, Edric entirely still. He doesn't move, his head bowed, arms stiff, hands knotted together. I wonder if he will speak if I should say anything; how long he will stand there.

"I want to go back to my room.," I finally break the silence., "I want to be alone." He raises his head., "You should stay up longer, let your body acclimate to the new time."

I have no desire to acclimate to this place. Instead, I glare at him. "Take me to my room."

He shrugs., "As you wish.," He takes a step, sweeping his hand around the dim room., "We'll be spending a lot of time in here."

I look around the dim bare room, curious., "Why?"

"Training.," His boots click on the floor., "You need to learn some basic skills."

He leads me through the double set of doors, and I hesitantly ask., "Do you know who's training me?" Edric looks over his shoulder at me., "Didn't you hear me say we?"

No, gods, no, I nearly groan before spitting at him, "Absolutely not."

"Talk to Dewain, Darcy," Edric chuckles., "I'm only following your father's instructions." My teeth grit, my hands fisting together. "I'll talk to him," I seethe at Edric., "And don't call him my father."

Edric raises his eyebrows, leading me along the outer edge of the terrace. We walk past the throne room. I know where my room is now. Edric speaks softly beside me, "You know I can't lie. And Dewain is your Father."

I open the door to my room, looking back over my shoulder to glare at Edric., "Just keep the truth to yourself, Edric. You're better when you're quiet." I don't bother waiting for Edric to reply before slamming the door. The walls don't shake, but I hit the door with the heel of my foot. A sudden thought crosses my mind, and I turn the doorknob. I'm locked inside.

Brendan

The healer works with Anya, carefully setting each bone, working the breaks back into place. Finally, she gives Anya a draught, keeping her asleep through most of the process.

When she's done, she summons me. "Her bones are all back in place.," The healer shakes her head, "But I can't heal her scars, erase her pain."

I look at Anya; she looks peaceful when she's asleep. The healer touches my elbow., "See her face?"

Of course, I see the girl's face, but the healer doesn't wait for me to state the obvious., "Her teeth.," She motions at Anya., "She's grinding her teeth."

"Is it painful?"

"It can be." The healer touches a finger to her green lips., "You should glamor her."

I look at the woman., "What do you mean?"

"Glamor her." The healer stares at me., "Help her forget what happened to her; whatever happened weighs on her. She suffers through her pain."

The healer can not know Anya was at the Finn Court, but it is obvious they tortured Anya. I look at Anya's hands, the fading bruises on her wrist. The bright, inflamed pink of her nails, the magic is working to dull the pain, to help her nails heal.

"Her nails will grow back, her bones will mend," the healer speaks quietly. "I've never seen someone so brutalized."

I don't look at the healer, and she continues, "But I have never traveled beyond the borders of my Court."

"Of course.," I give the woman a tight smile, evading her veiled question., "Has Brigit paid you?"

The healer glares at me., "Wherever she has been, you need to take her back to the mortal lands. Glamor her, make her forget what she's seen."

Almost Brigit's advice, though Brigit didn't suggest glamoring. However, I don't want to argue with the healer about taking Anya's memories, so I pay her and send her on her way.

The healer huffs, reaching down to gather her bags. She steps through the door, shooting me a dark look. The door barely closes when Brigit steps through., "You upset her."

I can't help but sigh., "She wants me to glamor Anya, make her forget what happened."

Brigit is silent, and I voice my question, "How much would a glamor work? Would I need to make her forget her cousin, her own home?" I turn to Brigit., "It doesn't feel right."

"It isn't.," Brigit surprises me by agreeing., "You can't erase pain like this girl has experienced." She squats down by the pallet, touching Anya's face., "Even with a glamor, her heart will always ache. It will just hurt her more."

Brigit looks up at me, her green eyes worried., "I don't want you to take her to court, expose her to more danger,

Brendan. She's been through so much already."

"I don't plan on taking her to court."

Brigit presses her lips together., "Then, what do you plan on doing?"

I pull a chair over, sitting in the rickety wood., "We need to reach the Finn, find Edric. Know the truth behind this mess."

Brigit nods slowly, and I continue, "We cannot enter their kingdom alone. The Queen has allies; we must work with them."

"Mermaids," Brigit breathes out the word, echoing my thoughts., "And if the Finn king has already bought their allegiance?"

"The mermaids and Finn have never gotten along," I press, my voice still low., "We must go travel to the Mermaid cove, ask for their help."

Brigit runs a hand over one of her braids, twisting the hair in between her fingers., "We can't trust the mermaids to speak with Edric."

I stare at Anya, keeping my voice quiet., "One of us has to go. Only one of us travels with the Mermaids."

Brigit nods, touching Anya's wrist., "She's starting to wake up."

Anya is stirring, her eyelashes fluttering. Her hands tug on the blanket, legs curling together. She sucks in a breath, then jerks awake, scrambling up, eyes wide and fear-filled.

"Anya.," Brigit touches her back., "You're fine."

I lean forward in my seat while Anya looks between the two of us, clutching the blanket.

"You're safe, Anya," I speak quietly., "We're friends, and we want to help you."

Her mouth opens, but she doesn't speak. Instead, she just looks between the two of us, her eyes darting back and forth.

"Darcy is not here," Brigit speaks quietly., "but she told Brendan to take care of you."

At the mention of her cousin's name, Anya straightens, her whole body rigid. Then, Brigit speaks again, "Are you hungry?"

Anya shakes her head, tangled hair quivering. Brigit touches Anya's hand, but Anya jerks it back, gasping. The first sound she's uttered since waking up.

"You don't have to speak to us," I assure her quietly., "We want to help you, and we also want to help Darcy. We aren't going to hurt you."

Anya curls her legs up, her body beginning to tremble. She looks down at her hands, the stubs of her nails the healer worked at growing back. She touches her finger, then looks at Brigit, her voice pinched., "Where's Darcy?"

Brigit's eyes dart to me before she sucks in a breath. "Anya, we want to help her."

Anya closes her eyes, body wavering. She fists her hands at her mouth, gasping a statement., "The Finn have her."

Our silence must be answer enough; Anya sits quivering, her body shaking. I look at Brigit, and she seems as lost as I feel. There are no words we can say to help, nothing we can do to genuinely comfort except working at reaching the Finn, at finding Edric and Darcy.

I finally speak, "We don't know what the Finn wants. However, we do know some friends who might be able to help us find them."

Anya finally looks up, tears coating her eyelash. I take in a breath before continuing, "We need to travel to meet these friends. We don't want to leave you alone."

She barely nods her head before sitting forward, leaning on her knees. Brigit touches her shoulder, and Anya stiffens., "You want to go with us?"

Anya nods quickly, her hair falling into her eyes. Brigit looks at me, frowning. I raise my palms, shrugging. Brigit speaks softly, "Why don't you eat something? We won't leave for another day; we all need to recover." She glances at me, her voice straining., "We all need to rest before taking flight again."

Darcy

If I were on land, I would be asleep. It's probably past midnight, but instead, I'm in the training room. Dewain insisted that I not sleep tonight, even though it's only my second night in this palace.

He wouldn't even let me go back to my room after the fancy meal, sending me with Edric. At least Edric was quiet, and he didn't gloat or remind me smugly that he mentioned something about training me last night.

We walk into the dimly lit room together, but Edric walks around the room, taking a torch, lighting the other torches. His boots echo on the stones, the room brightening some. Still dark, but I can see most of the room. The rack of swords, bows hanging on the wall, cases full of arrows.

Edric claims he's not good with a sword or any weapon. "If Flavian or Brendan were here.," He shakes his head.,

"Either of them would be much better teachers."

I don't know anything about swords or weapons, so I can't say if Edric lacks in technique.

As it is, we hardly do anything through our first lesson. Edric makes me work on sit-ups, casually watching, his arms folded. My muscles protest, but I do at least thirty repetitions. I'm panting by the time I hit fifteen, gasping by the time I hit Edric's required thirty.

More stretches. I stretch out on the floor, trying to reach my toes. Edric chuckles before sitting down, stretching quickly. His back leans over his knees, and I grit my teeth. He makes it look so easy.

Several minutes pass before Edric moves. Then, finally, he stands, holding out his hand, helping me to my feet,

"Good," Edric nods dismissively, "Next time, warm-up before coming to training."

I glare at him, "I didn't even know I would be here today."

"I mentioned it yesterday," Edric flicks his wrist dismissively, "No excuses. You should stretch on your own every dusk. Before the first meal."

It's not that I particularly mind that Dewain wants me trained. After all, the Finn Court is feral and violent. But it's horrible that I have to train with Edric, who I can barely stand the sight of. At least Flavian glowered and didn't hide his feelings.

Edric acts like everything is normal, his half-smiles, soft words. But, everything is certainly not normal, and it's all thanks to this Fae.

"I think we should see how you can handle a sword," Edric holds out a wooden stick, "I'll show you the pacing. Then, we'll walk through it."

I grab the wooden stick from him, surprised at how lightweight it is. I toss it up into the air, catching it in one hand.

"It's not a toy, Darcy." Edric frowns. "Set your feet apart."

I twirl the sword, "It's not going to kill anyone, Prince." Then, I slap the wooden sword against my leg, "I think that's the definition of a toy."

Edric bites his lip, nearly smirking., "You're not ready for real weapons."

I know I'm not ready for anything remotely dangerous, but his attitude, it's insufferable. I grip the wooden sword, huffing at him. "Well, I'm certainly ready for this."

Edric raises an eyebrow., "Are you certain?"

"Of course.," I jab at the air., "What else am I supposed to do with it?"

"Well, I thought I would teach you pacing.," Edric raises his wooden sword. "Or we could work through a simple parley."

I don't know what he means by pacing or parley. He makes both words sound above me, so I just shrug. Edric watches me before sighing., "Fine, if you want to parley, I'll let you."

He holds out his sword, one foot moving behind him. I raise the wooden toy, dragging my feet like his. Edric watches me, brow furrowed. "I'll try not to hurt you."

I almost shrug again, but Edric lounges too quickly. The sudden movement throws me off guard; I wave the sword fruitlessly—Edric bats against it, the wood cracking.

He's moving too fast, and I slide back, trying to get out of the way. Instead, he barks at me, ordering me to stand firm. I'm not that crazy, I swing with the sword, but Edric knocks it aside effortlessly. His blow unnerves me, and I yelp, dropping the wooden stick.

I jump back, not sure what to expect. Certainly not Edric, bringing the flat of his sword against my head. The wood cracks on my skull, and I gasp in pain and shock. Edric steps back, and I'm cupping my head, my ears ringing.

"You're not hurt," Edric says softly., "Most parlays are much worse."

That's hardly comforting, and my eyes are stinging. And my headaches horribly. I glare at Edric, running my fingers gently over my bruising scalp.

"Ah, Edric.," I stiffen at the unfamiliar voice., "We heard you were working with our mortal cousin."

I turn too quickly, nearly slipping on the stone floor. Edric's face is blank, while he executes a meticulous bow to the two figures standing in the doorway., "As I was asked, highness." His fingers touch the edge of his cloak., "My pleasure to serve."

I'm pretty certain it's not Edric's pleasure to serve, not since his voice has turned razor-sharp. If the Finns standing in the doorway pick up on the tense set of Edric's shoulders, they don't comment on it.

The two figures are taller than me, shimmering tan skin. They wear elegant dark cloaks, black shin guards laced around their scaled legs.

The girl steps into the room, lips parting as she gleams at me., "Darcy.," She gestures at me, her hand glittering with several rings, wide gold bracelets circling her wrist. "I've heard so much about you."

I steal a glance at Edric, but his face is so still, I can't tell what he's thinking. "Who are you?"

The girl laughs, tipping her chin back, elegant honey brown curls quivering. She takes another step, and I realize her dress isn't a dress. Trousers, the seams split to look like a skirt, "You don't know?"

"Am I supposed to know?" I nearly snap back, frustrated with her laughter, the arrogant tone of voice.

The male beside her grins wider, leaning against the wall. He wiggles his webbed feet, shaking his head slightly. His fingers slide into his waistband, thumbs hooking over the edges. Utterly relaxed. If it weren't for the sword strapped to his side, one could almost forget how lethal he is. That, and the sharp teeth he keeps flashing.

The taller girl steps towards me; the torchlight is reflecting off her plaited hair. Her blouse is seamless tight leather pulled taught around her stomach. Lacing pulls tightly at her chest, knotted above her breasts. A necklace of pearl-colored seashells hangs low, touching the edges of her breast.

Her hand rests at her waist, a silver sword strapped to her side., "I'm Princess Letitia.," She lifts her chin, nearly sneering., "Your cousin."

Dewain mentioned his sister was married to Murtagh; I blink, trying to think through this connection. Princess Letitia stands a head taller than me., "My brother.," She jerks her head at the male., "Prince Owen." "Highness," I start, unsure what to say.

Leticia truly sneers now, placing her webbed hand on my shoulder, "As much as I detest it, you're part of our family. My cousin." Her tongue darts across her red lips., "No need to use formal titles."

I risk glancing at Edric, but Leticia catches my chin with her sharp fingers. "Don't look away, cousin." Her violet eyes crease with amusement., "I suppose you feel betrayed that your Fae tutor never told you about me."

My heart is beating so fast; I'm sure this girl can hear it. What she says is true; Edric never said anything about cousins. Neither have I seen these two anywhere the last few days. They look so much like Murtagh, except for the lighter coloring of their hair. Hair like Dewain. If I had seen them, I would have remembered their faces. Leticia raises an eyebrow, her voice a touch softer., "I suppose you wouldn't know. You look so much like your mother." She taps my cheek., "Same flame-colored hair, same sea-green eyes."

I try to pull back, but Leticia's fingers hold stiffly around my shoulder., "You should know, I remember her. Stealing Uncle Dewain's heart, running away, pregnant." She sneers, "Ungrateful mortal."

"Humans are remarkably ungrateful," the male speaks from his place by the wall., "Especially when they steal things." Leticia drops my shoulder, shoving me back. I stumble, nearly falling to the floor. Her hands rest on her hips, fingers tapping on her sword., "If you ever want to hear about your mortal mother." She grins, leaning down over me., "Be sure to come to talk to me. I know more than Edric claims to know."

She sends a glare towards Edric, hissing, "Don't train her too well, Prince." She tosses her head, straightening away from me., "We don't need another one. I'm not entirely keen on thieves."

Then she storms away, her brother straightening from the wall. He grins wolfishly, curly dirty blonde bangs falling into his violet eyes. "Cousin.," He gives me a flourishing bow, twirling his long fingers, "They hadn't mentioned how pretty you are." His purple lips smack together., "I think we'll enjoy having you at court." He follows his sister, long strides, his purple cloak barely brushing the floor.

I'm shaking, still trying to understand what they mean. Edric touches my back., "I'm so sorry, Darcy. I didn't know they had returned."

It's a good thing Fae can't lie because I'm not exactly inclined to trust Edric. Especially not with random Finn royalty breathing down my neck, Leticia's veiled threats. Words about my mother, I suck in a breath. "Am I related to those two?"

Edric nods slowly., "As they said."

I brush my trembling fingers through my hair, wincing at the bruise forming., "What did they mean?" I clear my throat., "About not needing another one? Another thief?"

"It doesn't matter.," Edric lightly pats my shoulder., "Focus on training. Leticia will ignore you, for now at least." I purse my lips at his Fae answer, dodging the question. Practically untrue, but not technically., "That didn't feel like ignoring me."

"Leticia wanted to meet you." Edric finally meets my eyes, his blue eyes stormy, which makes my face heat. Edric's eyes are always so calm, but now, they look nearly black. As though they changed color., "She's Murtagh's heir, and she would make it her business to know everything that happens in court."

Murtagh's heir, I take in a breath., "What about Owen?"

Edric steps back, his dark bangs falling into his eyes again., "The Finn heirs are different from what happens in my own Court." He nearly stumbles over the words *in my own*, as though it chokes him to speak. His face pales, lips tightening., "They are chosen for their competence, their skill. As well as their blood relations to the crown."

"Leticia is more skilled than Owen?" I speak dumbly, thinking through Owen's slouched back and folded arms. "Owen doesn't want to challenge Leticia," Edric corrects my thinking, his words soft., "To take the throne, he would need to challenge his sister in hand-to-hand combat."

"Oh.," I nod slowly, tucking a loose hair back into my braid., "A fight to the death?"

Edric shrugs, brushing at his cloak., "A fight to defeat. The Victor chooses the consequences. Challenges are dangerous like that."

Leticia's teeth flash in my mind, the way her blood-red lips pulled back, rows of razor-sharp teeth. Her nails, already growing long. Everything about her presence announces what she thinks of herself as, the Finn heir. Only a fool would challenge her sheer ferocity. I've no doubt Leticia would turn any fight into a fight to the death.

"Don't be distracted.," Edric beckons me over. "As I recall, our parlay was cut short. Perhaps we should step through the pacing this time?"

I send him a scowl but follow in his footsteps. "Now.," Edric hands me the blunt sword., "Watch your pacing. I'd rather not crack your skull again."

Chapter Eleven

Brendan

FLAVIAN GRUMBLES ABOUT EVERY decision we make. I don't think Flavian has looked at Anya, at her hollowed-out cheeks and bleeding hands. If Flavian could take just one moment to stop fretting about Edric, then he might understand why we can't fly to Court and demand war against the Finn. Anya needs us. I'm surprised when Brigit agrees and insists that we have to rest with the human. I'm the one who promised Darcy to watch out for Anya, but Brigit orders her brother to be quiet. Finally, we're both tired of his constant grumbling.

Of all the places we could have chosen to rest, the Faun village is probably the best. The Fauns mother, Anya, feeding her rich stews, homemade slices of bread, steamed vegetables. Everything is calm, refreshing. I don't need to worry about anyone glamoring Anya or poisoning her with Fae fruit. I doubt Anya even needs salt sprinkled over her food; the Fauns don't have a single cruel thought.

Two days into our visit, I'm up early and pacing outside, unable to sleep. The sky is turning light blue over the peaks of the mountains, just barely a sign of morning. Then, finally, the cottage door creaks open, and Anya steps over the stone threshold.

I turn to her, surprised that she's awake and outside. She hasn't spoken to me the entire last few days. But now she looks at me and says firmly, "I want to go."

"Go.," I have no idea where she wants to go., "We can't wait any longer," she speaks quietly, a slight tremor to her voice., "They have my cousin." Technically, Darcy offered herself to the Finn. They didn't break the law and steal her from her village. Anya holds up her hand, the skin around her nails still pink. But it doesn't look raw, the healer's magic working quickly on her damaged hands. "I'll go mad if I stay here any longer."

I smile a little at that., "Let's eat breakfast, speak to Brigit and Flavian. We'll leave this morning."

I knew Flavian would be ready to leave, but Brigit doesn't look convinced. Instead, she looks between Anya and me, obviously thinking I talked Anya into wanting to go. I suppose I should be flattered that Brigit thinks I'm so deceitful. However, the Gods know I haven't the faintest idea how to skirt the truth.

I would offer for Anya to fly with me, but Brigit takes the lead. She folds Anya into her arms, and we stand together. Flavian looks at me, waiting for me to speak. I clear my throat, "Remember, we're heading to human realms." I glance at Anya, "According to the code of the Court, we have to stay hidden."

Brigit and Flavian step closer to me. I reach out my hands, touching both of their elbows. Close my eyes, think of the vast green hills above our Court. The human island. I breathe in, feeling my magic. Then, when I release a breath, I whisper the command.

The air shifts, our bodies shifting above the protective magic of my Queen's realm. We open our eyes to the soft breezes of the island. Brigit touches Anya's head, her magic hiding her. Flavian and I make sure our magic is in place before we all take to the skies.

The mermaids live far to the South; their coves stay hidden among the many islands dotting the landscape before the ocean swallows the horizon. The sun is high by the time we fly past the shores. We circle over the first set of islands before dropping to a landing on the beach. "One of their sentries should have seen us," I comment to Flavian and Brigit. "We'll see who decides to visit us today."

"We don't carry any court banners.," Flavian ruffles his feathers., "They'll know the Queen didn't send us." Flavian is right; we don't look anything like a Fae envoy. A Fae envoy would have more guards, an official from the Court surrounded by court glamours. A Fae envoy would especially not travel with a mortal girl.

We land on the beach. Anya leans down to the sand, cupping her hand around the damp dirt. Minutes pass, waves lapping on the sand.

I walk the length of the beach, waffling about taking my boots off. It's been ages since I've spent time at the ocean but taking my shoes off is too casual. My calves start sweating, my legs warm in my thick leather boots.

"I see something," Flavian calls out, and I jog back to the beachhead. We wade out into the shallow water, Anya's fingers clenched around Brigit's arm. She hasn't said a word since we left the Faun village. The water laps around my boots, pouring over the edge.

The Mermaid swims to the surface, pulling herself unto the rock. She tosses back her dark hair, grinning. A flash of white teeth against dark skin., "Brendan, son of Riordan. A pleasant surprise."

"Vivian.," I drop my head at the Mermaid., "A pleasure to see you once more."

"What has it been?" Vivian cackles, her brown eyes flicker with amusement., "Four years since I've seen you?" She gestures at me, her nails sparkling. Gold tips on each finger. "Much more handsome."

My neck heats, I can hardly look Vivian in the eyes, both of us remembering my last visit to the coves. The Mermaid's beauty is legendary, but despite my Father's warnings, I was star-struck. It was my first time seeing a mermaid. The Fae and Mermaid delegation met, and I couldn't keep my eyes off Vivian. My shy attempts at catching her attention earned me a whack from my Father. A slap across the face. Knowing she remembers me, the humor in her eyes. A slap was worth that.

"While I still admire your beauty, Vivian," I smile tightly, "my friends and I come on much more serious business." Her lips form a slight pout., "I admit to some disappointment, Brendan." She raises a dark eyebrow, her tail flickering over the rocks., "I always hoped to steal a kiss from you."

Brigit snorts, and this time, my entire face heats., "Perhaps another day." I smile again. "When the threat of war doesn't hang over our heads."

At the mention of war, Vivian's entire body tightens. Her neck snaps between the three of us., "Your Queen did not send you."

"No," I affirm. "We come from a meeting gone wrong with the Finn." Her lips pull back, and she hisses at the mention of the Finn., "No meeting with the Finn has ever gone well."

"She's right," Brigit mutters behind me. Anya visibly stiffens, Vivian's eyes dart towards her, but I can't read the expression swirling in her gaze.

I press on., "This one went particularly sour." Vivian rolls a finger around a strand of her curly hair., "We know the Finn have your Prince Edric."

"You do?" Flavian starts., "How could you know?"

Vivian's eyes narrow., "We are of the sea, Fae boy. The waters carry her secrets." Flavian sends a glance my way, obviously uncomfortable. Anya is still pale, her lips pressed together, fingers clenched tightly around Brigit's arm. "We need to reach the Finn court," I speak in a rush. "Contact our Prince. We have to know what's happening between Murtagh and our kingdom." Vivian's dark eyes move between Flavian and me, watching us intently., "I have no desire for war," I repeat., "But if Murtagh is planning anything, any hint of war."

She hisses at Murtagh's name, her lips parting, fangs showing. But she doesn't interrupt me, letting me finish my thoughts., "He will want us divided, able to conquer our peoples."

Vivian opens her mouth, eyes narrowing., "You speak of war, Brendan, son of Riordan, as though your hands are not tainted with blood." I run my hand over the pommel of my sword, tracing the outline of detailed metal., "I haven't fought for anything but peace."

Vivian's tail flickers., "What you're asking of me could destroy that peace." Her eyes flicker to Anya., "You carry around a mortal, taunting our peace with her presence." I don't look back at Anya while I fight to keep my voice calm.,

"The Finn stole Anya from her home, broke the ancient treaties. Her life is in danger."

"Don't lecture me on the mortals and danger.," Vivian leans forward on the rock, her skin shimmering in the sunshine., "Not when your very words invite war into our midst."

Vivian is nearly correct; when the Court realizes the Prince is in the Finn Court, many of the Fae will demand war. My Father will gather his regiments and loudly train every day in the courtyard. Fae courtiers will start wearing armor around the palace. Younger Fae will beg to join the units, and Fae families who've avoided the Court will travel to the Queen's castle to catch a glimpse of the army. It won't be about rescuing Edric as much as the taste for war. A war brings honor and a chance to prove yourself on the battlefield. My Father will lay out maps of the Finn kingdom, plan an underwater siege. He'll dream of gutting King Murtagh, nailing the king's webbed hands to his walls.

None of that will happen just because the Finn kidnapped a human. The Finn broke all the treaties ordering how the Seelie are supposed to treat humans. We're supposed to leave humans alone, take our annual offerings and help guard the human lands against magical threats. The treaties are clear, the Finn, the Fae, Mermaids and Fauns, all the Leprechauns, we're never supposed to harm a human. Breaking the treaty is a cause for war; the treaty outlines how magic demands payment for harming a human. If I tell the Court about what the Finn have done to Anya, most of them will shrug and ignore the story.

"But your people will go to war over your Prince.," Vivian tosses her mane of dark, curling hair., "Double standards, Brendan," she scolds, fingertips touching., "Broken treaties are broken treaties." Vivian's eyes linger on Brigit., "I don't trust you or your blonde friend." She grins. "But his sister has never been to Court. She's untainted by Fae trickery." I finally look at Brigit. She is glowering, her arms crossed, she's dropped Anya's hand. Anya stands next to her, shivering, eyes wide as she watched the mermaid talk. Vivian extends a hand towards Brigit., "Brigit, daughter of exiles, what should I do?"

Brigit doesn't look at me as she takes in a breath., "My brother needs to see Prince Edric and help him leave. Otherwise, the Court will insist on war."

Vivian raises her palm, gold nails catching in the sunlight., "You want me to take your brother to the Finn borders?"

Brigit nods while Vivian grins., "You don't like this whole idea, do you, Brigit?"

"No," Brigit admits, "I want my brother to stay here. It's a dangerous, stupid idea to travel into the Finn lands." Vivian slaps her tail on the rock, startling Anya, who jumps closer to Brigit. Brigit wraps her arm around Anya's shoulder., "I don't like it, but I believe it is necessary."

"I want to go," Anya falters, and I stiffen. She hasn't spoken anything in hours., "They have Darcy. She belongs to me.," her words catch, and she looks toward Flavian, speaking directly to him, "Just as your prince belongs to you." Flavian flinches., "I can't take Darcy back."

"I didn't ask for that.," Anya's words come in a strained rush., "I just need help reaching her. I don't need anything else from you."

"Anya," I interrupt, "we promised Darcy to protect you. But, unfortunately, we can't let you go."

"He can protect me.," Anya jerks a hand towards Flavian., "Can't you?"

Flavian's hands are trembling, his nerves fraying., "I don't know what I can do anymore. I don't know anything of the Finn court." Waves crash around us, Flavian's face pale as he shakes his head. Anya looks between us, Brigit trying to hold her back, fingers resting on her shoulder.

Vivian speaks, breaking all our thoughts. "Mortal, I cannot take you to the Finn borders."

Anya's lips quiver and Brigit squeezes her shoulder. Vivian explains, "My kind are sworn friends with mortals; we protect your ships, your shores as much as we can. I cannot take you, and I cannot allow you to convince your friends to take you."

Anya's eyes glisten with tears, her voice a hoarse whisper, "Can't you take me there and protect me?"

"No.," Vivian shakes her head., "It would break every oath my people have sworn." She glances at me., "But we can attempt to contact your cousin, Darcy. Watch over her as much as we are allowed."

Anya's hands unclench, and Vivian speaks, "We hear our rumors of Dewain's daughter. Of king Murtagh's plans. Even if she is not always a mortal, she still has a human heart."

"Not always a mortal.," I can't help interrupting Vivian's words with a quick question. She said the phrase so easily, *Dewain's daughter.* I don't need to look at Brigit and Flavian to know they've also caught the title. The Queen knew she was a Halfling; we all knew that no human could travel to our Court and feel magic as Darcy did. It was simple to say Darcy wasn't just human. But half-Finn? Dewain is a legendary Finn general, a warrior, my Father, told me about in stores. I have never seen him. My Father admired Dewain's cruelty; he's practically jealous of the Finn's stone-cold heart.

Vivian sends me a scowl, bringing my attention back, "My kind, you know we're sworn to guard the hearts of mortals. Darcy will always have a human heart, so Anya, daughter of Kian, we will watch over your cousin."

Anya takes a step closer to Vivian, her skirt caught in the water. She gathers her wet dress in her hands, twisting it., "They cannot hurt her."

"Darcy is as protected as she will ever be," Vivian answers quietly., "While the Finn are cruel, they will not hurt one of their own."

Anya jerks towards Flavian, crossing the water, grabbing his arm. He stiffens, surprise flickering across his face., "If you see her," Anya catches her breath, "please, tell her I love her. That I'm alright."

Flavian kneels in the water, meeting Anya's eyes. He places a hand on each of her shoulders., "I will try to speak to her.," His head dips, his blonde bangs falling into his eyes. "Her fate is intertwined with Edric, and he is my life." I know I must be staring at Flavian, stunned at his promise. But, if Brigit is surprised, she doesn't show it. Instead, she wades over to him, pulling him into an embrace, Anya caught between them. The three wrap themselves into a hug, Brigit kissing Anya on the cheek before kissing her brother's forehead. Flavian tips his head back up, brushing his lips across Brigit's forehead. They lean in close, and Flavian's lips move next to her ear. But I can't hear what he says.

Beside me, Vivian sighs loudly, "If you want to get there by dinner-time, you better hurry up."

Flavian nods, embracing his sister one last time. He touches Anya's face before stepping away. He walks up to me, and I grab his shoulder. "Don't do anything stupid."

His eyes are serious., "Of course, Brendan." I glance at Brigit before edging my face close to his. "What did you tell her?" His eyes tighten, and he snaps at me quietly, so no one else hears, "She's my sister, Brendan. You don't need to know everything. You're my commander, not my conscience."

I pull back, his quiet anger chilling me. I swallow, speaking a bit loud now, "Don't make bargains." I squeeze my fingers around his cloak. "Guard your heart. Don't rush us into a war."

"Dragging him into the Finn court is practically a declaration of war," Vivian snorts., "Oh, to be young and in love." I glare at her. "You're still young, Viv."

"Nearly a decade older." She waves her hand at me., "What is that thirteen centuries in Fae years?"

Flavian grins., "She has a point, Brendan."

"Not how time works," I growl back, shoving him a little bit. "Go, find Edric. Bring our Prince home."

Flavian steps further into the water; Vivian slides off the rocks, splashing into the water next to Flavian. He stands chest-deep before Vivian touches his head, ducking him under with her. Water laps around my boots, waves are rolling around the rocks.

We wade back to shore, and I glance at Brigit, biting my tongue. I should allow Flavian his secrets, but I don't like Brigit nosing around in our business. Whatever she tells her brother, Brigit serves herself first. She doesn't care about the Queen or protecting the Court.

"Your mermaid friend better bring Flavian back," Brigit snaps, catching me looking at her. "Or I'll peel your skin from your bones." She touches Anya, pulling the pale girl into her arms, as her wings flare., "I'm guessing you want to head to the Court?"

The Queen will know we've gone far beyond her instructions by now. I need to keep Anya safe, and hiding her from the Queen won't work well for either of us. I nod, "Perhaps my father will be on patrol tonight."

"Perhaps Flavian will dance with King Murtagh." Brigit raises her eyebrows, her disdain at my wishful thinking oddly comforting. At least one thing hasn't changed.

Darcy

I think I can count on one hand the hours of sleep I've been getting the last few days. But, despite my exhaustion, it's hard to sleep in the daytime. The room is filled with light, and apparently, it's not from the sun. You can't simply draw shades over a window when the light is magical.

When shadows start falling, I manage a few hours of restless sleep. But just as I fall asleep, Mara barges into my room. Time to dress for the night. Or day. I'm not sure what to call their time.

I'm at least awake for the meal. Mostly awake when Edric makes me walk through pacing. Do more push-ups. Walkthrough the pacing again. By that time, I'm constantly yawning. Finally, Edric gives me a pitiful smile and sends me to bed.

Only, the Finn Court is all still awake. I lay on the thick covers, wrapped in fluffiness, with jarring music sounding from every corner of the palace. The leprechauns played light, chipper tunes. The music at the Fae court was somber, majestic.

Here, the music is dissident. Harsh melodies scrape together—raucous laughter blending with the songs. I drift in and out of sleep, digging my head into the pillow.

When I finally manage to once again fall into a deep sleep, Mara bursts back into the room. Time for the third meal. Mara dressed me in a tight green gown, the sleeves cut away below the elbow. Like all the dresses I've seen, the sides split above my knees, the edges embroidered with golden thread.

"How do you like your training?" she Mara speaks around a mouthful of pins.

I wince as she twists my hair back tightly., "I'm sore all over."

Mara snorts, "Of course." She tucks the braids together, "Do you feel settled?"

At least, Mara likes to ask questions. She doesn't just order me around and sneer at my incompetence. I've had my fair share of mocking Finn faces. Though, not as often as Leticia. Leticia somehow always manages to sneak into my training, loitering against the wall and laughing at me every time Edric whacks me with his sword. I swallow, thinking through her query., "Settled?"

She stabs another needle-sharp hairpin into my mass of curls., "Into our court."

If feeling sleep deprived and bone-weary means settled, I push away that thought., "I'm learning."

"Good.," Mara turns me around, brushing her thumb over my cheek., "You will make a beautiful Finn."

I give her a tight-lipped smile., "Mara, I don't think I'll ever make a great Finn."

Mara's dark eyebrows knit together., "You aren't stupid, Darcy." She brushes my shoulders, picking her nails across the fabric., "Your beauty will rival Leticia. Far outmatch Owen's sullen face."

Her words leave me gaping; she pushes me forward., "On to dinner, Lady Darcy."

I look down at my calloused hand. The Finn don't have callouses, so I suppose my hands would look a lot better if I were Finn. That thought makes me shiver. Losing my callouses isn't worth a set of webbed hands and feet.

ψ

Dewain meets me before I reach the dining hall. "Have a pleasant day?"

Funny question since it's been a very long night. But I don't argue semantics., "It was alright."

His eyes scan my appearance, no doubt taking in the dark shadows haunting my eyes., "The hours still don't agree with you."

I almost yawn to prove his point, but that feels like too much work to annoy Dewain. He sighs when I stay silent, "You will understand our living choices better once you are Finn." He holds out his arm, and I take his elbow, walking with him into the vast hall.

We barely set foot into the room when Leticia approaches. She eyes my dress., "She looks almost Finn, Uncle." She grins at Dewain., "Your servants do a good job. Dressing her up."

Dewain doesn't say anything, but I feel his arms tightening. Leticia grins at me, flashing her teeth, "You really should visit my cove." She gestures., "I have so many human treasures, and I'd love to know how you use them on land.

Perhaps we could even find a dress that's more your size."

I'm wearing the dress in my size; I'm just not used to the long sleeves or low neckline. I want to snap at Leticia that I don't need her fashion advice when Leticia turns on her heels, clapping her webbed hands together.

I jolt at the noise, nearly tripping on the hemline of the evening gown, while Leticia spins back towards me, "They've brought in the Siren's tax. What stories we will hear tonight, cousin!"

Dewain noticeably stiffens next to me, crossing his arms and glowering. Leticia lays her webbed hand on my arm, yanking me forward. I want to pull away, but her sharp nails press into the soft velvet of my sleeves, and I still. "Do you see them?"

It takes a moment for my eyes to adjust to the darkness of the banquet room, the Finn only light a few sconces on the wall, and the room is far too large and dark to see anything very clearly.

I look past the king and hold back a gasp when I see the shadowy figures. Humans stand clumped together, their clothes ragged and hair matted into clumps of knots. Finn guards are dragging them into the room.

"The Sirens capture sinking humans," Leticia's voice is playfully lite, "We don't like to see anyone drown in the ocean, least of all humans."

She turns her head, meeting my eyes, "Don't tell me you're horrified, Cousin."

"Their families think they're dead." I speak without thinking, "If you've saved them from drowning, let them go back to the surface. To their homes. You don't need them here."

"Darcy," Dewain speaks firmly behind me, "This is our tradition."

Leticia presses her nails into my arm, leaning in close to me, "You know we couldn't have found you if your uncle hadn't fallen overboard."

Her words are a slap, and I instantly pull back. "Where is he?"

I look at Dewain, and he shakes his head, "Leticia, there's no need to bring up the past." he starts to step away, heading to his seat at the table. "Dewain," the words catch in my throat; he knows what happened to my Uncle. They all do. Dewain stops mid-stride and looks back at me. He takes in a breath, "I see no point in repeating the past." Then he turns and walks away.

"He won't tell you," Leticia sounds amused, "But he can't technically stop me from sharing."

Leticia is the last Finn I want to talk to. I don't want to hear what happened to my Uncle from her sneering voice. She drops my arm, and I slump away from her.

"If you don't want to know, you can leave." Leticia rests a hand on her hip. My cousin is right. I can walk away now and eat my dinner.

I can pester Edric during training and ask him what he knows. But if Dewain won't talk about it, he probably ordered Edric not to tell me. And Edric won't cross my Father to tell me any secrets.

I cross my arms, and Leticia takes my stance as her cue to tell the story, "The sirens brought your mother's brother here." Leticia tosses her lengthy hair, "Dewain knew him, had seen him before you were born, but of course, the Sirens had erased his memories when he'd fallen into the sea. He was next to useless."

My Uncle was here, in this throne room. While Anya and I mourned him, the Finn were busy trying to use him to find me. I'm not hungry anymore. All I want is to run. Away from this place and this Finn King and my supposed Father and these awful creatures.

"He was useless for us, of course. But Edric, with his unique magic could sift through any human's mind. We're lucky Edric has decided to work with my Father; otherwise, how else were we to find you?"

Leticia's words sink in, and I realize Edric must have led the Finn to Anya. They were looking for me and took Anya instead. The words are out of my mouth before I can think to stop them, "Edric wouldn't help you hurt a human. He's not heartless."

Leticia steps close to me, closer than when she grabbed my arm. Her breath is hot on my neck., "Sometimes, Darcy, you are more woefully human than I can imagine."

Leticia leaves me standing in the doorway. I can't sit down and eat dinner with Dewain while my head is reeling. I'm not hungry anymore. I turn, walking through the double doors out unto the portico. Edric is leaning against the railing; his arms crossed casually., "A bit early to leave dinner, don't you think?"

I don't want to speak to him. "Why are you here?"

His eyes screw together, lips pinching., "I saw the Sirens brought in the drowned ones. I don't think you knew about the humans at Court, so I was concerned."

"I don't need your concern.," I take a step, but Edric falls into step beside me.

"You're upset with me," he speaks softly., "What is it?"

The question makes my head spin, and I jerk to a stop, "You helped them." I grind my teeth at him. "Get information from my uncle."

His eyes flicker a bit wide., "I didn't know he was your uncle." I whack him, shoving him away. My fingers press into his soft shirt, even as my eyes burn., "He was a mortal, a human-like me. And you used him, helped the Finn use him. Just because you could."

"Darcy." He catches my arm., "Please, I never meant to hurt anyone. It was thoughtless of me." His voice is desperate., "A bargain I made without consideration. Please, Darcy, please, don't hold my actions against me." I look down at his slender fingers, the silver rings circling his knuckles., "You've hurt everyone I love." He doesn't answer, and I realize with a shudder that Edric is silent because he has nothing to say. He can't argue with me that he didn't help destroy the people I love most. Arguing would be lying, and as a Fae prince, he can't even lie.

Our eyes meet., "I can't just forget this, Edric." He lets go, his hand trembles. "I've lost everything because of you." His head shakes, bangs falling into his eyes. I think he's going to speak, but another voice interrupts.

"Darcy.," I stiffen at Dewain's voice., "Are you alright?"

I turn away from Edric, sucking in a breath. A stiff smile for Dewain, "We were just chatting."

"Chatting.," Dewain frowns at Edric. "I didn't give you permission to tell her anything."

I roll my eyes, wanting to laugh, "You don't need to worry; Edric won't ever dare disobey you."

Edric winces, and Dewain's eyebrows lift in surprise, "I can see Edric hasn't told you everything."

I almost look back at Edric. Edric chose to bargain with the Finn King for whatever reason. Edric, who had everything, so much more than I can imagine having. The entire Court rotated on Edric's whim. Even if he hated the Court, he had Flavian. Flavian would tear apart the world for Edric.

Eric didn't need anything. He chose to hurt Uncle Kian and Anya, and he didn't even bother telling me why.

At least Dewain hasn't hidden anything from me. Dewain let Leticia tell me the ugly truth and didn't try to stop her. Dewain did everything he could to find his lost family. My mother and me. I can hate him for it for now, but I can also understand. I would do the same thing to find Anya.

I shrug, "Apparently, I don't need Edric to tell me anything. We aren't friends."

Dewain looks down at me, "You are of the Finn, Darcy." He smiles briefly before frowning, his eyes narrowing. He looks over my shoulder at the Fae Prince, "We do not forgive."

I can almost feel Edric stiffening as he steps away. "I will see you at training.," He bows., "A good day to you." I watch his dark hair swallowed into the shadowed hallways as he retreats. Dewain takes a step, and I follow his lead back into the dining hall. I might as well sit with Dewain and drink rum and let the noisy dinner drown out my thoughts. Dewain catches my shoulder in his smooth hand, and he speaks firmly, "Do not feel any obligation to the Fae Prince." He looks down at me., "The Fae are peculiar about craving such things as forgiveness. But kindness is not the way of our Court."

Chapter Twelve

Brendan

O N ANY OTHER DAY, I'd avoid the slow journey through the ancient mounds to the Court. I've traveled beyond the Court borders half a dozen times, and each time I folded my wings together, reached for the Queen's tether, her magical hold on the Fae lands, and slipped across the border. I know you can bring others with you through the Tethering magic, but I'm tired. I don't have the strength to muster up the magic to transport us directly into our Fae Court. Brigit can't either, as the terms of her family's exile prevent her from reaching for the Queen's magic. I've grown up with the Queen's magic shaping through the lands, feeling the magic in the air we breathe in the Court, the ground we walk on leaching magic. It's hard to fathom how Brigit exists in a world where she's cut off from the Queen's touch. Since we can't use magic, we take the slower route and fly to the great mound.

The local villagers worship the old gods at the mounds, telling stories of the Fae who live underneath the banks. While not exactly wrong, we practically live under the giant mounds; the stories still humor me. Occasionally leprechauns use the mounds to gain entrance to the human world, probably because their hold on the Queen's touch is fleeting. The banks are simply gateways, not our homes as the mortals like to think. We land in the swaying grass of rolling fields, the green crops starting to turn into golden heads of spring barley.

Anya pulls away from Brigit's arm, falling to her knees in the grass. She yanks the plants into her hands, cupping her face with the stalks. "It smells like home." She raises her bunched fists, looking at both of us. "Darcy always wanted to leave the sea."

"Leaving wouldn't have protected you," Brigit answers quietly., "Nothing can stay the Finn's determination." Anya sways, pushing the stalks against her cheeks. I glance at Brigit, who raises an eyebrow as if to say., "*Well?*"

"I can't," Anya hesitates, green eyes turning to me., "I can't return home."

I step into the grass., "I can't guarantee your safety. Not as I can while you're with me." Her eyes are still focused on me while she twists the blades between her fingers., "What do they want?"

She doesn't need to say who she's asking about., "If the mermaid's spies are right.," I pause, watching Anya's face., "Darcy is related to the Finns."

Anya drops the bundle of grass., "I don't understand." I glance at Brigit, and she's smirking at me, amused but unhelpful as always., "We don't know much.," I turn entirely back to Anya, "Perhaps the Queen will have more answers."

"The Queen won't have answers," Brigit interrupts., "At least not answers worth our time."

"She's the Queen.," I send Brigit a ferocious glare., "You are remarkably talented at being disrespectful."

Brigit snorts, stepping close to both of us., "I'm respectful to those who've earned it." Her face is nearly gentle when she looks at Anya., "I don't want to see Anya deal with more monsters."

Anya's eyes dart between both of us, her lips parted. I want to reprimand Brigit, scold her for scaring her unnecessarily., "The Queen isn't a monster.," my words come in a huff., "And you aren't exactly very helpful."

Brigit grins, slapping me on the back., "Not sure when you started thinking I was here to help?"

"I don't know.," I hold back a snarl., "Maybe when you tagged along on a covert mission and wouldn't leave me alone for nearly four days?"

"You've been left alone too much.," Brigit tosses her head. "I'll take Anya under the mound."

Anya steps past me, tucking her fingers into Brigit's hand. I'm annoyed, and I can't quite explain why. They cut in front of me, weaving through the rows of wheat till we reach the mound. Perhaps because

Darcy asked me to watch Anya, and I don't need Brigit's help. I'll get more of a headache at Court if Brigit shows up. A lecture from my father, a least. His thundering speeches are always headache-inducing. For some reason, I think Brigit is going to enjoy that kind of headache.

We clamber over the rocks of the mound, Brigit kicking aside loose pebbles. She places her hand against the sealed door, and the stone trembles before shifting to the side. Anya gasps, jumping back. "It's true."

I can almost hear the smile in Brigit's voice, "Most things are true, Anya." She pushes aside a cluster of moss-draped over the now open door. She lays her hand flat against Anya's back, encouraging her forward. Anya sends a glance around, looking back towards the sky, before she ducks under the arched entrance. Her copper hair disappears into the darkness. I step over the stone entrance, running a hand over the runes. At my touch, the stone door closes, sealing us in the cavern's darkness.

My eyes adjust to the lack of light, the cobbled path that will take us to our kingdom. "Can you shine, Brendan?"

I jerk at Brigit's voice, and she continues, "Anya doesn't have Fae eyes."

Of course, she won't be able to see in the dark. I nod, closing my eyes, and focus on steadying my heartbeat, on the blood rushing through my veins. My bones ache, weary with constant flight, with worry, with transporting us through the kingdoms. The ache doesn't steal all my magic as my skin begins to glimmer. I hear Anya gasp again, Brigit's voice, a touch of humor., "The right kind of friends, Anya, and you'll get to see pretty much everything."

I open my eyes, finding Anya staring at me wide-eyed. She looks between Brigit and me, her head moving quickly.

"Can you do that?"

Brigit shrugs., "It's Brendan's special talent. His only talent, some might say," Questions lurk in Anya's gaze; Brigit is still holding her hand. They step together through the mound, walking down stone steps. Moss creeps down the wall, ivy tumbling over the rock floors. Anya asks another question, and Brigit starts ranting about the Court. It never takes much for Brigit to rant about the Queen or the Court.

While Flavian ignores his family's story, their history of treason that led to their exile, Brigit revels in it, wearing her family story like a badge of honor.

I've never heard what Flavian's family did, and Flavian won't ever say a word about his parent. I'm somewhat surprised when Brigit starts sharing details, her voice echoing against the stone walls, "Centuries ago, the Fae were divided. Two Queens. Each Queen ruled over her territories, magic courts. The Fae lands, all the magic lands were either in the Seelie Court or in the Unseelie Court." "I've heard of them," Anya comments.

"Most mortals have.," Brigit nods; she pushes aside a tangle of vines that have covered the stone stairs., "Most mortals don't know that the Unseelie waged war against mortals before eventually turning on their kind, attacking the

Seelie Court."

Silence passes for a few moments, the only sound our feet on the stone path. We duck under an archway, the plants now giving way to shimmering black stone.

"Eventually." Brigit's voice is so quiet; it's almost a whisper. "Queen Oona bound the darkness of the Unseelie, breaking the ancient pact between our two people." Her voice nearly breaks., "She broke the blood oath between her sister, Queen Mage."

I shudder. "Brigit," I choke the words, "that's only hearsay."

Brigit sends me a dark look; her lips pressed together., "Let me continue, Brendan. This is my story."

I can only nod, shrugging. Brigit looks back down at Anya., "My grandmother served Queen Mage. At the Unseelie

Court, far, far to the North. When Oona broke the Blood Oath, she shattered Mage's heart. Her island was doomed."

We duck under another arch., "My grandmother carried the sword of the Goddess Brigid, her ancestor."

I'm gaping at Brigit, frantically sorting through her words. I'm not even sure Anya can understand the importance of what Brigit is claiming, that she is a descendant of the Goddess Brigid.

"My grandmother fought her way into Queen Oona's Court, took her place as an advisor in the war against Unseelie bands. Roving

Unseelie bands who refused to acknowledge the Seelie Queen." Brigit drags in a breath., "The Queen trusted my grandmother; she was one of the few survivors of the wreckage of Mage's kingdom. My grandmother broke that trust."

Anya still clings to Brigit's hand, and I brush against Brigit's shoulder, my curiosity getting the best of me., "What did she do?"

Brigit bites her lip. "Only dark magic can break blood oaths. Using objects of intense power, objects forbidden to both Queens. I have heard." She turns to me, voice falling to a whisper., "I have heard my grandmother took that object. That is only a rumor, Brendan. A rumor without any proof, no truth to accuse my family with."

"Your sword," Anya speaks softly, "Is it the same sword?"

Brigit smiles, eyes beaming. She lets go of Anya's hand, unsheathing her sword. The silver glitters, the blade is double-edged. Ancient runes etched into the metal.

"Aisling," Brigit speaks nearly reverently., "The sword of gods," She holds it out to Anya., "My inheritance."

Anya looks at it, eyes wide as a full moon. "Go ahead," Brigit encourages, "touch it."

Her pale hands lightly touch the blade; she almost jerks back. Brigit stoops lower, holding the sword in one hand, touching Anya's shoulder, "I swear, Anya, daughter of Kian, as long as you breathe, I will protect you with my own life. My sword is yours; my honor is yours."

Anya touches the sword again, meeting Brigit's fierce gaze. Her voice is soft, so quiet I almost don't hear her. "I accept your oath, Brigit, daughter of gods." I hold my breath, my mind whirling as I stare at the two of them. Brigit, who boasts of being sworn to none, promising herself to Anya. A mortal who does not belong in Fae lands. A mortal I've already pledged to protect.

Brigit straightens swiftly, sheathing her sword. Anya reaches for her hand again, and I clear my throat., "We're almost to the palace." I jerk my chin., "I can see the last arch."

"Step across three stones to reach your heart's desire," Brigit quips, her heels tapping against the final three steps as the path opens into the Fae lands, "Though whoever thought our court was anyone's heart desire is beyond me."

Anya's lips quirk, the first hint of a smile I've seen on her face in three days., "I thought that was just a riddle."

Brigit's elbows her lightly., "Didn't they tell you? All the riddles come from the Fae."

Darcy

Edric and I can't avoid each other forever. So after I finish eating, I reluctantly walk to the training room. I'm not sure where else I would go, as I don't want to run into Leticia. She's told me enough.

Edric is stretched out on the floor, his cape tossed aside, sleeves pushed past his elbows. He glances up as I walk in, nodding slightly. "Did you stretch this morning?"

I sink unto the floor, folding my legs under me., "No, I slept late."

He jerks his chin., "You know what to do."

I wiggle my toes, stretching out my legs. The dress is tight around my arms, uncomfortable as I reach for my ankles.

"Try keeping your knees flat," Edric mentions, rolling to his feet., "You're cheating if you don't."

I grit my teeth, holding in my annoyance. He walks over, laying his hand flat against my back., "You need to get some proper training clothes."

"I know," I bite back, releasing my ankles, "I don't think they have anything custom-made for me yet."

"Probably not," he speaks stiffly, ordering me through some exercise. By the time I finish the sit-ups, my face is flushed, and my hair is coming undone. I randomly slap the loose strands back into the braid, huffing at my obstinate hair.

Edric hands me the training sword, but before I take it, I hold up my hands. "Can we make it short today? I'm starting to blister."

His gaze follows my palm, "How long will they take to heal?"

I rub my thumb over my sore palms, "I don't know."

"That's not a very helpful answer.," He shakes his head., "You wouldn't have to deal with them if you'd choose to become Finn."

I stiffen at his words, my neck heating., "That's none of your business."

He tips his hand, the edge of his practice sword raised towards my face., "So, wise mortal, tell me what my business is when I should not use my power to hold up a bargain. When I should exercise moral authority."

I lick my lips, fingers clenching around the sword, ignoring the discomfort of the blisters, "You don't need me to tell you right from wrong."

He leans forward., "Neither do I need you to scold me. You don't understand the ways of the Finn or Fae. Your mortal moral are next to useless here."

"Right is always right," I hiss back at him. "You can't change right from wrong just to fit your circumstances." He raises his arm, tapping his sword against mine., "I'm not arguing morals with you. Simply pointing out that you don't know everything."

"I know enough," I snap back, whacking his sword.

He slams his sword against mine, making my teeth clench., "Keep your feet apart," he scolds, whacking my blade again. I want to jump away, but I press forward, my legs shaking.

He swings back around, aiming a blow at my side. I jump, recklessly waving the sword in an arch. Another knock from him, nearly hitting my wrist. I let out a hiss, jabbing my sword towards his chest. He brings his wooden blade around, firmly whacking me on my exposed side.

I gasp, doubling over. The sword clutched in my hands, my breath gone out, my lungs burning.

"Keep your focus," Edric is scolding, his words a list of my flaws. He twirls the sword in his thin hands, his tattoos shimmering. I barely raise my hand, my body aching. Edric jerks his chin, "Again, Darcy. Let's walk through pacing." We step through pacing, Edric coaching, almost gently. My ribs still throb, but my breathing is calming. A blister on my hand is broken open, my palm burning with every flex of my fingers.

We've just stepped through the pacing twice when Leticia strolls into the room. I stiffen, wishing she'd leave me alone for a whole twenty-four hours. But for the first time, her eyes aren't focused on me. "Edric, dear.," She clicks her tongue., "My father's men just brought in an intruder."

Edric hardly looks her way, "Every kingdom has vulnerabilities."

"Yes, of course.," Leticia threads a finger through her twisting hair., "But this fellow is Fae."

Edric immediately stiffens, almost pausing in our faux fight. "Ah, hum.," Leticia smirks, "Perhaps you know him? Blonde, I believe."

"Flavian.," The words drop from Edric's lips; he drops the practice sword., "Is it Flavian?"

Her eyes gleam at his response, "That does sound familiar."

He tears across the room, knocking the practice sword out the way. I glance at Leticia before throwing the blade down and racing after him. We run down the dark hallway, Edric feet ahead of me. He shouldn't run into the throne room; interrupt this. I yell at him, but he doesn't stop, turning the corner, heading straight to the Finn King. Edric darts ahead of me into the throne room, running past the guards, standing alert. I pull up short at the door; guards have Edric in their arms, holding him back. My hands tremble at the agonized cries, the lash of whips against flesh. Edric starts screaming, yelling the King's name. He twists in the guard's arms, lashing out at them. His hands are balled, and he brings his boot down on one of the guard's feet. The guard sputters, yanking back. Edric twirls, bringing his fist against the other guard's nose. The guard howls, stumbling around as Edric breaks past them both into the throne room.

The guards stumble to their feet, one holding his hand to his bleeding nose. They ignore me as I step into the throne room. Another guard has grabbed Edric, twisting his arms behind his back. Edric is straining against them, his eyes focused on Flavian. I follow his gaze, horrified at what they're doing to Flavian. His hands are bound in chains, two Finn Guards holding whips in their hands as they pace around him. They've beaten him bloody, the skin of his back chewed through to the bone. His blonde hair is matted in blood, and his body sags against the floor.

King Murtagh lounges on his throne, arms crossed, picking his teeth with a knife. Then, finally, he beckons his guards forward, and they drag Edric with them.

"Prince of the Fae," Murtagh drawls lazily., "You know this fellow?"

Flavian groans, head lifting a moment before falling forward. Edric's eyes are wide, his eyes darting between Flavian and the King., "Why is he here?." It's not exactly a question but a desperate statement.

I jump as a hand touches my back, Dewain. He leans down, his voice a whisper, nearly identical to Edric's question, "Why are you here?"

"Edric was training me.," I nod towards the Prince., "I followed him."

Dewain frowns., "You don't have the stomach to watch this, Darcy."

"What are they going to do to him?"

Dewain looks at me, his shoulders slumping., "This is the way of the Finn, daughter." His fingers brush a loose strand of hair back from my face, "You shouldn't see this."

Our eyes meet., "I know Flavian," I protest quietly., "I can't leave him."

His face draws together, jaw clenching. He doesn't object, doesn't order me gone.

"Dewain," Murtagh calls out, and my father stiffens.

"Eminence." he steps away from me.

"Edric would have us keep the prisoner alive." Murtagh waves a hand towards Flavian. "I promised him that you would give his friend a swift, clean death."

My fingers crush together; of course, Dewain doesn't want me to see him. He's going to execute Flavian.

"Please," Edric stands ramrod straight before the throne, "Let him go; I will give you anything."

"Anything.," Murtagh's brows lift., "Surely not."

"His life is worth everything to me," Edric pleads, his voice strained., "Whatever you want, whatever I have refused, I will give it to you."

Murtagh leans forward., "Edric, you offer a promise I cannot ignore. Anything I ask, anything of your court, and you will tell me?" Edric is quiet a moment, his hands clenching and unclenching. I step closer, holding my breath. Edric is practically promising betrayal, anything Murtagh asks. It is a ridiculous bargain, wrong, evil, playing strictly on Edric's fear for Flavian's life.

Edric finally speaks., "I cannot tell you anything. But I can answer one question, one question about my mother that you hunger to know."

Murtagh flashes his teeth, spinning the knife in his hands. "You are too wise, Prince Edric of the Fae. You know my desires far too well."

From his place on the floor, Flavian groans, "Don't Edric," he lifts his head, blood running from his lips, "It's not worth my life; don't give him an answer."

Edric looks back at Flavian, his lips colorless, "You don't know what you're worth, Flavian. I will not throw away your life."

The King laughs, the sound echoing around the room. I shiver, pulling my cloak tighter around my shoulders. "You will not play with lives, Edric. Not with lives that matter to you, loyal to your core." He raises his hand, black nails flashing., "For your answer to my question, I will release Flavian."

"Unharmed and unchanged," Edric speaks firmly., "Unbound to your Court returned to the Fae lands; I will answer your question."

Murtagh's eyes narrow., "You're too clever with bargains, boy."

Edric bows and I can almost hear a touch of a smirk in his voice., "I had a clever teacher."

"Don't," Flavian moans again. "Don't bargain with him."

Edric's knuckles are white, his back to Flavian. The King holds out his hand, and Edric climbs the seven steps of the throne. They hold each other's wrists, and the King begins., "For an answered question, I return Flavian, unharmed, unchanged, unbound to the Fae Court."

The chains around Flavian's wrist snap, and he sags forward, falling against the pearl floors. Edric steps back from the King, walking backward down the steps. He turns to Flavian, crouching next to him and holding him in his arms.

"Dewain," Murtagh calls out, "escort Flavian back to his own country."

My father bows, stepping forward, grabbing Flavian's arm and pulling him to his feet. Flavian's feet are in shreds, and my stomach turns. Edric catches his arm, clinging to him. One of the guards grabs Edric, pulling him back. Flavian leans against Dewain, his face pinched and pale. He raises his eyes, breathing something in Fae. In the guard's hold, Edric stops fighting. His shoulders slump, and he yells something—another string of Fae words.

My father starts to drag Flavian from the throne room, streaks of blood trailing him. Edric falls forward, landing on his knees. He presses his hands against the stones, his hair tumbling around his face, "Ah," Murtagh chuckles from his throne., "Our Darcy doesn't know how we treat Fae trespassers here in the Finn Court. Tell her, Edric, won't you?" I wince at the King calling me *Our Darcy* as though I belong to them. I may be trapped here, but they don't own me. The King glances at me, his lips curling around his sharp teeth, "I hear you enjoy teaching Dewain's daughter."

Edric pulls himself to his feet, turning to face the King. He stands ramrod straight, his hands clenched at his side. The King waves him away, "Be sure to include this lesson in today's teaching, Prince. Then, I will find you to answer my question."

Edric turns on his heels, his cloak smeared with Flavian's blood. The guards step away from the door. I fall behind him, turning back to glance at the King. But Murtagh is already gone; the throne sits empty.

I turn on Edric as soon as we step out of the throne room., "Why are you here?" He walks beside me, silent. He doesn't even blink at my words or even looks at me. My father just carted his boyfriend away, Flavian nearly died. His back was torn to shreds. I could see his bones; the guards beat him nearly to death. Fury builds in my blood; I grab his arm. "Murtagh could have killed Flavian, killed him right in front of you. And you still choose to stay in this palace!" Edric yanks back from me, his face still pale, but his eyes are livid., "I made a mistake," he snarls at me, brushing past. I nearly need to jog to keep up with his furious pace., "A mistake?" I try to catch up to him, grabbing at his arm, "Why can't you fix it?"

He looks back at me., "Are you still so pitifully human, Darcy, Daughter of Dewain?"

I cringe at the anger in his voice; he flings the words at me., "You can't fix bargains."

"You just bargained with Murtagh," I reply quickly, "Can't you give him something he wants?"

Edric pauses, his eyes darting past me., "I barely have anything Murtagh needs. Information is my last resort and won't fix my mistakes."

The question burns through me, "Why can't you return home?"

"I'll be an ass," he spits at me, snarling., "Is that enough? Will you leave me alone now?"

His words leave me more confused., "You'll be an ass?"

"An ass." He lets out a rushed breath., "The moment my feet touch land, I turn into a braying, long-eared, ignorant ass."

I'm gaping at him, trying to understand. He shakes his head, turning his eyes away from me. "I made a bargain with Murtagh, and I wasn't careful enough. Murtagh twists words as he likes."

I think through exactly what he says before clarifying., "You can choose to go home, but you'll turn into an ass." Edric doesn't answer, shrugging his shoulders lightly, his lips quirking. I stare at him, still making sense of his words.

"What?" Edric hits my shoulder lightly with his elbow., "Thinking I should be an ass all the time?"

I blink, attempting to disagree, but I can't help it; I start laughing., "An ass, Edric?" He flushes, and I whack him lightly on his shoulder, "Couldn't Murtagh be more creative?"

Edric rolls his shoulders., "I always thought Flavian was an ass.," he looks at my face, smirking, "though, obviously, you think it fits."

I roll my eyes, catching my laugher. I haven't told Edric how his boyfriend hated me, blamed me for him disappearing. Flavian is an absolute ass, "Edric, you're pompous. And I don't know that I'll ever forgive you for what happened to Anya." I pause, swallowing., "But you don't deserve a twisted bargain. Flavian," I can't unsee what I saw in the throne room, Flavian's skin in tatters., "Flavian didn't deserve to be beaten nearly to death."

Edric is quiet a moment., "I left my court, Darcy. Of my own free will." He looks past me., "You saw what Flavian endured for me. I don't deserve that. I left him; I left my court."

"You thought you could return.," I hate the guilt ravaged on his face, the despair in his words. "King Murtagh tricked you."

"Darcy.," He shakes his head., "I shouldn't have trusted Murtagh. I shouldn't have thought he could help me; I was foolish. Now my Flavian," he practically chokes on the word, "My love is paying for my mistake."

He turns away from me, walking swiftly down the terrace. Edric may be free to roam the court, free to enjoy dinners with the King, free to do as likes within the walls, but he's still trapped. He doesn't have to fear for his own life and safety, but he can't possibly return to his home. Though he refused to talk about Flavian, I know he loves the blonde.

He'd willingly trade his life for his boyfriend.

Yet, Edric has managed to look as though he is living here of his own free will. I think of all the times he has chatted with Murtagh, the head nods, courteous bows, polite laugher and practically chained to the King, sentenced to eternity under the sea. Separated from his court, apart from his boyfriend, yet Edric acts as though he is content. A mask of relaxation.

My promise comes back to me with a horrifying jolt. Edric is trapped, and I promised the Fae Queen I would return him to his home. Goosebumps line my neck; I know what I need to do. I curl my fingers through my hair, pulling at the waves.

I step forward, my bare feet chilly on the pearl terrace. The door to the throne room is still open, though the seat is vacant. I glance at the guards, who are both watching me. Only moments ago, these guards nearly beat a man to death. At least Edric broke one of their noses. They deserve worse, but for now, I can at least try to free Edric from them. Breath fills my lungs, my voice echoing through the throne room, "I need to speak to the King. I'm ready to bargain with King Murtagh."

Brendan

My father steps forward, meeting us at the doorway. His face is hard, his dark eyes narrowed, "Brendan," he speaks my name coldly, "has the night stolen your days?"

I keep my body still, my voice forcefully calm, "I was serving the Court, Father." I bow respectfully., "All I do is for my Queen and Court."

My father's eyes dart behind me, his lips curling as he takes in both Anya and Brigit. One a human I brought into Fae lands. The other a political exile, banned from the Court. His eyes narrow, his words filled with disgust as he demands why I've brought them both.

My father sneers, "I don't pay you to rescue damsels in distress." I can hear his men chuckling, lips curling at me.

Scorn. My cheeks flush., "The treaty isn't a fairytale."

My father must decide it's a waste of time to keep questioning me. He looks at Brigit., "Why are you here, exile?" I don't think he's ever spoken to her, and she's never visited the Court before. You wouldn't know this from the way Brigit steps forward, her back straight as she leaves a hand on her sword. Her chin lifts, her words calm., "I don't answer to blood traitors, Riordan."

I nearly stumble back at her words, the accusation that my father betrayed a blood oath. My father's face turns almost purple., "And I don't dally with exiles."

Brigit's words are cold, and she doesn't flinch away from my father's glare., "Your family was sworn to Mage. You broke your oath, broke my grandmother's heart. For gold. Your pride."

"Nonsense," I rush to speak, stepping closer to Brigit., "Take your accusation back." I've never heard anyone at Court mention Mage or my father working with her. Mage has been dead for years. I try to grab Brigit's arm, pull her back from my father. Brigit shakes off my touch, "Stay out of this, Brendan."

The words tumble from me, and I wince at the tremble in my voice, "You've no right to hurl accusations. You can't say this," I nearly choke, fighting for the right words; it doesn't matter if Brigit's claims are valid. She's accused my family of treason, called my father out.

Brigit doesn't wait for me to collect my thoughts. She reaches out, laying a hand on the cool leather across my chest,

"I don't want to fight you, Brendan. Your father's lies require vengeance."

Brigit may insist she's not fighting with me. But my father won't duel her; he'll demand I stand for his honor. I've fought in his place twice in my life; both fights were quick and straightforward. I didn't even know the two soldiers who had insulted my family's honor. My father had just placed his sword in my hands and told me to deal with them. I glance between Brigit and my father; his face has turned stoney, removed.

"You've insulted my honor," he speaks steadily, "When the Queen is done with you, Brendan will stand in my place." Brigit's eyes narrow, but before she can protest, we hear the Queen coming. I turn back towards Anya, remembering how Darcy had gotten sick on the throne floor. But Anya's face is just scrunched; like all of us, she hears the tingle of bells as the Queen walks our way.

My father turns away from us, walking towards the front of the line of his guards. Brigit and Anya stand on either side of me; I can almost hear Brigit thinking. She can't take back the words she spat at my father, and all of his guards heard her. Before I can say a word to her, the Queen walks in. Her light is nearly blinding, as the room is crowded with her radiance. Out of habit, I fall to my knees, the cold stone biting into my legs. Her heels echo on the floor as I keep my eyes trained on the marble. I don't look, but I realize that Brigit hasn't kneeled, and she kept a hand on Anya, keeping her from bowing as well.

"Brendan, son of Riordan," she says my name faintly, "I crave your answers." The Queen's words may be gentle, but her eyes are icy. She might be less cold if we had returned directly to Court instead of traveling to the Mermaids and avoiding the Court for a few days. I'm hopeful that the Queen will understand our choices as I begin to tell the story. There's no flicker of surprise from my father as I talk about the Finn. My father's lack of reaction can only mean that he knows most of my story. He must know the Finn didn't let Edric come back and that I've been traveling with a mortal girl for days. I try to keep the story brief, explaining how we traded one human for another. Or not quite, since Darcy wasn't wholly human.

The Queen looks at us, her hands folded together, "Did you learn what Darcy is?" I'm tempted to evade the truth. But even if I hide the truth, my father is bound to find out sooner or later. I take a breath, unable to find a way to hide the truth, "Darcy is Dewain's daughter."

The Queen's eyes widen slightly., "King Murtagh's niece, then? A missing heir." Silence passes, the Queen looking at all three of us. She steps past me., "Brigit," her voice is sharper., "You cross my threshold." "Only to protect," Brigit answers shorty.

I don't turn to look behind me, though I hear the Queen turn away from Brigit., "You are Anya."

She doesn't wait for an answer, turning back to speak directly to me., "Why haven't you returned the mortal?" Before I even open my mouth, I know my words are weak excuses. The Queen and my father won't understand a promise to protect a mortal. My father has already mocked me for wanting to help Anya. Both of their faces darken, the Queen's eyes narrowing as I try to explain. Anya hasn't done anything wrong, and while I know Brigit is banished from the Court, she is only standing here to help protect the human. All my life, I've learned that the Queen upholds justice in the Fae lands and unites the Court against the danger of a divided Seelie land. Hating a human just because she isn't Fae, that isn't justice. But as I try to explain, the Queen's glare grows icy, her eyes sharp as glass.

My explanation hangs in the air. Anya shifts on her feet next to me, nervously looking between the Queen and me. My father snorts, lips stretched thin in a sneer as he keeps glaring at Brigit.

The Queen finally speaks, "Fulfill your oath and get rid of them both. Neither of them belongs here." Her words are clipped, "Erase the human's memory."

I know this is a command, directly from my Queen. But taking Anya's memory, that will be a living death for her. She will be haunted by what the Finn did to her while unable to heal without her memories. Brigit stiffens, her wings flaring in anger at the Queen's order. My father and the Queen are still standing still, expecting me to jump into action. Next to me, Anya has frozen, her breathing turning silent with fear.

"You heard the Queen," my father spits, "take the girl's memory."

I turn slowly, avoiding meeting my father's stare. I pull out a knife, holding it in my hand. I'll need to cut Anya's arms, take her blood to perform the magic rite to erase her memory. With the knife in one hand, I grab Anya's hand with my other hand. I barely feel her fingers cold and thin before I jerk her around, slicing my hand with the knife. It cuts through my palm, the knife clattering to the stone floor. Then I grab for Brigit's arm, the magic spell a torrent of rushed words. I hadn't spoken this spell in years, not since my mother taught me the phrase before I left home for the Court. My vision narrows as the air thins around us, the stone walls retreating in a gold rush of light and heat. I can hear my father roar, as a moment too late; he realizes what I've done.

Chapter Thirteen

Darcy

THE GUARDS LEAD ME away from the throne room, taking me down a hallway I've not yet seen. There are also guards here, more numerous than in the throne room and dining hall. Every few feet, there's another Finn guard, spear in hand. Their eyes stare straight ahead, unblinking.

The door at the end of the long hallway is open, the king standing on the threshold. "Darcy, daughter of Dewain.," he grins, flashing his rows of sharp teeth., "I admit, I wasn't expecting you."

"Majesty.," I bow slightly, rubbing my sweaty palms over the pleats of my dress., "Thank you for seeing me."

The king motions the guards away, gesturing for me to follow. I glance at the guards one last time before following the king into the room. It's smaller than I expected, just room enough for a table, chairs slid haphazardly around. Unlike other rooms, there are no windows here. Just a dark paneled wall, a few candles burning.

"My council room.," Murtagh shrugs, pulling out a table., "I'm wary of the throne room. And I presume you'd rather not have a public meeting."

I swallow. "Thank you," my fingers are still fiddling with the pleats of the skirt. "Sit.," The king edges a chair with his toes., "No need to be formal."

I drag the heavy chair across the stone floor, wincing at the sound. The king waits until I'm seated before raising a hand., "Your father sits right there." He taps the chair next to his., "I remember him the night your mother absconded."

His eyes meet mine, dark amusement., "He was beside himself. Nothing like I've ever seen him. Frantic, grief-filled." He shrugs., "You might call it hopeless."

I still don't speak, and Murtagh continues, "Now you've returned, and my brother-in-law is more alive than I've seen him in a decade." He chuckles, "Should have realized his refusal to remarry meant he always believed he would see his firstborn again." His eyes study me, and I fold my hands nervously in my lap. Another toothy smile., "You aren't here to hear about your father. What do you want, Darcy?"

I swallow, my voice more nervous than I would like, "I promised the Fae Queen I would help return her son to her." Murtagh slaps his hand on the table., "A foolish sort of promise."

"Since I've been here," I press, trying to steady my voice., "I thought Edric stayed in your court by choice." The king's grin makes my stomach turn, "I realized otherwise today."

"It is a choice."

"Hardly," I gasp at him. "He can't return to his home as an ass."

"He wanted to be left alone, to be safe from his court's fighting." Murtagh leans forward, his breath hot on my face.,

"Is he not safe, Darcy? Protected in my Court, unrecognizable in his own?"

"That's not what he wanted," I bite back., "He can't return like this."

The king shrugs., "And what would you have me do?"

I can't stop my voice from shaking, no matter how much I try. "I want you to release Prince Edric, let him return home as himself."

Murtagh raises an eyebrow., "You might be mortal, but you're not stupid. You have a price in mind."

"Yes.," I drag in a breath. "Me."

His hands clasp together, nails black against his pale skin., "Your mortality for Edric's freedom." I don't trust my voice, even as my heart-beat speeds up, my fingers quivering as I bunch my hands into fists. Murtagh's dark eyes gleam., "You have an affinity for bargains, Darcy."

I almost laugh, "I've gotten used to them lately."

Murtagh smiles widely, stretching his skin over his sharp cheeks. I didn't know his skin could lake paler, but it does, his teeth gleaming as he speaks again, "Perhaps, you don't know bargains well enough."

My cheeks flush, but the king doesn't seem to notice my discomfort. He taps his nails against the wooden table, scratching mindlessly at the wood, "The Fae prince is obnoxious, and his court will be restless until he returns home." Another flash of his teeth, "You're a much finer replacement."

I force myself not to look away from his glimmering eyes, "Your mortality for the Fae prince's safe return, complete freedom from his bargain with my court." I don't need to answer, so I simply nod. Murtagh holds his hand out, and I touch his webbed palm. His fingers clasp around mine, his grip firm as an eagle's talons. He speaks firmly. "I will free Prince Edric of the Fae from all of his bargains to my court in exchange for the mortality of Darcy, Daughter of Dewain."

I take in a breath, my words mirroring his promise, "I give my mortality to King Murtagh of the Finn in exchange for the freedom of Prince Edric of the Fae."

His fingers squeeze even harder, and my breath chokes in my throat, "As soon as Prince Edric's feet touch the dry ground, Darcy, Daughter of Dewain, you will return to the sea that gave you life. Shedding your mortal skin, you will be one of the Finn Folk forever."

I gasp as he releases me, my hand throbbing. Murtagh's chair scrapes back as he stands, "Take Edric to land at first light. The prince has been absent from his kingdom for too long." He walks away, leaving me hunched over, my hand still tingling in discomfort. I cradle my head in my arms, forcing my breathing to calm. My eyes are burning with unshed tears, but I can't cry at my choice. My promise with the Fae Queen was my choice. I swore to do everything I could to return her son to her. I left Anya in Fae's hands, battered, terrified Anya. I made all these promises for her, and I'll keep making promises even if I never see her again. Once Edric gets back to his Court and Mother, he'll make sure Anya is fine. He knows what the Finn did to her, and he'll make sure she heals.

"Darcy.," I jump at my name, knocking my head on the side of the table. I yelp before I can stop myself, and I catch my forehead in my hands, wincing at the instant pain, my burning tears slipping free. "Darcy," Dewain speaks just behind me, placing his hand gently on my back.

If I were stronger, I'd pull away. A day or a night ago, I might have straightened and shrugged him away. Now, I can barely lift my chin. If I push him away, the sob in my throat will break free. He kneels, his knees touching the stone floor., "You spoke to Murtagh."

I nod at his words, pressing my eyes closed. I feel Dewain's slender hand touching my hair. He runs his webbed fingers through a tangled curl. "I bargained.," The words come in barely a whisper., "With the Queen. I had to keep my promise."

Dewain catches my hand in his, tipping my chin up. I blink my eyes open, looking into his dark green eyes. Worry creases his face. His fingers tighten around my wrist before I even answer., "It was for Edric," I whisper, "so he can return home." I look down, my fingers tight around his cold hand. It feels strange to touch him after carefully avoiding this man for so long.

I finally raise my eyes, blinking at my father. Murtagh must have told him. He hasn't asked me what I bargained away, and the lines across his face, the heavyweight across his shoulders tell me he knows. His eyes are downcast. "Darcy.," his voice catches, he swallows before finally speaking, "Let me talk to Murtagh; you should not do this." His words are confusing. Ever since he first saw me, he called me his daughter. The Finn will never accept me until I lose every trace of my human nature. He can call me his daughter and promise me the world, the ocean, but his people will still despise me. "Don't you want me to be like you?"

"No.," His answer is fierce., "Not for you to give yourself for a Fae prince." He drops my hand, leaning back away from me., "This life should be your choice. Not forced on you by promises and bargains."

"It is my choice.," I grab at his arm, desperate to make him believe me., "It's my choice to live here." His breathing is heavy as he studies me, and his following words show how little he believes me., "It is hardly a choice if you bargained with Murtagh."

I want to smile because, of course, he's right. I can't let him know how right he is. My stomach turns at the idea of being Finn, losing my feeling and my tears, and even the sunlight. Whatever Dewain knows of my feelings, he doesn't want me to follow through on this bargain. Even though I know, he longs for me to belong to his Court, to be his daughter forever. He wants me to choose him, not bargain my life away. He'll hate himself, hate me, for this bargain. I lean forward., "You're my father.," my voice almost breaks, the tears I'm fighting catching in my voice as I force the words out, "I don't want to fight my future with you." He remains stiff as I plead with him., "I am choosing this."

"Darcy.," He finally lets out a breath., "I might not be able to lie, but I can taste deception."

I'm stung, pulling away from him. I put as much of my strength into my voice, forcing my words not to shake with my unshed tears., "If you want me to be able to make my own choices, let me choose this. Let me make this choice."

He touches the arm of the chair, fingers tight around the wood., "You've made your choice," he sighs, standing up, "Bargains are twisted paths that destroy as easily as they are created."

I follow his lead, standing., "I don't plan on making more bargains." I twist my fingers together, tipping my head back to look at him. "Once Edric returns to land, I'll have kept all my promises. I'll be through with bargains."

His lips twitch., "I hope so, Darcy." He pats me on the shoulder, awkwardly tense and suddenly unsure., "For your sake, I truly hope so."

We walk out of the small room together, but Dewain is restless. His hands twitch, and he glances around as though we're being followed. I'm not sure if he's upset I didn't listen to him and wouldn't let him argue with Murtagh. Or maybe, he's as unsure as I am about talking with me. Since I've arrived, we've navigated careful small talk and avoided talking alone longer than he a few minutes. We pass through the rows of armed Finn guards before he makes a babbled excuse about He leaves me to walk alone, searching for Edric. I keep yawning, sleep biting at my thoughts. If I stay awake until I take Edric to land, it will be the first night I've been able to stay awake the entire time.

But at the rate of my yawns, I know I need to catch some sleep.

Edric is in the first place I check, the training room. He slashes at a dummy, cutting slashes across the straw figure's chest. Then he advances again, cursing as he slices, stabs, slashes again. I step into the room, but he doesn't hear me. He cuts again, his cloak billowing behind him. Another whirl and he lops the head off. The stuffed skull falls to the ground, and with a hoarse cry, Edric throws his sword to the ground. The metal skitters across the floor; the racket is making my teeth clench.

"Edric," I speak softly, "are you quite through?" He stiffens, fingers fisting at his sides before he turns slowly towards me., "I didn't hear you come again."

I don't answer right away, stepping closer to the prince. His eyes are red and swollen, his nostrils flaring., "How many of those straw dummies have you destroyed?" He shrugs, rolling his shoulders in his casual way, before stepping in to pick up his sword. He bends down in a smooth motion, deftly slipping his blade back into his sheath in one fluid motion., "Not enough."

"Perhaps I'll whack apart a few more for you." He nods, still not looking at me. His teeth drag across his lips before he speaks again., "I thought you'd have gone to bed."

I shake my head, trying not to yawn., "Actually, no. I spoke to King Murtagh."

His dark eyebrows scrunch., "Whatever for?"

Now or never, I sputter. "You're free to return home." A moment passes, Edric finally looking at me. His puffy eyes are widening. "At first light, I can take you to the shore. Murtagh's magic won't keep you here."

"Murtagh didn't say anything about this," he answers softly., "I saw him not a half-hour ago." Of course, Murtagh wanted to have his question answered. Though I'm surprised he didn't tell Edric about the deal, congratulate him on his new freedom. I don't have an answer, so I shrug, yawning again. Edric stares at me., "You're telling me, I can just return to the shore. Return home as me."

"Yes.," I nod decisively, rubbing my tired eyes. "I'll take you to the shore at first light."

He turns away, fingers tapping on the hilt of his sword. The silence stretches before I clear my throat. "I'll see you at dinner."

He inclines his head, looking at me., "Dinner, then, Darcy." Black hair falls into his eyes, his lips quirking., "What is that now, a dozen yawns in less than two minutes?"

I roll my eyes, knowing I'm about to yawn again. My brain is far too tired to come up with anything clever. I start to walk away, barely stepping over the threshold when Edric speaks again., "I want to know why Murtagh is releasing me." his voice is strained., "You must have bargained with him."

I lean against the threshold, closing my eyes, "It doesn't matter, Edric."

"Doesn't matter because the mortal needs to sleep." A voice sneers too close. I jerk awake, Leticia standing just a few feet away. Not alone this time, her brother Owen is right behind her.

I stiffen., "Cousin.," nodding my head at them both., "I was just about to leave."

Leticia raises an eyebrow., "Really?" She leans towards her brother. "Can't quite stay awake an entire day yet, or does she still call it a night?" My cheeks flush, I hear Edric's boots behind me. Walking closer. "Edric.," Leticia smiles., "I heard you'll be leaving us."

"As I heard.," Edric's voice is just behind me., "I was just informed."

Owen picks at his sleeves, surprising me by speaking., "My sister is disappointed." Leticia sends him a nasty glare, his lips puckering as she pouts., "Edric is good company."

"As you said.," Owen's sneer matches his sister., "Good with a sword."

I can't tell if Leticia is blushing or angry. Edric is so close; I can practically feel him still. It's strange to feel the legendary Fae stillness, Edric's skin turning into stone. "I'm not near as good as my friends," Edric speaks softly, "But if this is my last day in your court, I would be happy to cross swords with you, Leticia."

She brightens, elbowing her brother before sauntering over. I skitter out of her way; she hardly looks at me, aiming to choose a sword from the rack. I should be going to bed, but it's too tempting to stay and watch the two duel. Edric's blade is long, thin. The sword Leticia chooses is wide, not quite as long. She slashes in the air, shooting me a nasty smile. Or perhaps her brother. Owen has moved close to me; I was too distracted watching Leticia and didn't notice him move.

Owen places a hand on the wall beside me, leaning down to whisper., "She rather hoped to make him her consort." My cheeks redden as Edric and Leticia pace, setting up against each other. Edric stands nearly frozen while Leticia advances on him. Hacking, heavy blows, which Edric side steps. His cloak billows behind him. Leticia snarls.

"Now," Owen whispers again, his face so close to mine I can feel his breath on my neck., "The Fae prince runs away.," He pauses, his voice slithering. "Leaving her alone. Without a chance."

I don't want to be watching this. Leticia barks at Edric, raining heavy blows on his thin sword. He twirls out of her reach; lips pressed thin. He can't keep dancing out of her reach like this. She won't have it.

Owen's fingers move closer to my face., "My poor sister has nothing, no one worthy of a match." I glance at my cousin, his deep blue eyes. "And you're better matched?"

His red lips quirk., "I think so. Especially if my father bargained well with you."

I hold back a shiver, the hairs on the back of my neck cold. I smile politely, turning to look back at the fight. I catch a breath as Leticia assaults Edric, jumping at him. Edric steps to the side again but thrusts out his blade as he sidesteps. The point of his sword drags across Leticia's wrist.

She yelps in pain, falling back. Snarling. Edric bows swiftly, slipping his sword away. His cloak dances as he speaks, "Well met, Highness. A fight I shall always remember." He turns away, walking toward us. Stopping, staring at Owen., "Darcy wanted to rest, Highness. Surely, you don't object?"

Owen slinks away from his spot beside me, hands slipping into his pocket. He grins at me., "Want me to take you to your room?"

"No," I fumble, stepping away from them both., "I quite know the way." I don't wait for Edric or Owen to answer, jumping away down the hall. I can hear the two of them exchanging words. I don't care what Owen is saying, and I don't want to talk to Edric. I just want to crawl into my bed, find some rest before the morning.

Before, I can't even finish the thought. *Before everything changes.*

I round the hallway, stepping back unto the portico. I stop, looking at the wall of water—mere feet from where I stand. My breath quickens, and I close my eyes, leaning against the railing. This is what I feared my entire life—the ocean. In a few hours, I'll be bound to this darkness forever. "Are you afraid of the water?" I stiffen at Edric's voice, opening my eyes. I could lie to him, but I'll probably never see him again. Lying seems terrible right now, even if I hate answering his question.

"If you see my cousin," I decide to say instead, "will you make sure she is alright?"

"Of course.," Edric comes beside me, thin arms resting on the railing., "Anya is strong. Wherever she is now, I am certain she is well." I want to believe him, but I have to ask., "Why didn't you stop them?"

"The Finn?" I nod. Thinking of Flavian, beaten, bloodied. Edric would do anything for him, but he did nothing for Anya. A moment passes before he speaks, "I did as much as I could. I tried to show Murtagh she didn't know anything. Murtagh doesn't like to be wrong."

"You violated her," I choke out the words, the thoughts I've not been able to keep back., "She didn't deserve you pawing with her mind, treating her as a toy."

"I was wrong.," I close my eyes at his answer., "I will live knowing I wronged Anya the rest of my life. I can barely stand that." He breathes sharply., "All I want is to hear your voice, to hear your forgiveness. A chance for me to live with your forgiveness."

My fingers tighten around the railing., "No," I breathe the answer out softly., "I don't think I can. You can ask Anya's forgiveness; perhaps she may. But," fresh tears sting my eyes, "I cannot."

He pushes away from the railing, voice low as he speaks, "I didn't want to ask you. Not after all that you've said, I didn't think it would be possible."

"Then why did you ask.," My voice is burning with tears, and I'm angry. Angry that he wanted to ask, that he forced me to choose to hate him. It reminded me of what he did to Anya.

"If I return to land, will I ever see you again?" He answers so softly, and I almost don't hear. "Leaving an unpaid debt to anyone is dangerous. I want to leave no debts in the Finn Court." I struggle to control my tears. I can't tell him that I will probably never return to land. Never see his glittering Court or my beautifully simple home again. With a sharp breath, I rein in my thoughts, thinking of his other words. His question about debts., "There will always be the debt of Anya's blood." I wipe my tears away., "When she is happy, truly at peace, your debt is paid."

Our eyes meet before he bows., "I promise to pay my debts, Darcy. I will leave no path untried, no road unpaved to pay this debt." My throat burns, and I barely manage a nod. He holds out his hand, and I reach for his slender fingers.

My skin brushes one of his rings. He clasps my hand., "All I ask is your forgiveness when this debt is paid. Your complete forgiveness."

I manage a nod, swallowing. "Restore Anya's peace, her life, and I will give you my forgiveness." He bends towards me, and his lips brush against my knuckles. He drops my hand suddenly, walking swiftly away. My vision is clouded with tears, the weight of my words: my refusal, his promise.

"It's not a bargain," I breathe to myself, stepping into my room. Not another bargain. A promise. For Anya's sake. A promise I made for her.

Brendan

"What the fuck," Brigit gasps the words, laying a few feet away from me. Anya is on the other side, her body in a crumpled heap. I can hear her breathing, heavy gasps of air. They're both still alive. My Mother created the spell to take me far away from the Court. I'd never used the magic words before, never teleported through the magical barriers with two lives in my hands.

I push myself to my knees, the earth still spinning a bit around me. I take a deep breath, biting back the feeling of nausea filling my throat. "I'm sorry," I manage to gasp, "I didn't have a chance to warn you; we just had to get out." Brigit pulls herself to her knees, pushing hair back from her face. "Fuck," She narrows her eyes at me, then turns to Anya, laying a hand on the girl's back. Anya barely lifts her head, her hand covering her mouth. Her shoulders jolt as she heaves. Anya heaves a few more times, then grabs Brigit's hand and gets pulled to her feet. Brigit wraps an arm around her shoulder, pulling Anya's hair back from her face.

Brigit looks my way, and I can see the demand for an explanation in her eyes. Before I cans peak, she starts, "Well, you dragged us out here, but I'm sure the Queen will just send your father to chase us down."

I'm not surprised Brigit assumes the worst about my decision-making; I haven't exactly made the best set of choices the last couple of weeks. "We're actually at my mother's estate." My words are little comfort, which is again no surprise. It's not like I ever sat Brigit down and explained my family's complicated history. "My father always said he banished my Mother to the North," I start explaining, "The land has always belonged to her family. He can't cross into the Estate without her permission."

Brigit tips back her head, chuckling, "So your father is the one banned from the estate." I nod, my neck heating as Brigit smirks. I've never told anyone the true details of my Mother's exile. Not even Flavian, who used to bug me with questions about my Mother and childhood. I trusted Flavian with my life, but risking my father's anger to share the secret seemed like a bad idea. One slip and my father's fury would have rained down on me in a storm.

Anya pulls back from Brigit, her eyes darting around the green space around us. We've landed just inside the edges of my Mother'sMother's lands, on a cluster of cliffs a distance from the house, behind us the sea stretching out in billowing waves. Anya stares at the water, crossing her arms before asking, "Where are we?"

"A long way from the Court," it's hard to explain the Estate. It's north in human lands, on the last bits of land before the island dips into the sea. I spent most of my childhood here, but it's been nearly a decade since I've seen my MotherMother or the rest of my childhood home. I glance towards the house; I can barely see the gates around the entrance, the metal grating glinting in the midday sunshine. Brigit touches Anya's arm, grasping her hand, and they follow me towards the gate and graveled pathway.

We almost reach the gate when it opens, the metal squeaking before my MotherMother steps out. I knew she would have felt us land, the disturbance in her magical guards. Still, it's strange to see her.

Brigit lets out a short gasp, "Damn, Brendan." She spits behind me, "You didn't tell me."

Maybe I should be annoyed that Brigit expected to know. My mother crosses her arms, webbed hands showing her identity. Anya pulls up short, and Brigit speaks softly, "She's not a Finn," she explains, "Brendan's Mother is a Selkie. She won't hurt you."

"Brendan," my Mother's voice is at once soft and sharp, "I wondered if I would ever see my son's face again."

"Mother," I dip to my knees, "Please forgive me, I didn't know I'd have to drop into your land uninvited."

"Bother," She lifts a hand, tossing her long blue-green cords of hair, "You're always invited. I gave you the magic words, did I not?" She holds out her hand, and I take it before she pulls me into an embrace. My Mother's arms are always a strange mixture of warm and cold. She pulls back, running a hand through my hair. "Brendan, it's been too long." She lets out a sigh, "I suppose I always knew you'd only be back when you needed to run from your father." I nod, unable to begin explaining the mess I've made of my life. Somehow, she knows that I did what I thought was right, and my decisions didn't live up to my father's expectations. Her eyes flit to Anya and Brigit. "You have a Human and Fae lover? I always thought you were more prudish than that." Brigit snorts, and my Mother's lips quirk, "Ah, I see, bold of me to assume my boring son could get one lover, much less two."

Chapter Fourteen

Darcy

I PAUSE OUTSIDE OF my room, leaning against the palace railing. Music echoes from somewhere; the clanging cymbals are mixing with deep bass. I take in a breath, stretching my fingers to touch the water. I haven't seen the stars in days.

When I become Finn, I shiver at the thought; I might swim to the surface at night and finally get another look at the stars. At least, that will be a comfort. Something I can enjoy while trapped here forever.

"Darcy.," I stiffen, leaning back away from the railing.

My father walks toward me., "It is almost dawn." I hadn't even realized how much time had already passed. The shortest night I've spent here., "Would you like for me to accompany you to the shore?"

I jerk. "No.," I shake my head., "That's kind of you to offer, but I'll be fine."

He nods., "A few of my men will still need to accompany you." He gestures forward., "Edric is probably waiting at the gate." I follow his lead, walking with him along the portico. He clears his throat., "When you become Finn, I can take you to my home."

"This isn't your home?" I look up at him. "I thought you lived here?"

"No.," His lips curve slightly., "A dangerous choice to choose to live permanently with the King."

I wipe my sweaty palms against my skirt, searching for the right words. "I look forward to seeing your home.," My words are flat, and I wonder if I'll be able to lie so quickly when I become Finn. Dewain is silent, only our feet making noise, though the music is still echoing around us.

I catch his arm before he turns to go, "What of the blonde.," I swallow, letting go of his sleeve, "Flavian, is he alright?"

He turns toward me, his face now unreadable., "He is of the Fae, Darcy. You shouldn't concern yourself with the Fae." I swallow back his words, wetting my lips before speaking again., "I knew Flavian." I press on, avoiding the tightening around his eyes., "At the court, he was almost a friend."

The air is heavy between us before he speaks, "You're not with them anymore. You should forget the people you knew, the Fae creatures. You belong to the Finn now. It is best to forget the past and those friendships." I'm taken aback by his words, the idea of forgetting everything that has ever mattered to me. My home, Anya, everyone I met at the Fae Court, Brendan, and Flavian, Brigit. I sputter, "The sirens didn't kidnap me; I still have my memories. You want to steal everything from me?"

He nearly flinches, blinking and looking away., "No. I would not want the sirens ever to touch you."

"But you want me to forget."

"I would have you choose not to remember. To not think of the past."

I force in a deeper breath, biting back my anger and frustration. All that Dewain has said to me, I think I can understand what he wants. He hasn't mentioned my mother once since our first meeting, and he never came for me until he realized I was alive. I cross my arms, fidgeting with the sleeves of my tunic., "Have you chosen to forget?" His eyes come back to me., "Forget?"

"My mother," I can barely ask the question., "Did you choose to forget her?"

His eyes close, and he rubs his hand over his face., "I could never forget your mother. Never."

Questions bubble inside me, everything I want to know, his feelings toward my mother, how he found her, why she was here if she remembered her home. But I can't ask this all now, so I force myself to focus on what I need before taking Edric to the surface., "Why can't you forget her?"

His eyes flicker open, and he steps closer to me, reaching for my hands. I slip my hands into his calloused fingers, his grip tightening as he holds unto me., "She was my life, Darcy. Your mother." He chokes out the words, his eyes closing again. I am sure I would see tears on his cheeks now if the Finn could cry. A deep breath before he speaks again. "My life was complete with her."

I squeeze his fingers, stepping into his embrace. "Father," I speak softly, "No one could ever ask you to forget your past. You have never chosen to forget my mother or your feelings. How can you ask me to choose to forget?" His fingers are still tight around my hand, but his eyes open. I can't read what he thinks before he speaks, "It is for your protection, Darcy." My eyes must reflect my confusion at his words because he continues, "I have given up most everything to protect my feelings. I don't want you to become what I am." He gathers me into an embrace, hands on my shoulder., "Take the Fae prince to land. Leave your memories on the shores." He tips my chin up., "We must leave the past behind, or it will only hurt us more."

I can feel tears gathering, and I force my eyes not to blink. I can't cry, not now when my Father and his guards would just see my tears as a sign of human weakness. I can't imagine even beginning to do as he's asking. I turn out of his arms, touching my fingertips to my eyes. Catching my breath. Thinking of something else to ask, anything to change the subject., "How far away is your home?"

Dewain speaks softly, "Half a day, perhaps. Closer to the shore." Close to the shore, I almost breathe a relieved sigh.

Close to Anya, my throat burns. In a few hours, he wants me to forget her. Not think of her anymore. "Being close to land, I was able to meet your mother," Dewain speaks quietly, pulling my thoughts back., "She enjoyed the ocean more than any human I've ever met." I certainly didn't inherit that love. My face must give away my feelings because Dewain studies me before asking., "Have you always hated the water?"

"Yes," I fumble for words, hoping he understands this at least., "The ocean has always frightened me."

Dewain reaches out, fingertips light on my shoulder, his voice calm., "Your mother grew frightened of the water, Darcy. She feared it more than anything, more than our love." He drags in a breath., "Her fear poured itself into you, protecting you from what she dreaded most."

I want to ask him what made her fear something she supposedly loved. But before I can begin to form the words, Edric's boots click on the smooth walkway. Dewain releases me, looking up at the Fae Prince.

"Dawn," Dewain speaks with a grim smile., "Time to return." I turn away from Dewain, taking in the prince. Edric's eyes are bloodshot, his hair a rumpled mess. Dewain snaps his fingers, and three Finn guards come. I look around, the light glittering off the stones of the palace. Dawn's light is just beginning to fight against the ever-present darkness, the candles starting to gutter out. "A safe journey," Dewain speaks softly, patting my shoulder., "And all the god's blessing."

I give him a tight smile before following the guards onto the walkway. The stone walkway stretches out into the ocean, a wall of water on each side. In the end, we'll step into the water. Swim to the shore. Edric falls into step beside me, silent except for his clicking heels. We walk to the edge of the palace, and I take a final step. The cold water jolts through me, and I gasp before being dragged into the murky depths.

I can't describe it any other way, but the water sucks you in. Weightless, you can't resist it. My eyes are screwed shut, my breath caught in a tight gasp.

Edric touches my shoulder, and I cringe, forcing my eyes back open. We are floating in the dark depths, the stone walls of the palace fading from view. The guards surround us, gesturing for us to begin swimming. I reach out my arms, pulling myself forward. The water ripples around me, tangling in my hair, pulling at my heavy dress. Finn magic keeps me breathing.

The darkness of the water fades into seaweed greens and blue shades as we swim closer and closer to shore. Plants sprout around us, fish darting in and out of rock formations. We paddle past other groups of Finn, their gazes cold and wary.

"Darcy," Edric grabs my arm, pulling me to a stop as we near the shore, the ocean floor mere feet below us., "You don't have to do this." His blue eyes pierce into me; he touches a thin hand to his hair, brushing back the dark waves.

I glance at his pointed ears, repeating the promise., "You'll be free once we reach the shore."

He squeezes my shoulder, repeating his words, "You don't have to do this, Darcy."

I look past his thin face and Fae ears. Edric supposedly knows so much and yet refuses to face the truth. Freeing Edric is my only choice. If I don't, I'll be human and miserable with him as a prisoner forever. The Finn guards behind us shuffle, stabbing at fish with their spears. My stomach tightens., "I promised your mother."

He grabs my arm, twisting me. I yell out in surprise, but he clamps a hand over my mouth. The guards step closer, but I feel his eyes glaring. Those royal blue eyes, so charged with life. The guards still uneasy but held back by his dagger-like glare. "I know your promise.," His words whisper into my face., "You did what you could. If you do this, I'll be with my mother."

He pauses, lifting his hand from my mouth, but his fingers trail on my lips. I try to step back; his every touch is weakening me. My heart is pounding in my ears, and his breath is warm against my cool skin. "If you do this," he repeats, the words silvery., "I'll be with my mother, but I will lose myself. Abandoning you. Another wrong to blight my life."

I do the only thing I can. I close my eyes. Flavian's hands run down my arms, touching my wrist. "I can't bear the thought," he murmurs., "You sentenced to this life forever. Losing your kindness and compassion for Finn cruelty and spite."

"I don't have a choice," I force myself to meet Edric's eyes, "I can't go back home." And I can't imagine refusing the Finn much longer. Dewain is not only my Father; he is the king's most trusted advisor. Uncle to the Finn heir. He can't afford to let me return, to lose me after finally finding his child. I grab at Edric's hand., "We're almost to the shore." I spit the words, "And you'll be free." I feel his body deflating, his disappointment weighing on his shoulders. I lean close to him, my cheek brushing his shoulder. "Edric, you'll be free. Free to be with Flavian. Free to protect my cousin and rule your kingdom and live."

He looks down at me., "My freedom for your slavery? What a cruel choice you offer," he runs his hand over his face., "You are no mortal to be so cruel."

His words eat into me. I pull my shoulders tight. My toes still wiggle; my lungs still move. The magic that keeps me breathing, I am still human. I press ahead, moving my legs purposefully. I spread my fingers; I will enjoy these last moments. The water is growing shallow; sand scrapes against my toes. I wince as shells dig into the arch of my foot.

Beside me, Edric is stiff even as we wade through the water.

The water is now more transparent, a window to the world outside the Finn kingdom. The sky breaths warmth with spring blue colors. A view I've seen for years but never breathed in as pure life. Seagulls pass overhead, their calls vibrant. I blink back tears as sunlight dapples my eyes. My hair sticks to my neck, salt clinging to my skin. If I could just stand here for a moment longer, the sun will dry my hair. Heavy and crusted with salt, but dry and warm. I can't keep soaking in the sunshine and spring ocean air. The Finn guards catch my attention, grousing at each other as they wait for me yards away. They're avoiding surfacing, their tails breaking in angry splashes against the water.

Edric surfaces, gasping in the fresh air. He gapes at the sight of the land, the rocky green hills, and dark brown sand.

His mouth is open, his lips almost blue. The magic must be wearing off; soon, he'll be freezing.

"When you touch the shore," I fight to talk loud enough, my voice catching in my stinging throat, "you'll be free." I wait, but he still gapes. I cross my arms; my dress drags in the water. I look at the golden threads, the buttons running across my chest. The sleeves hang heavy, and I fidget with the seam, rolling it up closer to my elbow. Then I spread my fingers again, looking at my wrinkled fingertips. Trading a slight annoyance for webbed hands, I suck in a breath at the thought, feeling tears prick at my eyes again.

Edric takes a step. He looks down at me. Now that we're standing on sand, instead of floating in the water, he's a full head taller than me. His shoulders are broad, his pale skin shimmering. He's been away from the sun for so very long. He touches his hair; the salt is starting to grow crusty. He grins, his entire face softening. Then he leaps, splashing into a smaller pool of water. The tides wash around us, foamy sea catching at Edric's ankles.

Loud laughter. "I can hear myself." He roars his words, then he shouts, pounding on his chest. He falls forward, knees landing in the shallow water. Then he looks back at me, nearly pleading., "I could still stay. You could be human."

I shake my head, refusing to think of Edric returning to the murky darkness of the Finn King's castle, "Go ahead, Edric. Return to your kingdom. Be free."

He looks down at the water, skimming his hand over the cool surface., "No matter what, Darcy. You are not of the Finn. A true Finn does not wish others happiness. Does not sacrifice themselves. Does not fear."

I suck in a breath: fear, *happiness*. Will I even feel these things? The thought ends in a void of panic. Then, Edric takes a step. I watch his pale feet drag through the muddy sand. And then a final step and his toes touch the rocks, pulling him to shore.

Pain radiates in my stomach; I tumble forward. My body convulses, my ears pounding. I can hear my name. Is it Edric? Someone is screaming. My body twists, pulls, and yanks. I bundle forward, curling into a ball. My chest explodes as my blood vessels splinter. It's like glass pressing into my heart, my chest squeezing, convulsing. I spread my hands, clutching for anything as my bones cry out in agony. And then I'm screaming; I dig my fingers into the sand, sobbing, shrieking, heaving. And just as quickly, the pain is gone. I'm shaking in the shallow water. My eyes pressed closed, my head spinning.

"Darcy.," the voice is still calling. It's so very far away.

I force my eyes open. The sun is far too bright; I hiss in pain. The air burns my skin, more hissing. I sink back into the water, floating on the surface.

And then I look down at my hands. The wrinkled tips are gone, replaced with smooth, long nails. Purple webbing spreading between each finger, translucent but catching the water. I can't stretch my fingers out. I touch the webbing, my chest shaking.

I'm sputtering, trying to find the surface. I need a breath; my chest is burning, my stomach heaving. I break the ocean surface, gasping for a breath. But the air is colder, and my body gasps as knives press into my skin. I flop into the water, forcing my head past the tidal foam and waves. Another wave breaks around me, air meeting my skin again. The pain is instant, heat, and burning. I clamor in the water, forgetting about breathing and my nauseous stomach. I just need to dive deeper. The water pushes around me, and the waves carry me as I fight my way further out to sea. "Darcy," the harsh Finn tones of the guards jolt through me, one of them must have grabbed for me. I twist away, the water working with me. I accidentally release a breath, my mouth opening and cold seawater rushing in. But my lungs don't fill up, the water passing effortlessly down my throat. My fingers find their way to my neck, to the gills I realize must be there. I touch the broken skin, shivering at the feeling.

I can't bear it; I simply can't look down at my missing feet. I know my legs have molded into scaled limbs, a shadow of my former life. As if to confirm this, I shake, my feet jerking against the water. The guards surround me, their words a jumble of orders, telling me that we need to leave. We're too close to shore, the sun is a danger to any Finn, and the shallow water means we're exposed to the sun.

I've already felt the sun, thousands of pinpricks of knives scraping at my new skin. The guards are right; we do need to leave. But I can't just follow them through the water back to the Finn palace. "Wait," I speak too loud, not used to the way my words can now carry through the water.

The Finn guards stare at me, "Wait," I repeat, spinning in the water, my new Finn feet propelling me higher; I break the surface, holding back a gasp of pain. I can barely open my eyes, the air cutting at my skin. I fall back to the ocean before clamoring up a rock. Every second is more pain, but I hold unto the sharpness of the rock, knowing I can't leave without one final look at the land. I let go of the rock, long enough to hold my hands up to my face, shielding my eyes.

I blink. The land is just a few yards away, the green grass mossy, the sand glistening in the daylight. Edric is still standing there. If I lift my chin, I can see him. For weeks, I've lived surrounded by water. But I never heard anything through the water, the ocean walls blocking any sound outside the palace.

My new pointed ears twitch, catching the sound of his voice. He turns long enough to see me, and I gasp, my scaley legs scraping against the rock. I bring my long fingers to my pointed ears, stopping them from hearing his voice. Then I let myself slip from the rock, falling backward into the cold arms of the water. The waves cover me, blocking out Edric. I push myself deeper, my webbed feet propelling me deeper, deeper into the inky darkness of the sea. My body soaks up the water, the new, strange blood in my veins running faster. The Finn guards swim alongside me, and I easily keep pace with them. Even as the water grows darker, land and sunshine now more distant, I can still see my new home—the schools of fish and towering seagrass dance around me. Hidden behind crops of rocks, the faces of my fellow Finn, their eyes narrowed and ears twitching. My new ears can hear their hissed words, the bits of my story repeated, "Not a human anymore. Bargained with the King. Dewain's spawn."

We're close to the palace gates now. I know Dewain will be waiting, the entire Finn court judging me. They'll take in my new body, the way I swim, and walk on my new, strange feet. I'm not a human anymore, and now, my promises have sentenced me to this new life. I clutch my webbed hands together, my throat burning. My heart feels shattered into a thousand sparks. Still, not a single tear comes to my eyes.

I am Finn. One of the Finn folk forever. I can have no tears, but I will suffer all the more.